THE RAINBOW
CONSPIRACY

First published by Muswell Press in 2017

Typeset by e-Digital Design Ltd.

Copyright © Stuart Hopps 2017

Stuart Hopps has asserted his right to be identified
as the author of this work in accordance with the
Copyright, Designs and Patents Act 1988
Printed and bound by Clays Ltd, St Ives plc.

A CIP catalogue record for this book is available from the British Library

ISBN 978-0-9954822-2-7

**MUSWELL
PRESS**

Muswell Press
London
N6 5HQ

www.muswell-press.co.uk

THE RAINBOW CONSPIRACY

STUART HOPPS

MUSWELL
PRESS

ACKNOWLEDGEMENTS

I would like to thank my Deal friends for their help
and encouragement:-

Frances, Jenny, David, Sylvia and Ryan.

Court Miller 1952-1986

CHAPTER ONE

SPOKE ASSOCIATES MONDAY

Spoke Associates was one of the top five leading theatrical agencies in the UK, and Shirley Morris had worked there for many years. She was familiar with the way her boss, Clive Spoke, liked things done, and had personally reserved a ticket in his name at the National Theatre for that night's 1984 London premiere of the new musical *Marilyn,* making sure he had a very good seat in the stalls. Miss Morris had originally worked as a secretary for British Lion, one of England's most important film companies. However, she soon became disenchanted with sitting behind a desk all day, where there was little opportunity for her to rub shoulders with glamorous film stars, let alone get to know the big names that mattered behind the scenes.

She had decided therefore, to change tack and get herself a job in a theatrical agency, where she thought she would come into contact with leading actors on a daily basis. But her first job at the Bobbie Kelly Agency proved disappointing, since Shirley was only employed as a secretarial assistant. However, it was there that she first met Clive and, when he broke away from that establishment and formed his own business some five years later, Shirley decided to join Spoke Associates. There, she started off as the receptionist, but she was ambitious and soon worked her way up to becoming Clive's personal assistant. In a way, they had both looked after each other, had developed more than just a professional relationship, and had finally become close friends. Some thought too close, but there was always bound to be a certain amount of jealousy in 'the show business' as Mr Spoke liked to call their line of work.

Clive fully recognised that Shirley had contributed a great deal to the success of his agency and together they had become a formidable team, their professional life forcing them to spend a good deal of time together, working as well as socialising. True, Shirley was at times overprotective of Clive and although he usually benefited from this form of attention, he was perfectly capable of politely disengaging himself from her maternal clutches when he felt smothered, which of late did appear to happen with somewhat greater regularity.

Spoke Associates now represented some very big names in the industry and Clive was enjoying the esteem in which he was now held. What infuriated him however, was how long it had taken him to get to where he was and how slow producers, directors and casting directors had been to recognise his ability to spot real acting skills, and be respected for what he had always believed was the obvious quality of the artists in his stable.

He knew he could smell talent a mile off and liked to think of himself as a good judge of character, and other people in the business had slowly begun to realise that he had a particular nose for sniffing out a potential star. As well as assessing the artistic worth of his actors, he had a genuine flair for measuring the honesty of his clients as human beings, as well as their ability to own up to the pressures of the profession they had chosen.

Clive loved the excitement of first nights and was particularly looking forward to the one he was off to that Wednesday evening.

One of his most talented actors, the young and beautiful Miranda Martin, had landed the lead in the latest musical at the National. Having read the script, Clive openly announced that *Marilyn* would be a huge flop, although he also believed that Miranda would shine through, confirming her star quality, and demonstrating the calibre of the artists that Spoke Associates now represented.

He had been on the verge of leaving the office when Michael's call was switched through to him. Such was his tearing hurry to cross the Waterloo Bridge, take his seat before curtain-up and prove himself right by the end of the opening number, that he very nearly refused to take the call at all, and barely recognised the name Shirley had yelled through to him from her adjoining office. Michael's news was brief: Dennis was dead. He'd developed AIDS.

It had been ages since Clive had heard from either of those American friends, and truth to tell, he had simply drifted apart from them and lost touch. However, geographical distance was not the main reason: rather it was Clive's obsession with Spoke Associates, and what Shirley and others had recognised as his delirious love affair with show business, coupled with the undoubted success of his clients and the growing reputation of his agency. This infatuation had caused him to drop many of his former friends and acquaintances, with whom he now had little in common, and that telephone call, coming from out of the blue, had really knocked him for six.

In addition, the details of Dennis's death made Clive feel uneasy about his own state of health. Only a couple of years before, in the early eighties, one or two of his New York friends had died of AIDS, and only last year, when he'd attended the premiere of *Night for Day* on Broadway, he'd bumped into his old friend, the American actor Morgan Fleming and barely recognised him. Shortly afterwards, he had not been surprised to read that the actor was dead. But an ex-lover was a much closer call and he knew that this relatively newly diagnosed disease was a killer. It made him feel more than a little fearful for his own life, as well as for Michael's, who had sounded so distressed on the telephone. So after Clive's diplomatic attempts at consolation, he assured Dennis's partner that he would leave for Columbus the next morning and be with him as soon as possible.

Clive replaced the receiver onto its cradle and slowly eased himself back into his chair, his own life of glittering first nights and star-making quickly receding into the background as he was suddenly overcome by an intense sense of loss. He buzzed through to Shirley and asked her to organise his travel arrangements to fly to the States the next day. Shirley was well aware that Columbus, Ohio did not feature anywhere in the Spoke Associates' diary of engagements but was sensitive to how agitated that call from the USA had made her boss feel, and went straight ahead and did as instructed.

She ordered a black cab to collect him from his home at nine-fifteen the following morning, at least thirty minutes earlier than was really necessary. Clive's views on punctuality were so engrained in her that she made premature arrangements as a matter of course. That way she knew he would arrive at Heathrow in good time to catch his plane, have some airport fruit juice if he liked, and make any last-minute phone calls before his flight was announced. Gone were the penny-pinching days when, in order to save on expenses, Clive would have carried his own bags down to the end of Ladbroke Terrace and picked up a cab at the corner of Holland Park Avenue. Taxis were relatively frequent along that stretch of the main road, so it was easy to hail one there and, living in the west side of London, his journey out to Heathrow Airport could be achieved in no time at all.

But that was then and, let's face it, Shirley knew all about the early days of Spoke Associates. Things were different now, and she had the authority to deal with what she feared might be her boss's current crisis in a manner more appropriate to his present status.

She was very well tuned in to Clive's mood swings and had become a dab hand at smoothing the waters when the going got rough. Her sharp antennae had become expert in registering the least change of pitch in his voice and at moments such as these, Shirley had only one tactic. She would allow fifteen minutes for fallout, then would move in and commence the rescue operation.

So, having made the necessary plane reservations for the following day – first class of course – she set about putting the coffee on and let the dust settle for a while before finally entering Clive's inner sanctum. She checked herself in the mirror, applied a little more lipstick, straightened her pleated skirt and put her navy blue jacket back on.

'Do you want to talk about it, Clive?'

'No! Not really.'

'And are you going to sit there all night in your overcoat?'

'Shirley, I'd like some coffee.'

That signalled the end of round one, but Shirley was by no means certain that round two would reveal the reason behind his sudden need to go to Columbus. Although they were close, Clive was curiously uncommunicative about the life he had led pre-Spoke Associates and had related absolutely nothing about his university days. Likewise, Shirley, although once married, had decided to use her maiden name professionally and had volunteered little information concerning her private life or upbringing, and Clive, discretion personified, had duly respected her need for privacy.

When Shirley returned with the coffee, Clive had removed his bulky outer garment and was deep in thought and drawing on a Balkan Sobranie, something he only did when under stress. Shirley placed a small tray on his desk, poured a cup for Clive, adding milk and one sugar, then crossed to the drinks cabinet and helped herself to a large Scotch. She held out the bottle towards him, knowing full well he would take a shot in his coffee.

'Not having seen them in ages, Shirley, makes it all seem

somehow less real. Does that make sense?'

'Of course it does,' she replied, still not knowing who the 'them' were.

'Dennis is dead, and I'm sure Michael could do with some moral support.'

'It's all taken care of, connecting flights and a taxi out to Heathrow.'

'Shirley, darling, thank you. What more can I say?'

That phrase usually heralded another silence, and Shirley consequently sat herself down opposite him, quietly nursing her drink. She wasn't at all sure who Dennis and Michael actually were but understood Clive well enough to know that he would take advantage of the pause and come round to filling her in about them in his own good time. After a while, Clive stood up and stretched. 'I don't think I can face tonight.'

'For goodness sake, don't even think about it. I'll stop by at the National and hang around till the show comes down. Miranda will understand when I explain that there's been a death in the family. I am right, aren't I? That is what's happened?'

'Yes, it's Dennis, Michael's lover. He's dead. He had AIDS.'

'Clive, I'm so very sorry. No wonder you're so upset.'

'Shirley, you can't imagine how fit and strong he was. But I've seen this happen before. You remember the actor Morgan Fleming? Well, I saw what became of him last year when I was in New York. That young man had aged so much I hardly recognised him. He looked so ill, had to walk with a stick, and had enormous trouble breathing.'

'Yes I remember you telling me. I suppose I know so little about AIDS.'

'It seems to be getting closer and appears to be targeted just at gay males. In fact my very dear friend Susan Carlsberg told me last year, when I was staying with her in New York, that two of her closest hairdresser friends, Simon and Mike, were infected with it.

She didn't understand why it was attacking so many young gay men in America, causing so much suffering and so many deaths. Susan felt that there was something sinister about the whole business and when I pressed her further she said she'd heard a rumour that her government might be involved.'

'Is that so? You haven't mentioned that before, although I do remember how upset you were about Morgan Fleming.'

'I was shocked!'

'But it hasn't really hit us over here yet, has it?'

'Yes it has, but not to the same degree,' Clive continued. And what about Alan Humphrey? He died of it this year following his season on Broadway ... and Shirley ... I'm scared for myself: it's a killer and Dennis and I were an item long before he met Michael, you know.'

Hearing this latest confessional made Shirley feel more than a little uncomfortable, to say the least, but she tried to hide her anxiety with: 'You've not mentioned these American friends of yours much before.'

'I met them a hell of a long time ago, Shirley.'

'When, exactly?'

'Actually, I met Dennis on my first trip to the USA, after I had completed my first year at university.'

'How was that, then?'

'I was hitchhiking around the States like a lot of English students back in the sixties; I set off for Chicago, then travelled around a bit, and finally ended up on Cape Cod in a resort called Provincetown.'

Clive had found Chicago in total chaos. Thousands of young Americans were converging on the Windy City determined to disrupt the Democratic Convention which the city was hosting. Student solidarity encouraged him to join the protestors, but what had started off peacefully ended up in bloodshed. Mayor Daley's thugs had tried to disperse the crowds and set upon the students who, of course, had retaliated. Clive got caught up in the rioting and witnessed at first hand the brutal beatings, which resulted in many casualties and even some fatalities. In all his twenty-two years he'd never been so scared, and it made him aware of his own impotence in the face of physical violence. However the summer of '68 was to present many new experiences, not least his visit to Provincetown, which was to provide him with a life- changing one.

'So tell me ... Provincetown is on Cape Cod?' Shirley asked.

'Yes, it's the New England equivalent of Key West.'

'Oh, I remember. The one claimed Sean O'Casey, the other Tennessee Williams,' Shirley beamed back.

Shirley certainly knew her playwrights, which was hardly surprising, since she came from quite a theatrical background herself. Most of her family had been in the film industry: her father Alfred had been a props master and had met her mother Mimi on a film set. Mimi had worked her way up to becoming a very successful continuity girl, while Shirley's Auntie Flo, her mother's sister, had been a Gainsborough Lady and a real beauty. The Morris family lived in Grange Road, opposite Ealing Studios, and very handy for work. Mimi's mum and dad lived only two doors away, which made Grandma Lucie an ideal childminder and surrogate mum. It was Lucie who took great pleasure in parading her granddaughter Shirley around Ealing Studios from a very early age, much to the admiration of casts and crews alike. Shirley had started doing extra work when only five years old and so you could also say that 'the show business' ran through her veins too.

Clive hadn't a clue that Shirley had grown up surrounded by a family who worked at Ealing Studios home to the famous Ealing Comedies and the Carry on Films. Shirley had not felt the need to volunteer any such information, and was most certainly not in the habit of bragging about her own life in the movies. She sat patiently as Clive continued to reminisce about Provincetown, explaining that as well as playwrights, it also attracted actors and directors, and stressed that it was a really beautiful seaside town, particularly after

Labor Day, when all the crowds had gone back to work, leaving the sandy beaches almost deserted in the warm September sunshine.

'It all sounds too perfect and rather romantic.'

'Shirley, it absolutely was, but a lifetime ago, and my memory plays tricks and then I get rather confused about dates.'

Shirley knew Clive well enough to realise that there was nothing wrong with his memory and allowed another silence to descend. Then he started up again.

'You know, Shirley darling, I had no idea how old Provincetown was.'

'Really?' she replied, pouring herself another Scotch and checking her watch: it was only half past six, and she knew she had masses of time before the curtain came down on *Marilyn*.

'Yes,' Clive continued, 'the American Indians used to summer there, long before the white man came. It got so hot inland that they moved out to the coast with their wigwams and cattle so as to enjoy the cooler air and sea breezes. They found the dunes tree-lined and that provided them with adequate fuel and shelter.'

'Didn't the Pilgrim Fathers land there too?'

'Yes, that's right ... and the Vikings before them. I remember visiting the Viking Wall, at the west end of town, a sort of monument to the explorer Leif Erikson. But all those foreign invaders chopped the trees down to build shelters and soon the dunes began shifting and that changed the entire nature of the place.'

'I suppose that's what drove the Indians out?'

'Yes, eventually, but what is fascinating is that the Pilgrims didn't stay there long either. They went south and founded the settlement of Plymouth, but they continued their association with Provincetown by shipping their "deviants" back there. It became a refuge for criminals and pirates and anyone else who didn't quite obey their rules or fit in with their ways ... if you know what I mean?'

'And I suppose you're going to tell me there has been a gay

community there for centuries.'

'Yes, in a way that is probably the case. I was told that by 1680, two settlements had been established, and there were probably "deviants" living in both of them. One was at Long Point and the other was out at Herring Cove, where the gay beach is now located. That settlement was then known as Hell Town, and it's certainly turned into one hell of a gay paradise now. It was in the thirties that the artistic set started to move in. In those days it was relatively inexpensive to live there, and the sort of place struggling creative folk could well afford. Nowadays, the holiday crowd tend to hang out at the rather posh, and I think somewhat overrated, Atlantic House.'

'So where did you stay?'

'Oh, back in the sixties I couldn't afford anywhere there on Macmillan Wharf. So I wandered along the seafront and found a guesthouse called Reveller's Den and booked a room.'

Clive remembered it was cheap and cheerful, clean and comfortable enough for the student he was then. A typical New England affair, built in wood, with a veranda that seemed to encircle the entire building. The owner, a beanpole of a man who answered to the name of Ned, showed him to a room that looked right on to the beach. Ned told him that he had missed the crowds and that after Labor Day there wasn't much action of an evening. As things transpired however, Clive was to prove him quite wrong.

Ned suggested he stop by for a drink when he'd finished unpacking and have a beer on the house. Clive travelled light in those days and so in no time at all found his way back to the front door, where there was a bar just next to the office. Ned made him feel most welcome, poured him a glass of lager, and introduced him to the three men sitting on bar stools. However, one of them, a handsome blond who'd made an immediate impression, unfortunately announced that his lunch break was over, and that he had to get back to work. Clive bought a round of drinks for the two men remaining, but the absentee soon became the main topic of conversation. Needless to say, the fellow on his lunch break was Dennis, Provincetown's resident lifeguard, and he was on duty.

'Shirley, that's where I saw my first lifeguard in the flesh, and he was such a handsome blond hunk. The sort of Adonis you know exists but whom you never actually meet in real life. I just couldn't take my eyes off him, even though I knew it was rude to stare. Anyway, he didn't stay long and nor did I, since I soon realised it was well past my lunchtime.'

Clive had only eaten a muffin with his morning coffee before boarding the Greyhound Bus to Provincetown, and was absolutely starving. So off he trotted into town, found a sandwich bar, and ordered a triple-decker and another beer. The weather was nice and warm, so he sat outside to enjoy the New England sunshine, while munching his way through his enormous sandwich.

'I must have been feeling a bit tipsy after so much to drink, so rather than explore the bars Ned had told me about, I made my way back to Reveller's Den and decided to take a nap.'

'So Dennis was a blond?' asked Shirley.

'We all had such long hair in the sixties, and his framed his bright blue eyes and button nose, and hung down the back of his thick bull of a neck.'

In all the years Shirley had known Clive, she'd never heard him be so animated about another man's sex appeal. Whether by choice or accident, Clive had now settled into a celibate lifestyle and, like so many gay men of his generation, was far too cautious to engage in any casual brief encounter. The same could be said about Shirley, whose first and only husband had been killed in a car crash some years ago. At work, she had kept quite quiet about that side of her life and, apart from Clive, Shirley was never known to be seen on the arm of another man and it was clear to everyone at Spoke Associates that Miss Morris had no intention of getting hitched again. So, in a way, they had much in common. The Clive Spoke she knew rarely got involved and neither did she, for that matter. Her boss was also too professional to allow any of the fine specimens currently on his books to impinge on his emotional radar. Consequently, Clive's new display of total frankness was giving her a good deal of vicarious pleasure, so she urged him on further.

'And the bod?'

'Your classic "V" shape. Muscular arms with broad, tanned shoulders tapering down to a tiny waist, and narrow hips that stood firmly on good strong legs.'

'Not at all like your average lifeguard then,' she chuckled.

'In a place like "P"-Town, I suppose showing off the beauty of your maleness was an everyday occurrence in the daily routine of a lifeguard. I figured that anyone who worked out that much must have wanted to be admired and, for once in my life, I conquered my English lower-middle-class sense of guilt and simply enjoyed staring at him.'

'Clive, you're such a Brit!'

'To us in the sixties, working out seemed rather ridiculous and besides, I was such a weed myself: barely five foot eight, with no muscle definition to speak of. Seeing Dennis look like that made me realise that I had to get myself into shape and do something about my skinny little self.'

'So Dennis is responsible for your regular visits to the gym?'

'Absolutely, and I have to thank him for the Mr Muscles you now see standing here before you.'

'You're a caution!' giggled Shirley.

'Oh, you may laugh, but working out did improve my chances on a Saturday night back in London, in the good old days of the Huntsman. That basement Soho club was a really popular meeting place for us gays after the law changed in '67, and it provided me with a regular supply of admirers, I can tell you.'

They both burst into uncontrollable laughter. Then Clive sat upright and what had appeared to be laughter evolved into what

Shirley took to be a coughing fit, until she realised that actually he was quietly sobbing. Shirley simply took Clive's cup out of his hands, stood behind him and put her arms around his shoulders, comforting him as best she could.

'I think you need a Scotch and I need the loo,' she said, and briefly bade leave of him.

It struck Clive how deeply he regretted having lost touch with his 'Columbus boys' and the rift that he had largely engineered. He had been devastated by the death of his mother two years previously, but suddenly discovering that the man who had played such an important part in his emotional development had died of AIDS made him realise that he had lost a dear old friend and that his own life could now also be in the balance.

Shirley interrupted his reverie, and as they embraced Clive volunteered: 'Listen, Shirl, I think I'll head home.'

'Do you want me to call you a cab?'

'No, I need to walk for a bit. I'll pick one up in Saint Martin's Lane.'

'Are you sure you don't want to go to Joe's for a bite?'

'Now, Mummy dearest, I'll have some soup when I get in … then it's early to bed for me. I'll be fine, really; I just need to clear my head a little and think things through before the morning. This awful news has really knocked the stuffing out of me.'

Then, almost out of the door, Clive turned back, blew Shirley a kiss and whispered: 'Don't worry. I'll call you from the airport.'

CHAPTER TWO

PROVINCETOWN REMINISCENCE

Clive left his office in Cecil Court, and as he turned into Saint Martin's Lane he hailed a taxi and was back home in Ladbroke Terrace in no time at all. The shock of losing his ex had affected him badly and, try as he might, he just couldn't drop off to sleep. Memories of his first encounter with Dennis in Provincetown kept going round and round in his head and so he decided to get out of bed and fix himself a cup of cocoa. As he sat nursing his hot drink, his mind went racing back to the summer of '68. What a time he'd had on that first visit to the United States, when he had found the country in such turmoil.

He had gone out West on the pretext of visiting relatives, but in Chicago he'd got involved in a big student rally. Thousands of young Americans had converged on the Windy City, determined to disrupt the important Democratic Convention which the city was hosting. At the time, the war in Vietnam was polarising so many U.S citizens, and the youth of America had galvanised itself and come in their thousands to protest against the war and hold a demonstration there.

President Lyndon B. Johnson had become so besieged by the anti-war movement, he had encouraged the CIA to launch Operation Chaos, a domestic surveillance scheme devised to investigate any expected protest meeting and enable city police to receive several days' advance training from the US government's Clandestine Services Division, which equipped them to deal with rallying protestors. The emergence of the Black Panthers and the upset caused by the two Kennedy assassinations had contributed to the breakdown the sense of idealism that had existed in the States during the early sixties. Then, to cap it all, there was the murder of Martin Luther King Jr., which had led to rioting in many American cities, adding racial unrest to the general mood of disenchantment.

But back in Ladbroke Terrace, it was his memories of Provincetown that held his attention, and he soon pictured himself back in his room at Reveller's Den. He remembered that from his open window there was an excellent view of the sea in two directions and, as he looked along the beach that day, he found it almost deserted, and the cool sea breeze on his cheeks helped sober him up a little. The details of his first afternoon came back to him so vividly, he felt he could actually see the chair on stilts where Dennis was perched on lifeguard duty. It was an easily recognisable landmark, and with the surrounding flags flapping vigorously and the sea getting a lot rougher, it occurred to Clive that Dennis should be keeping a watchful eye just in case any of the last few remaining bathers got into difficulty. However, Clive did notice that although on duty, it didn't prevent said fellow from being deep in conversation with one of the guys Clive had met in Ned's bar at lunchtime: a well-built, good-looking man, about thirty, with a rather charming smile.

Clive reflected that in those days he'd been rather timid and so, after taking a quick shower and attempting to conquer that Englishman's self-consciousness of his, he finally decided to pluck up the courage and take a closer look at the two men. He soon packed a canvas bag, left through the door that led directly out onto the veranda and, skipping down the wooden staircase adjacent, he jumped onto the pure white sand that stretched down to the sea. Turning south along the beach, he headed towards the lookout post but walked along the water's edge, in order to maintain a safe distance and avoid giving the impression that he was interested in joining the two men he'd just spied.

As they came into sharper focus, Clive could see that the taller of the two appeared to be grinning and shuffling sand from one foot to the other, while the lifeguard, now down from his perch, had begun to swing his left arm backwards into ever-increasing circles, keeping his right hand firmly attached to one leg of that high chair of his. His arm-swinging grew more and more energetic until it suddenly propelled his body up into the air, culminating in a graceful descent, which climaxed in an acrobatic finale of deep knee squats. Clive's vivid imagination led him to believe that the athletic display had been intended for his benefit alone, such was his continued captive rapture. It certainly could not have been idle conversation that held the other man's attention, any more than it was that tall chair holding Clive's.

Even though he was back in his bedroom in Ladbroke Terrace, that great Spoke visual memory enabled him to relive his afternoon in Provincetown, and he felt as though he was fast-forwarding a film. In it, he could see himself keeping close to the waves breaking along the beach, and finally pitching his site on a raised dry sandy mound a fair distance away from the lookout post. He emptied the contents of his bag onto the towel he'd spread out and stripped down to his red and white swimming trunks. The ritual of smothering his puny body in suntan oil over, he collapsed onto his knees, turned onto one side and faced directly into the sun, benefiting from the last of the day's rays, which most people believe gives the best tan. To read or not to read, that was his dilemma, and he finally cast his copy of *Last Exit to Brooklyn* to one side and sat up again. It was then he noticed that his two men had split up and the darker of the two was walking away along the beach in the opposite direction.

Then the lifeguard suddenly threw himself down from his chair, broke into a fast run and made straight for the sea, his great thighs cutting through the waves, and galloping over them before hurling himself headlong into the ocean. At first, Clive had thought the lifeguard's sudden action heralded the likelihood of a swimmer in distress. Then, through his binoculars, he could see that was indeed not the case and, with his aided field of vision, he began to focus on the powerful overarm action of the chap who had captured his admiration. He could see that Dennis was now racing far out to sea, and had become a mere speck on the horizon in no time at all. As a result of all this excitement, Clive felt he needed to cool himself down, and although not really at home in the sea and consequently not a strong swimmer, he nonetheless decided he would take a dip. The water was warm and inviting and after splashing around for a token five minutes, he dried off, felt refreshed and was able to return to his *Last Exit*.

He soon realised the sun had shifted and so had to alter his position in order to acquire the maximum benefit of its dying rays. It was then he noticed his lifeguard coming along the beach in his direction, now wearing a faded pair of denims, a white T-shirt, and had a duffle bag slung over one shoulder. Because the chap sported a pair of reflector sunglasses, Clive found it difficult to determine whether he'd been spotted or not; however, as Dennis approached he gave a friendly wave, and Clive's reciprocal wave back encouraged the lifeguard to change direction and make straight for him. To this day, Clive had never forgotten the exchange that followed.

'Hi! How are ya?' the lifeguard asked.

'I'm very well, thank you.' Clive replied. 'It's just lovely here.'

'So you really are English.'

'Yes, from London. Where are you from?'

'Columbus ... Ohio.' And without prompting, he threw his towel down onto the sand, right up against Clive and sprawled out, clearly enjoying soaking up the last of the warm September sunshine. 'You know, I've never been to London.'

'And I'm ashamed to say, I don't know exactly where in the USA Columbus is. I mean, geographically speaking.'

'Oh, it's due south of Detroit, about seven hundred miles or so. I'm only here lifeguarding during my summer vacation.'

'So you're a teacher?'

'Close! I'm studying to be an elementary school teacher … You're probably thinking I'm too old to be a college student, but I only quit the military last year.'

In fact, other thoughts were occupying Clive's mind, while at the same time he fought hard not to brush up against Dennis's powerful shoulder.

'In England we call that primary school. We have an excellent approach called the Montessori method, which I know a little bit about,' added Clive, in an attempt to keep his mind focused on educational issues.

'Oh yeah! I've heard about that system. You know, we may speak the same language, but we sure as hell don't use the same terminology … I suppose I always wanted to teach, but for personal reasons I decided to join the marines and then went ahead and signed up for six years. Crazy, I know, but it seemed right at the time. Anyway, that's enough about me. What do you do?'

'I'm still at university too. I don't really know what I'm going to do when I leave. I've still got one more year to go. Sometimes I think I'd like to be an actor, but doesn't everybody? If I had the talent, I suppose I'd try to get into RADA – the Royal Academy of Dramatic Art.'

'You Brits with your royal this and that,' Dennis smiled.

'Look here, I'm very proud of our royal family!' Clive responded with what he hoped came across as mock indignation. He didn't want to spoil their first meeting by having an argument; it would have been terrible to have fallen out over the Queen.

Fortunately, Dennis didn't seem to want to be drawn into a political discussion either. 'Say, what's your name again? Oh yes, of course, it's Clive.'

' Yes, Clive Spoke. And you're Dennis, I remember.'

'That's right, Dennis Montrose,' he said rather formally and they both shook hands.

Then, looking up and down the beach, he observed, 'It gets pretty quiet out here now after Labor Day. In fact, I finish my duties the day after tomorrow.'

'I suppose there can't be too many stragglers left to save right now,' Clive agreed jokingly and changed his position in an attempt to avoid contact with that well-formed torso, which had brushed up against him.

'I plan staying out here till my money runs out. I need a vacation too, y'know, and school doesn't start up again until October tenth. How long are you staying for?'

'A couple of weeks I think. This is my first day.' And Clive put his T-shirt back on.

'Once the sun goes down, it does begin to get a little chilly. I suppose it's time to make a move.' And with that, Dennis sprang to his feet.

'Yes, it is getting a bit nippy ... actually, I saw you earlier on in the bar at Reveller's Den. That's where I'm staying, by the way.' And then Clive plucked up the courage to ask: 'Would you like to come back for a drink?'

'Sure.' Dennis's reply came back without hesitation.

As they walked along the beach, Clive tried to steer the conversation towards the many differences that exist between the British and American educational systems. The temperature had dropped quite a bit, and a shiver went through his body, which Dennis was quick to pick up on.

'Now, you should take a hot shower as soon as we get there. In fact, I wouldn't mind one myself.'

Clive remembered thinking that he couldn't get over how easy it had been to get his new acquaintance back to his room. At the time, he admitted that he was also entertaining other thoughts about his new friend, such as getting him under that hot shower and then into bed.

However, he also recalled that the cold seemed to have taken over his senses and by the time they finally reached their destination and climbed the stairs up to the veranda, he was actually shivering.

'Yes, I do feel rather cold.'

'That's only natural. In the daytime, your body temperature builds up a good deal, and that's why you now feel the cold more keenly. In future you should remember to pack a sweater. Now, just get straight under the hot water. Go on – and that's an order!'

'There's a bottle of whisky on the dressing table,' Clive yelled out from the bathroom. 'I wouldn't mind one myself,' he said, thinking that it might help steady his nerves.

'That's a great idea,' Dennis shouted back, then after a moment he arrived with a glass of whisky in his hand and pulled the shower curtain gently to one side. 'Here, this should warm you up.'

Clive laughed as the water streamed down into the glass.

'Better drink it quickly before you drown it,' Dennis advised.

'Where's yours?'

'I couldn't find another glass.'

'It's over there by the washbasin.'

With such vivid memories of that first encounter flashing past him, Clive sat up in bed and was now wide awake. He could visualise Dennis letting go of the shower curtain and walking away. However he also remembered how aroused he had become, and, on reflection, he wondered whether it would have been better to have taken a cold shower instead, to cool his ardour. Dennis, on the other hand, appeared not to be in the slightest bit interested, removed the extra glass, went back into the bedroom and poured himself a Scotch.

'I feel a lot better for that. It's your turn now.' And Clive handed Dennis a spare towel as he breezed back into the bedroom.

'No worries, I'll use this one,' and Dennis waved his beach towel as he disappeared round the bathroom door.

Clive had tried hard to contain his excitement that day, because in less than twenty-four hours of arriving in Provincetown, he had pulled, and he just couldn't quite believe his luck. With someone who was almost the embodiment of a gay myth; a nude Adonis who could have walked right out of one of those physical culture magazines he'd always been too uptight to buy. Now fiction was fact and this sexy ex-marine had come back with him to his room, and was now in the bathroom. However, Dennis didn't seem to want to spend long under the spray, unlike the Englishman for whom a hot shower was still something of a real treat, if not an indulgence.

'Now I feel all warmed up too,' said Dennis as he re-entered the bedroom, sat on the only chair in the room and was more than happy to receive a top-up. 'Say, what are you doing about dinner?'

'No plans,' said Clive. 'I hadn't thought about it.'

'Why don't we have a bite together?'

'That's a splendid idea.'

'Then we can go to Vanessa's.'

'What's Vanessa's?'

'It's a gay bar that's still open after Labor Day. My girlfriend Marianne knows Vee, the owner, real well. We always go there. You'll love it.'

'Is Marianne from Columbus too?'

'No. I just met her last summer. Marianne has a house out here, but she packs up after Labor Day like most folk in 'P'-Town, and she went back to New York a few days ago.'

Then Clive remembered how confused he'd been at the time: the chap wasn't gay after all and this Marianne was his girlfriend. Suddenly the thought entered Clive's head that Dennis might be bisexual. Clive had never been able to decide whether men like that were simply queer but were unable to come out of the closet completely. Consequently, it had crossed his mind that if that really were to be the case, it meant that the American was in the fortunate position of being able to enjoy the best of both worlds, and that made him appear even more desirable to Clive.

'Tell me Dennis, why did Marianne buy a house here? Everyone knows that Provincetown's a well-known gay resort.'

'She bought it after she divorced her husband. She has a lot of gay friends in 'P'-Town. They're a great laugh, and I guess she likes being around them. For that matter, so do I!'

The conversation had now become thoroughly ambiguous and Clive didn't know where he stood with his ex-marine. He just couldn't decide whether he was being led up the garden path or whether Marianne was just another fag hag.

'Look Clive, I need to get back to my rooming house, change into something warmer and pick up some dough.'

'That's fine ... I don't feel like eating too early.'

'Me neither.'

There then followed the first uneasy pause between them since they had met, and Clive wondered whether Dennis was wavering under pressure. On the other hand, he felt the lifeguard was big enough and more than able to extricate himself from what might have become an uncomfortable situation. Clive averted his gaze towards the window, noticed that the light outside had been fading and, realising that they had almost been sitting in the dark, he reached across and switched on the bedside lamp in an attempt to ease the atmosphere.

'Look Dennis, I'll understand if you change your mind about dinner. Anyway, I'll see you on the beach tomorrow.'

'No worries! I'll be back .– I'll see you in an hour.'

Dennis picked up his bag, and as he went to say goodbye, Clive wasn't at all sure whether he was going to take him in his muscular arms, or shake him by the hand. In fact he did neither, and gently tapped him on the shoulder, swiftly turned and walked out of the veranda door, leaving Clive in a mild state of shock.

It still struck Clive that it had been one of the most exciting encounters he'd had that summer. Such typical understatement: it had been *the* most exciting.

Nevertheless, there was a possibility that Clive might be dining alone that evening, such was his uncertainty about his new beach buddy. He recalled that this line of thinking led him to take his time and dress slowly for dinner, and, after a while, he made his way to the bar for another Scotch and invited the owner to join him. So. deciding to steer the conversation away from lifeguards and the like, he asked Ned: 'What other tales do you have to tell me about Herring Cove Beach?'

'Say, did I mention the Mooncussers?'

'The what?' spluttered Clive, almost choking on his drink.

'The who, actually. It was the name given to the folk who lived here when it was called the Province Land. The Mooncussers used to go out at night carrying lanterns up and down the coastline, in an attempt to lure ships to their doom. Some stupid ship's captains would think that these lights signified that they had found a safe harbour and then they would steer their boats in that direction, only to flounder and perish on the rocks. These local guys were no amateurs, you know. They were brilliant at stealing floating cargo while watching the ships go down and sink with their crews still on board.'

'But I still don't understand why they were called "Mooncussers".'

'That's because whenever there was a full moon, it was bad for business and the Mooncussers could be seen swinging their lanterns to no avail and cursing at the moon as its beams guided the ships away from the rocks.'

'It sure wasn't known as Hell Town for nothing!' Clive laughed.

Then, as he entered the bar, Dennis interrupted Ned's tale with:

'It sure as hell wasn't.'

'So Dennis is your date! You English may come across as all shy and retiring, but when push comes to shove, you sure do know how to get your act together.'

'Honestly Ned, I'm only trying to do my bit for Anglo-American relations,' Clive responded in his poshest English accent.

It was well after nine and Clive was starving, so he was relieved when Dennis declined Ned's kind offer of a drink. They were thus able to beat a polite but hasty retreat from Reveller's Den, leaving Ned to think whatever he damn well liked and not be too offended that they had declined his hospitality. Clive remembered that, once outside, he began to take in the local architecture as they made their way along Town Beach towards Macmillan Wharf.

'I love those turrets you see on top of a lot of the houses along here.'

'Yes, they're quite a feature in New England,' Dennis replied. 'They're called "widows' walks".'

'Oh, really! How did they get to be called that?'

'The story goes that they were built for the wives of the ship's captains, so that they could get a good view of the sea while keeping watch and waiting for their husbands' boats to return. All too often they didn't come home and many of the wives were left widowed, and that's how these lookout turrets got their name.'

'Well Professor Montrose, you certainly know your local history.' To which Dennis, sensing that Clive was sending him up, changed the subject and pointed to a restaurant.

'Say, why don't we go there. Do you do fish?'

'I love fish, and it must be good here on the Cape.'

'It sure as hell is. There's been fishing on Cape Cod since the American War of Independence. They used to salt the catches and ship them out to Europe.' Now Dennis was clearly playing Clive along, and enjoying the role of Professor Montrose.

'So please mister teacher sir, what else can you tell me about the

Province Land?'

'Well, that all depends on whether you allow me to give you an examination later. Of course, I mean in order to test your knowledge of local history.'

'Please sir, can we eat first? I'm ravenous.'

'Certainly, my boy. I hoped you'd say that.'

As they tucked into a delicious dish of roast cod and baked potatoes, Dennis refilled their glasses, and continued his history lesson. 'By 1840, the inhabitants here became rich and very respectable. They exported salt, whale oil and dried and salted fish all round the world and the Town Beach was used as a road, and this became a very busy and prosperous port. Then a most mysterious thing happened.'

'I say, the plot thickens!'

'Yes, as a matter of fact, it did. The town records suddenly disappeared without trace.'

'How extraordinary! But why?'

'It was suspected, but never proven, that the old families that had become so rich and powerful from the whaling industry wanted to cover up their criminal ancestry. So they conspired to get the town records stolen so that they could never have their respectability challenged. Anyway,' Dennis's lesson continued,'by the end of the nineteenth century, the so-called leading families took a slide because the kerosene lamp had been invented; the whalers went out of business and the town became very run down.'

'So when did the faggots start coming here?'

Clive had caught Dennis in the middle of a mouthful and he almost choked on his food. He took a large sip of wine and fixed Clive with his piercing steel-blue eyes. 'Why did you use that word? Surely you must know how coarse it is. And, besides, aren't you gay yourself?'

'Yes of course I am. Aren't you?'

'No, Clive … I'm sorry to disappoint you, but I'm not!'

CHAPTER THREE

PAN AM FLIGHT 101 TUESDAY

In Ladbroke Terrace, Clive woke early, he had breakfasted on tea and toast, and was ready and waiting to go with his luggage all packed. Despite several nightcaps before turning in, he had not slept at all well and it showed. Memories of Provincetown had been swirling round in his head, preventing him from having that good night's sleep he so cherished. Without his habitual eight hours, he could be thrown into a foul temper, which was known to upset him for the rest of the day.

Shirley had become very practised at reading such sleep-deprivation signals, and often, on arriving at the office and having taken stock of the state her boss was in, would make herself scarce after a quick cup of coffee, and leave the rest of the staff to deal with Clive. After all, Spoke Associates had by now assigned a number of artists to her guardianship and her occasional disappearances were consequently a matter of course, although, truth to tell, on a really bad Clive day she was more likely to be found at the hairdressers. Not that her gorgeous auburn locks needed too much help, you understand, although she was in the habit of encouraging her

French coiffeur, Olivier, to liven up the colour from time to time.

Clive could go on and on about the problem of lack of sleep to the point of obsession and, such was his self-control, he was even known to drag himself away from an event he was particularly enjoying once the clock had struck one, thus creating his own brand of Cinderella vanishing trick. Mr Spoke maintained that an orderly lifestyle produced healthy results and believed that his youthful forty-year-old appearance was due to self-discipline, exercise and moisturiser, but not necessarily in that order of importance. He also freely admitted that Shirley's strict attention to his dietary needs, as well as her shopping tactics, ensured that he ate well and regularly, and this, combined with his daily visits to the gym, resulted in his keeping in such very good shape.

The black cab that Shirley had ordered pulled up outside 18 Ladbroke Terrace slightly ahead of time and, as Clive opened his front door to the smiling cabbie, he could smell the fresh spring morning air and noticed that early rain had left a fine patina of glossy moisture on the road surface outside. He was travelling fairly light that day but still couldn't get everything into one case, so the London taxi driver helped him get his large suitcase up front, into the driver's area, while Clive boarded the large passenger compartment behind with some hand luggage, and stretched out along the roomy back seat. Hours of travel lay ahead: first to New York, then changing planes at Kennedy Airport for Columbus, Ohio. The traffic out to Heathrow was reasonably light that morning and he was more than confident that he would arrive in good time to catch his plane. Such was not always his experience, since only ten days previously, he'd nearly missed his flight to Los Angeles because of a bottleneck on the Hammersmith flyover.

Lately, he'd got to know the West Coast well and he really enjoyed the laid-back atmosphere he found in California. His frequent LA visits were largely due to Anthony Pollard, one of Spoke Associates' most cherished clients, who'd become the toast of Hollywood that year following his Oscar-winning performance in *The Butler*. This had clearly boosted Clive's own reputation no end and so, once again, that Spoke nose had paid big dividends. This resulted in what some of his colleagues admitted was the beginning of a burgeoning international career for both him and Mr Pollard. In addition to this, recent Broadway seasons had recognised the success of several West End plays, and, due to a healthy reciprocal agreement between British Equity and its American counterpart, it was now quite commonplace for London productions to transfer to New York, and this had proved quite lucrative for Spoke Associates and several of Clive's clients.

The English had landed.

However, at present, Clive was much more preoccupied with the notion of take-offs. No matter how many flights he'd taken, he still experienced minor panic attacks as his plane raced for levitation and he felt his own life was in the balance. He had to will himself to relax, and lessened the tension in his fingers by forcibly releasing his grip on the armrest of his seat. There was that terrible moment when he seemed to leave his stomach behind him and had to wait for it to return to its rightful place once the aircraft had levelled out and attained the horizontal. It wasn't until the seat-belt sign had been switched off and the first dry martini was safely in his hand that he felt he could tell himself that, provided there was no turbulence, the worst was over.

As his taxi swung past the Hogarth Roundabout, fears of flying were replaced by thoughts of Dennis and his first visit to Columbus in '76. Although it was eight years since they'd last met, Dennis had invited Clive to his home town and even paid for his airfare. He also remembered now that it was on the pretext of Clive meeting Michael Poledri, who had become Dennis's partner. Then he recalled the time when Dennis had invited him to join a skiing trip to Aspen, but that had been in the spring of '79, some three years later. Up till then, there had been almost no communication between them whatsoever, and at the time, Clive had been really surprised to hear from Dennis, who was apparently travelling without Michael.

So it was decided that Clive would join his Columbus buddy in Colorado and, because the pressure of work at Spoke Associates had been building up, Shirley encouraged her boss to take a break. However, she had absolutely no idea that he was meeting up with his Dennis and had just assumed that he had gone on a skiing holiday on his own.

Clive remembered that in Aspen he had found Dennis in a rather agitated state. It transpired that his life had got rather out of control of late, and that he had got mixed up with a very fast crowd. After they had finished dinner, Dennis told Clive that there was a very important matter he wanted to discuss with him, but that he didn't want to spoil their first evening together and said it could wait till the following morning. However, by the next day, the American seemed much more relaxed and when Clive reminded him that he thought he had something pressing to tell him, Dennis laughed the whole thing off, said he was just feeling a little depressed and left it at that. Nevertheless, before Clive flew back to London, Dennis did ask him to promise that should anything untoward happen to him, Clive would always keep an eye out for Michael. Now in retrospect, the thought crossed Clive's mind that Dennis must have got into some sort of trouble but, at the time, Clive never found out what it might have been. He was sure his chum could not possibly have anticipated that he would develop AIDS, since the health problem didn't really begin to spread until well into the eighties. At any rate, a promise was a promise and he was determined to keep his to Dennis: in a crisis, he would always be there for either him or Michael.

As his taxi headed out to Heathrow, Clive recalled that his first visit to Columbus had also been in the month of April, only at that time, he was already in the States, visiting his dear friends the Carlsbergs, who lived in New York on West 89th Street. He had known Susan and Martin for years, and like so many New Yorkers, they were great fun to stay with, most generous and very hospitable. The fact that they lived in a very glamorous penthouse on the Upper West Side may also have contributed to how much he relished staying with them. On that occasion, he was flying to Columbus from La Guardia Airport, and although crossing town had been quite straightforward, the moment he reached the Hudson Freeway, he had hit thick traffic all along the East River and his taxi was reduced to a snail's pace. True, it was the Easter weekend, but according to the yellow cab driver, the hold-up was due to the Jewish holidays. He explained to Clive that thousands of folk were making their way down from Queens and heading out to Long Island in time to celebrate Passover. For the moment, it had slipped Clive's memory that these two religious events often coincided, but he was even more surprised to learn that the 'Paschal Feast', as his driver called it, was what was almost bringing the highway to a complete standstill.

When his taxi finally reached La Guardia and pulled up outside the American Airlines terminal, he found that the Bicentennial celebrations were in full swing and the entire building was decked out in red, white and blue. Souza marches blasted out from every loudspeaker and there was a carnival atmosphere throughout the terminal building. Clive loved visiting the States and that particular year of the Bicentennial made him sense an even closer affinity with his American cousins. Also, the deep passion that Dennis had awakened in him years earlier had made him feel eternally grateful to that 'Land of the Free', which had contributed to his own new sense of liberation. So, amidst the slogans, banners and razzle-dazzle, Clive had boarded his Dallas flight, AA175, and the party atmosphere continued in the plane until the first stop delivered him up in Columbus.

Clive's reverie was interrupted with a jolt as his black cab came to a halt outside Terminal Three. He was soon checking his luggage through to its final destination and collecting his boarding passes.

Then he made his way to the Pan American passenger lounge and there, without any warning, sat Shirley. She was wearing a stylish tailored Jean Muir suit in charcoal grey over a very simple white cotton blouse, tiny gold stud earrings and had her late Auntie Flo's mink jacket draped loosely around her shoulders, adding a degree of prosperous elegance to her entire ensemble.

'Hello, Clive darling, I'm also on my way to New York. Roberta needs sorting out and you know what she's like when she embarks on a Broadway run. At least I hope it's a run, and a long one at that. I didn't think you'd mind, but honestly, darling, we don't have to sit next to each other on the plane. I'll totally understand if you need to be alone.'

'Don't be ridiculous Shirley. And besides, I can sit on your lap, you know how much I hate take-offs.'

'By the way, before leaving for the National last night, I took the liberty of calling Michael back and giving him your flight details.'

'Oh thank you, I was going to call him from New York and let him know my arrival time in Columbus.'

'He sounded utterly charming and, after expressing my condolences, I suggested that if ever he felt like a change of scene, I would be only too happy to book his flight to London and take care of all arrangements, following your instructions, of course. After all, he is family.'

The lack of response from Clive made Shirley think that she had probably crossed the line yet again, despite her well-meant intentions. This was a common occurrence at the office, and she was just about to attempt an apology when their flight was called. Once they had boarded their plane and the self-imposed drama of the take-off was over, Clive reached down for his briefcase and took out some reading material as he heard the rattle of the drinks trolley down the aisle. They had both brought work with them to help pass the time, but as he leafed through the pages of a script, the words met his eyes but simply failed to register, and so he finally turned to his fellow passenger.

'Shirley, you know I'm just not in the mood for reading this script.'

'And, you know what? This contract can wait.'

'Maybe they'll show a good film?'

But Shirley had already double-checked: 'I'm afraid it's *The Butler.*'

So, there being no escape, a silence descended; Clive retreated back into his inner world and was reliving the dinner date he'd had with Dennis in Provincetown, that first night they'd met.

They had left the restaurant and retraced their steps, walking slowly along Town Beach. As they approached Reveller's Den, Clive made some trite remark about the lateness of the hour, which to his utter astonishment Dennis dismissed and invited himself in for a nightcap. This request threw Clive yet again, since he had decided the ex-marine was surely a lost cause. He remembered how he had attempted to disguise his confusion by performing a deep and exaggerated bow and then, in the most affected of English accents, pronounced: 'Oh, you must forgive me, Mr Montrose, but I seem to have mislaid my manners. Won't you please come in?'

To which Dennis had responded with an equally florid American Southern drawl: 'Why, kind sir, I'd be *dalighted!*'

The wine having obviously aided their performances, they raced round to the beach, climbed the veranda steps, giggling like a pair of giddy schoolgirls, and entered Clive's room through the back door so as not to be noticed by Ned.

'There's only whisky, I'm afraid,' said Clive as he poured two good measures, and they once again clinked glasses, this time reversing places with Clive taking the chair, leaving the bed free for Dennis to relax and sprawl out as he drank his Scotch.

Dennis apologised for getting so moody over dinner and went on to explain that he just couldn't stand the word 'faggot'. It reminded him of when he was in the marines and explained that whenever they went on leave in Boston, one of them would return with a story of how he'd picked up some gay and then robbed him after beating him up. It was like a terrible game they all played and it made him feel truly ashamed of himself. He insisted that the word brought those times back to him and made him feel angry with his younger self and, at the time, Clive had naturally accepted his apology.

Clive's current flashback was interrupted by the air-stewardess's eager-to- please request to her passengers: 'Would either of you care for another martini before lunch is served?'

It was a needless question, and they both politely accepted the offer graciously.

'Now come on. Tell me more about your Provincetown escapade with Dennis.'

'You know, I was just right back there myself.' And Clive explained that when dinner was over, Dennis came back to Reveller's Den; he went on to admit that things between them got rather complicated.

'In what way? Did you or didn't you?' Shirley asked.

'Well,' Clive replied, 'after making it abundantly clear that he was not gay, Dennis suddenly leaped up, pulled me out of my chair, kissed me fully on the mouth, and pushed his tongue between my teeth. He squeezed me so hard, I thought my ribs would crack. Then he let me go almost as suddenly as he'd seized hold of me and told me I was the first man he'd ever kissed.'

'You're kidding. Did you believe him?'

'Not for a moment, but I was completely nonplussed because he started to take his clothes off. So I took myself off to the bathroom and cleaned my teeth. When I came back, he'd turned out the light and was already under the covers.'

'So you did get your American dream after all?' Shirley was clapping.

'Not exactly, Shirley darling. Dennis made it quite clear that although he wanted to spend the night with me, there was to be no sex.'

'I know what I would have done.'

Clive confessed that at the time he was very inexperienced about such matters and stupidly thought that Dennis would change his mind. He didn't dare ask his new pal to leave, and simply suggested that they try to get some sleep. He then described how he had grudgingly moved over to the other side of the bed, and added that, since the two of them had only just met, he wasn't at all sure whether his new American buddy had been deliberately putting him through some sort of third degree or whether Dennis simply just couldn't help himself. 'And remember, Shirley darling, back then … I was still a virgin.' She made no response to that remark, but took another sip of her martini.

After a slight pause, Clive continued. 'I was very relieved when he got up early and crept out, trying hard not to disturb me. I must have dozed off after that, and the next thing I knew it was gone eleven o'clock and the sun was streaming through the crack in the curtains.'

'But you did get him in the end?' Shirley eagerly asked.

'Yes, actually … eventually. I have to admit that I did lose my virginity in Provincetown to that Adonis of a man.'

For once Shirley was speechless, but Clive clearly wasn't.

'He changed my life and there's not much more to tell. We continued our friendship but the basis of our transatlantic relationship was correspondence, and, I'm afraid to say, it only lasted for a couple of years. Dennis wrote wonderful letters – almost poetic, and I've kept every single one of them. But it wasn't until he invited me to visit him in Columbus in '76 that we saw each other again. You see he'd met Michael by then, and claimed his excuse for the invitation was that he wanted to know what I thought of his choice of partner and so I went … and I haven't been back to Columbus since and now I'm really dreading it.'

'I'm sure you must be.'

'Naturally I'm also very worried about this AIDS business and I'm finding it hard to get my head around it. I can't understand why it's hitting so many of my gay friends in America and for all I know, and because of my affair with Dennis, I may be in the firing line myself. You know something else, Shirley? I'm also beginning to think there's something very worrying about the way it's spreading.'

Shirley brushed his last remark to one side and assured Clive that his doctor in Hammersmith could test him for AIDS.

'Yes, of course … you're right. We'd better make that a priority and arrange an appointment as soon as I get back to London.'

Flight Pam Am 101 touched down smoothly and Clive had to admit that Shirley's lively banter had helped the time just fly by and take his mind off things. Shirley, for her part, had enjoyed being taken deeper into Clive's confidence, and she relished finding out more about his Columbus boys and what Dennis had meant to him.

She could see how anxious Clive was, so insisted on waiting with him until his Dallas flight was called, and, knowing how much he detested fond farewells in public, she swiftly took leave of him in a businesslike manner. By the time his plane had taken off, Shirley's taxi was already speeding towards Manhattan and, once over the 59th Street Bridge, she soon reached her destination: 242 East 72nd Street, between 1st and 2nd. Spoke Associates had shrewdly leased an apartment in that building on the East Side and it served as the headquarters for all its New York operations. The flat was very central and a great base, offering comfortable accommodation, as well as ample office space for all those company members who now needed to commute regularly between Broadway and the West End. This classy address provided Shirley with an impressive venue to meet her client the next morning: the up-and-coming actor Roberta Blackman.

Clive continued on the second leg of his journey, which flew him non-stop to Columbus and although he hadn't bothered to adjust his wristwatch to all the time zones he had flown through, once his plane had reached its stand he set it for 6.35 p.m., American time. He was determined to be as supportive as possible to Michael.

CHAPTER FOUR

MICHAEL POLEDRI TUESDAY

The rousing Bicentennial send-off from La Guardia in 1976 had fuelled Clive's feelings of hopeful expectation. Back then, he'd positively brimmed over with excitement as his first visit to Columbus drew near and the much-anticipated reunion with his Provincetown lifeguard and the introduction to Michael became a reality. On entering the arrivals hall he was met by a sea of expectant faces, but there was no mistaking those unforgettable piercing blue eyes and that compact muscular physique waiting for him. In the intervening years, Dennis' physical appearance hadn't changed much apart from the fact that he seemed to have lost his long blond locks. However, what really surprised Clive was that Dennis was sporting a bright pink T-shirt, showing his torso off to great advantage, signalling that he had finally come out of the closet and wanted all the world to know it. Quite a brave statement for an elementary school teacher from the Midwest.

Now, in 1984, although a similar sea of expectant faces greeted Clive, those bright blue eyes weren't there to receive him. Instead it was Michael's turn to welcome him and his gaunt, solitary figure stood there waiting. Although Clive had anticipated an emotional reunion, he was not at all prepared for his friend's open display of grief.

With his eyes brimming over with tears, Michael greeted Clive. 'You know Clive, I really am happy to see you, honestly I am. It's just that at the moment I don't seem to be able to control myself and then I get that sinking sensation and I just go. I'm so sorry, but I simply can't help it.'

Clive's body language clearly expressed what he was feeling and no words were necessary to convey the depth of the emotion he felt as they stood and hugged each other tightly. Now tears were rolling down both men's cheeks as they held each other. Finally the moment passed, and they were able to head for the airport car park, where they stopped in front of a dark brown Ford sedan, so very unlike the vehicle Dennis had come to collect Clive in on his first visit to Columbus back in '76.

That car had been Dennis's pride and joy: a bright cherry-red hard-top convertible which, he explained, he'd bought off an old friend who'd moved out of town. At the time, he didn't attempt to own up to how he'd managed to acquire the extra cash in order to afford it, but he later came clean about that side of his life. Back in the seventies, Clive had expected Dennis to own some big flash American job but was delighted at the sight of the sleek European Mercedes-Benz convertible that awaited him with its roof down. Clive's enthusiasm for the car obviously delighted Dennis, who confessed he had christened his automobile Benjy, and it must be said that Benjy's bodywork was kept in almost as pristine a condition as Dennis's.

Now, some eight years later, Michael was in the driving seat of a very different car, this time travelling east from the airport along the motorway that skirted downtown Columbus, with its tall concrete Manhattan-style skyscrapers looming up in the distance. Then they swung off the highway and took the exit leading to the

German Village section of town and Clive finally broke the silence.

'Had Dennis been in hospital for a long time?'

'No, not really, but he'd been feeling awful for months. Nothing serious exactly: nothing you could actually put your finger on, just a general malaise. Then he got this bad cold that he couldn't shake off. It was so very unlike him to be sick, so I suggested he go see Dr Levitt. Dr Levitt moved to Columbus fairly recently; he's a charming young gay man.'

'I'm afraid to say,' admitted Michael, 'with both of our lifestyles being as they were, we were often susceptible to getting "the clap" and so we made regular visits to see Allen Levitt for the cure. He became a good friend of ours, he's a Reform Jew with a busy social life so he didn't hang out with us very much. Now, with Dennis gone, he and I have got to know each other a lot better and I see much more of him.

'So, tell me Michael, what did your Allen suggest when Dennis got sick and went to see him this time?'

'At that point not a great deal, but he did insist on giving Dennis a thorough going over and a blood test. Then, weeks later, Den began to notice that his glands had swollen up. One time when I stayed over, he woke up in the middle of the night dripping with sweat. So I made him go back again the next morning and Allen gave him a further examination and took another blood sample.'

'Call it sissy, Michael, but I have to say I detest needles.'

'So did Dennis, and he loathed the idea of being sick even more.'

'What happened with that blood test?' Clive enquired.

'Allen summoned both of us to his office, and told us that AIDS had been diagnosed.'

'That must have come as a terrible shock.'

'To start with, we just couldn't take it all in, especially as Dr Levitt reckoned it had probably been dormant for some time.' Michael continued, 'In those days, neither Den nor I knew much about AIDS but, fortunately for us, Allen immediately got us an appointment to see a specialist at our local hospital here in Columbus. Dr Norris is a urologist involved in AIDS research.'

Then after a brief silence Clive responded. 'Poor Dennis.'

'You know what Dennis was like, always so fit, working out an' all. For him, being sick was a real downer and, in a way, I think he suffered more mentally than physically to start with. Finally Dr Norris told us that Dennis had a form of pneumonia, and his health deteriorated quite quickly. Shortly afterwards he was admitted to the Columbus General Hospital, where they put him on an intensive course of drugs, and, for a while, it seemed to do the trick.'

'I see, so his health started to improve?' Clive asked.

'Yes, it seemed to ... for a while. Later they discharged him with a whole batch of medication, which he took assiduously, and we just hoped for the best. That was the worst part about it – like living on borrowed time. A prolonged and difficult illness like AIDS can have a profound effect on you, mentally speaking, and it did start to make him feel like he was going crazy.'

'It sounds as though he was very courageous, which makes me feel all the more guilty for not getting out here sooner. Michael, I just wish I had known he was so unwell.'

'Honestly, Clive, there was nothing any of us could do. We just had to sit tight and wait it out. There's such a big epidemic here in America, and I'm only just beginning to get a handle on it myself. I mean, how much do you know about AIDS? I hear that back home, you've only had a few cases reported.'

Clive told Michael that he'd read only the other day that there had been about forty cases reported so far in the UK, but he understood that was quite a small number compared with the situation in the United States. He added that, while working in New York the previous year, he had become aware that a number of his gay colleagues had died of it but, at that time, it was the first he'd really heard about the damned thing. The little he'd managed to find out is that it was a relatively newly diagnosed disease and rather difficult to identify.

Then, in an attempt to lighten things up a bit he added: 'As a matter of fact, an actor friend of mine told me in all seriousness that he thought it had flown into the UK from the States on the Skytrain.'

For the first time during the journey from the airport, Michael took his eyes off the road and looked at Clive incredulously.

'No joking!' Clive continued. 'He blamed Freddie Laker's cheap flights to the US, which have been tempting us gay Brits to hop over to New York and San Francisco in droves, and gorge ourselves on the kind of bathhouses and tea rooms that don't exist back home.

'And do you think he might be right?' Michael enquired.

'Well, it's obviously an exaggeration, but what I do know for sure is that a lot of the English cases have been chaps who'd come over here and had sexual contact with men they met on holiday … and that's why I'm so worried.'

Michael's mood changed and he became rather intense and, with a formal tone to his voice, stated that AIDS stood for Acquired Immune Deficiency Syndrome. He maintained, that as far as he was aware, it was caused by some sort of transmission agent, and he indicated that evidence suggested that the so-called agent that caused the known symptoms was either a virus, bacterium, protozoa or some form of fungal substance.

'Michael, I'm afraid now you've lost me, it all sounds a bit too technical. I really don't know the difference between some of the things you're describing.'

'Yes, it is rather complicated,' Michael admitted. 'But you see I have had to get on top of all of this. Whatever this so-called agent is, it seems to cause a complete or partial breakdown of the body's natural ability to fight off disease. Apparently it can lie dormant for a long time and then, for no obvious reason, the most minor of infections can come along and this agent takes hold and can pull you right down, and ultimately kill you.'

Clive didn't really want to ask the next question but he just couldn't stop himself. 'Is there a high mortality rate?'

'They reckon it really is quite high: over eighty per cent. So, ultimately, what steps in and takes advantage of the breakdown of defences and becomes the major cause of death is either a form of skin cancer known as Kaposi's sarcoma or a rare form of pneumonia, which is what killed Dennis.'

'So in the end he died of pneumonia because his immune system was so fucked.'

'Yes, in a nutshell, but they weren't able to nail the agent that caused it. Apparently they still haven't been able to come up with a positive solution and find a cure, and it seems that not every AIDS patient shows signs of the same root cause. You know Clive, there is still so much uncertainty as to why some people have more severe immune disorders than others and some live longer than others.'

'But Michael, you did say that they treated Den with some drugs.'

'Yes, that's so, and for a while it did seem to attack the pneumonia. In hospital they gave him morphine, which alleviated the pain but gave him terrible nightmares. As hard as he tried to fight back, the virus just grew stronger and finally it won. That powerful, muscular body of his just seemed to disintegrate before my very eyes and I watched him shrivel away and become an old man. I'd never seen anything quite like it and, in less than a week, Dennis had aged so badly that he was barely able to walk; he seemed to just shuffle about, constantly attached to a drip that he wheeled behind him.'

Michael's description of Dennis' last days proved too painful for Clive who, now overcome with grief, started to sob quietly.

'Honestly Clive, I didn't mean to distress you, and I realise how selfish I'm being, but you see I've had no one to share all this with, not even my own parents. Oh, don't get me wrong, my folks have been great and loved Den as a son. But there are still certain things I just haven't been able to talk about yet.'

'Michael, I totally understand and that's why I'm here. Look, you're my friend and Dennis's partner and you know I was in love with him too. I needed to know how he spent his last days. You see, I've never had to sit by the bedside of a friend who was dying, and I wasn't here to see him suffer and pass away as you were. So I need to know what he went through and I want the truth. I made Den a promise that if ever anything happened to either of you, I would always be there for you both.'

'And here you are and now you have it. He was really brave and you need to know that too.'

'It all seems so very unfair.'

'It most certainly is and that's why the current research is so important. You know they still haven't found a vaccine that can actually help restore the underlying immune deficiency that finally leads to death. We need to get to the bottom of what's causing this epidemic and why it seems to be decimating our gay community.'

'I absolutely agree with you and now at least I feel a little better informed about what we're all dealing with.'

'You know Clive, some people are calling it the "gay plague" and believe that nature is having its revenge on us for having enjoyed so much sexual freedom during the last decade.'

Michael's last remark made Clive remember the rumour he'd heard going round New York: that it wasn't nature's revenge but something a lot more sinister, and that there were even some people who thought it had been instigated by the American government. At the time, he just put it down to the kind of homophobic gossip you hear in any big city with a large gay population. Now, sensitive to Michael's distress, he was sure that this was certainly not the right moment to discuss such matters, and consequently Clive applied a much more conciliatory approach to the discussion at hand.

'But Michael, according to the little I've read, at least a quarter of AIDS patients worldwide are not homosexual men. I understand that some people receiving blood transfusions have developed it because they were given infected blood.'

'Yes, yes! I'm only too familiar with all the facts. Drug addicts can pass it on sharing needles and haemophiliacs seem to be at an even greater risk, since they often get infected by anonymous donors, and the chances of the blood banks being contaminated must be high. I suppose we should all be much more responsible and refuse to donate our blood. But the fact remains that over seventy-five per cent of the men who contract this disease in the US are gay, and this high percentage troubles and alarms me'

Michael was clearly getting upset and Clive tried to calm the situation: 'I was only trying to suggest that it's not just a gay illness, that's all and let's face it, we can't be entirely blamed for spreading AIDS and causing this epidemic. I've read somewhere that it's been going on in Africa amongst heterosexuals for a long time, and that it's only now that doctors in the West have been able to recognise it for what it is. I know it's easier for me, coming from the other side of the pond where there aren't so many cases, but it is important for us not to get all guilt-ridden and panic about it.'

'I'm sorry to have to say this, but it is easier for you, Clive. And you're right, I am panicking. Specially when they told me that because my lover had it, there is a strong likelihood that I may have caught it too. The little they do know is that it does appear to be sexually transmitted and I was told I was a high-risk candidate for catching it. Listen, buddy – I'm scared shitless!'

The brown sedan had pulled up some time ago, and they both just sat in silence in the parked car. Their discussion had once again flashed up the fact that Clive could also be at risk himself and that succeeded in distracting him momentarily. Then, when he looked back at Michael, saw the terror in his friend's eyes and the anguish he was going through, Clive became much more concerned for him, and was completely overcome with a sense of helplessness. He tried to be reassuring and silently placed his hand firmly on Michael's, which was still clutching the steering wheel.

This time it was his friend who broke the silence.

'I guess I've been wanting to let this out to somebody … and

I'm just sorry it had to be you.'

'Well, I'm not. You're why I've come to Columbus, and I wanted to be with you,' Clive responded, as he squeezed Michael's hand even tighter.

One thing's for sure, Clive, if I do have it, you couldn't catch it from me socially. I mean, not just from sitting next to me in the car, with me breathing all over you. Apparently they don't even recommend quarantine: it's fine for us to use the same towels, cups – and even toilet seats seem safe enough. However, the latest research does indicate that whatever this agent might be, it has to be carried directly into the bloodstream by other bodily fluids such as saliva, semen or piss. So transmission would almost certainly have to be through direct sexual contact. And I can assure you, I'm keeping celibate at the moment.'

'Michael, darling, that's you and me both.'

The AIDS discussion had exhausted the two of them, and they both needed to get out of the car and get some fresh air. Clive noticed that they had parked in the very same spot that Dennis had chosen the first time he'd been taken to Michael's house. Clive just stood there for a while, gazing up at the familiar two-storeyed semi-detached wooden building, but his bout of nostalgia was interrupted by the loud sound of the car boot being slammed shut.

Michael approached, carrying Clive's luggage: 'I guess it hasn't changed that much, apart from the odd fresh coat of paint.'

'It's funny how things come back to you,' said Clive, 'but I remember thinking, when I first came here with Dennis, how strange it was to enter your house by the back door, rather than using the main door to the front porch.'

At this point they both broke into laughter for the first time since Michael had collected Clive from the airport.

'Clive, let's get some dinner. I'll just go and dump the bags inside and come straight out.'

Michael lived near Ohio State University campus, and there were a number of local eateries to chose from. He selected one he usually frequented and, on entering, they were greeted by an overkeen, tall, blonde waitress, who showed them to a table for two in an empty section of the restaurant. Having seated her two customers, she brightly introduced herself.

'Hello there, my name's Heidi. Now what would you two gentlemen like to drink today? The dinnertime offer is tequila sunrise at a dollar and fifty cents.'

She almost seemed to sing the information at them and showed a great deal more enthusiasm than Clive was used to back home and so, in his most affected English accent, he responded: 'Well, I haven't had one of those in *yaarhrs* and that would do me perfectly.'

'Make it two, miss,' added Michael, and with both her customers so easily sorted, Heidi turned on her heels and went back to the bar.

'Michael, I'm sure you know that my love affair was with America, as well as with Dennis. It's so good to back in the jolly US of A.'

'I'm so very glad you've come, especially under the circumstances. Speaking of which, I wanted to ask you what Den was so mad about when he brought you to my house that first time? He was in such a temper and his face looked like thunder.'

'Actually, it was me who was furious, because he'd told me you wouldn't be at home. So when he put his key in the lock and the door was suddenly sucked inward, we were both surprised to see you standing there.'

'Oh, I get the picture.'

Dennis had taken Clive out to lunch and they'd had a bit of a row, which Clive admitted to Michael was mainly his fault. He confessed that at the time he was still infatuated by Dennis, but because his American idol had refused to sleep with him the previous night, he had started to behave badly and was having a bit of a sulk. Dennis, on the other hand, in his soft-spoken, let's-be-reasonable tone of voice, had tried to win his English buddy round, but Clive just wasn't having any of it.

'You really did know him very well,' said Michael.

'Yes. He told me how I had meant so much to him in Provincetown, and that the last thing he wanted to do was to hurt me. Back then, he actually confessed that I was the first man he had ever kissed.'

'And did you believe him?'

'I didn't know what to think and you know, in those days, I was virtually a virgin myself. But with those appealing blue eyes of his, who wouldn't believe him? But over lunch he played his ace card by telling me that the problem was that I represented a threat to his relationship with you.'

'That was so typical Dennis. As much as I loved him, I hated the way he could soft-talk his way out of an awkward situation.'

'Dennis made me feel so guilty that I just felt unable to meet you that day.'

At which point the drinks arrived with the overzealous waitress: 'Now, gentlemen, don't these look delicious? Would you like to order your food?'

'We'll have the cocktails first ... Heidi,' Michael said firmly.

'Oh, no problem sir. Enjoy! Just call me when you're ready.'

'To be honest, said, Clive, 'I just couldn't admit to myself that I'd come in search of a lost ideal, and I suppose I was behaving like an immature teenager. But what had really pissed me off was that he had given me such a warm welcome, made me feel he still cared for me, then showed me the spare room and worst of all, went off into the night and dumped me. If he'd have been going to see you, I would have understood. But no. He even told me he was off to the local gay disco to meet his friend he used to call Disco Dick. He was such a number, but you know what? I forgive him for everything, and I'm finding it very hard to believe that we've lost Dennis for ever.'

After an awkward silence, Michael admitted that Dennis was a mass of contradictions and confessed that he did know that Dennis wasn't coming over to see him that night, since he'd told his lover that he was going to stay with his parents for Easter, and they lived on the other side of town.

He went on to explain that he'd had to alter his plans because he'd gone into his studio and lost all track of the time. He had put off visiting his folks till the following day and was finishing off a painting he was working on, and was genuinely not expecting Clive that afternoon.

'Dennis had told me you were an artist and he was so very proud of your work. I remember he was quite curious to know what I thought about your paintings.'

'He was my greatest fan and encouraged me to exhibit.'

'While you were busy making coffee in the kitchen, I sidled up to one of the pictures on display in your living room, and guessed you'd painted it. Dennis followed me over and told me it was your latest work. He was as pleased as punch when I told him I genuinely liked your use of colour and texture … and I really did.'

'Yes, I remember the kind things you said. And then I asked you if you wanted to see my studio.'

'And I guess we both remember what happened next.'

'Yes, I'm not too proud about that. I seem to remember we both wanted to entice you into a threesome. It wasn't just Den's idea, you know?'

'And at first, I was just too inhibited to accept the offer. I think I said something stupid like: "Sorry chaps, but threesomes are illegal in my country," and then I ran into the bathroom and pretended to wash my hands.'

And once again Michael responded with a long silence, which Clive broke. 'I can't wait to see what you're working on now.'

'With all that's been going on lately, I haven't been able to concentrate much in my studio, but of course I'd love to show you the abstract stuff I was into last year – that is, before Den got sick.'

At this point Michael summoned Heidi over and suggested that it was time to order food.

'I can recommend the special: silverside of beef with roast potatoes at three dollars fifty,' Heidi beamed.

'Actually , I haven't had a decent hamburger since I was last in the States, and I'd really love one.'

'Wouldn't you prefer something more filling? Dinner's on me, you know.'

'Honestly Michael, I'd love a cheeseburger with fries.'

'Then that's what you shall have.'

Heidi seemed disappointed, but her face lit up when Michael ordered the silverside of beef, jacket potato, squash, horseradish sauce, salad and Jell-O, along with a good bottle of Zinfandel. 'Good choice, sir,' she announced as she disappeared to get their order.

'You must know, Michael, the last thing I wanted to do was to come between you and Den. Nevertheless, I stupidly thought that by inviting me to visit with him he simply wanted to continue our affair.'

'And he probably did. Just in case you didn't realise, Dennis and I had a pretty open relationship, especially at that time. We both had tricks on the side you know, but I suppose we never got involved with them; in my case they were just for sex. With Den, it was a little more complicated.'

'Yes, I did come to realise that, but I suppose I was just too naive and English and far too narrow-minded to get my head around all the sexual freedom you guys enjoyed here in the States.'

'I wonder,' Michael mused. 'Do you suppose those days will ever return?'

'I sincerely hope so.' Then, steering the conversation back to Dennis, Clive continued: 'I have to say I knew that Dennis had come out with a vengeance since we met in Provincetown, and that he had become aware of how attractive he was to other men. Anyway, when I woke up in his house that next morning, I did feel differently about him and realised that I had been able to shake off the power he had over me and I sensed that he hadn't quite expected that.'

'Did he act all wounded and rejected?'

'Yes, he tried that one on, and I was well aware that he had a genuinely vulnerable side, which was very endearing. But you know,' Clive continued, 'I really had grown up overnight and even surprised myself with the adult way I handled Dennis the following day. He had spent almost the entire lunchtime trying to make amends and show how fond he was of me.'

'And then I added to everyone's vexation by still being at home when you arrived.'

'Spot on ... I really thought Dennis had planned the whole thing and knew you were going to be there all along. Now I realise it was a genuine surprise for him too and that he'd been completely taken off his guard. Honestly, Michael, I wasn't upset with you, although I have to admit that I did view you as competition, but I also knew full well that you would always come first for Dennis.'

As they sat opposite each other and tucked into their dinner, which Heidi had served far too eagerly, Clive recalled the first impression he'd had of Michael. He was struck by the distinctive colour of his eyes: they were blue-green, and he still had thick dark brown curly hair and masses of it. He was also reminded that he had judged Michael highly on their first meeting and he remembered thinking how fortunate Dennis had been to find such a bright, handsome and intelligent partner: Clive could always trust that Spoke nose.

'You were in your late twenties when we first met, and because of your colouring, I remember thinking you must have been of Irish or Italian descent.'

'And you were right.' Michael proudly responded. 'Italian!'

'We were so different, not just in looks but also in temperament. I tended to blurt out the first thing that came into my head, without giving myself time to think things through. Whereas you expressed yourself in a much more considered way and were more slowly spoken. I could have been the Yank and you the Limey.'

'Clive, what I still remember about you is your zest for life and your great sense of humour.'

'You were a very striking tall young man and still are.'

'Well, that's very sweet of you to say, but I'm really not feeling my best at the moment.' Then, changing the subject he asked, 'And how's that hamburger, by the way?'

'Delicious – the best I've had in years.'

Michael poured more wine. 'This certainly is a much more relaxed meeting than our first.'

'Yes, we seemed to stand on your back porch for ages, but once the embarrassment had subsided, you graciously invited us in and offered us tea.'

'And I remember you asked for coffee.'

'I think, in my head, I was playing the Cecily–Gwendolyn scene from *The Importance of Being Earnest.*'

'The what?'

Clive didn't need to answer the question. Instead, they both burst into laughter again and clinked glasses as the wine helped them unwind.

'Look, I hope you don't mind, but I've taken the liberty of inviting my dear friend Steve Leggard over for lunch tomorrow. I don't think you met him on your first visit to Columbus, but I've known him for years, and he's one of my closest pals. Dennis told him a lot about you and he's so very keen to be introduced to you. I feel sure you two will hit it off.'

The name Steve Leggard struck a familiar chord in Clive's memory and although he was beginning to feel the effects of jet lag, his manners were still intact, and so he assured his host that he'd be delighted to meet Steve the following day. Michael picked up on the fact that Clive was beginning to fade and called for Heidi, who was devastated that her two gentlemen were going to pass on the strawberry cheesecake and coffee on offer. Clive explained he'd only just arrived from London and was exhausted, which appeared to pacify her somewhat. His host picked up the tab, left a handsome tip and as they drove back to Michael's house, Clive asked to know more about this Steve Leggard character.

'I think you'll really like him. Steve's a social worker by day and he's been very committed to assisting us in establishing a self-help group here in Columbus at what we call the Men's Center. Because of the current crisis, our main aim there is to educate the entire community about AIDS and give maximum support wherever possible.'

'And how many cases have there been here in Columbus?'

'About a dozen, so far.'

'Really! That many?'

'That's nothing to speak of, compared with Cincinnati or Chicago.'

'No, I suppose not.' And Clive tried to change the subject by asking more about Steve.

'What can I tell you? He's such a great guy and has been such a terrific help, and because he's got a lot of experience in dealing with bureaucracy and working the system, the Men's Center has benefited enormously from having him on board.'

Clive told him that there was already something similar in London, called the Terrence Higgins Trust. He explained that it was a voluntary organisation set up with the help and advice of doctors and social workers and was named after one of the first Brits to die from AIDS. Michael said he was glad that the UK was getting itself organised and agreed that it was really important to get the message across without scaring the shit out of everyone.

Back at the house, they went through the kitchen, then finally settled in the room that looked on to the street, which Clive remembered as a comfortable lounge. There by the side of one of the sofas, he noticed another pair of suitcases next to his own.

'They're mine. If you don't mind, I thought we'd stay at Dennis's old house. We'll be a lot more comfortable there. Here, there's only one bedroom cause I still use the other as my studio and besides, you can help me with all the packing up I have to do at number 257.'

Clive tried to camouflage how uncomfortable he felt about returning to Alexandria Colony Court so soon after arriving back in Columbus but assured Michael that he was there to help in any way he could. Then he added: 'I don't know about you, but I could do with a nightcap. There's some duty-free in that plastic bag, and a quickie might help me sleep better.'

Michael thought it an equally good idea and the two men drank a toast to friendship and downed their shots in one.

'The Colony has a leisure centre available to residents, and I can easily get you a pass,' said Michael.

'Yes I remember the gym and its facilities, but I'm not a very strong swimmer and will pass on the pool, if you don't mind. I never really gained my sea legs.'

Then, reminded of what a strong swimmer Den had been, Michael broke down again. Clive hugged him close and told him that he could cry whenever he felt like it and insisted that there were to be no barriers between them. 'Are we agreed?'

'Agreed! Let's get straight over to Alexandria Colony right now, and get some shut-eye.'

CHAPTER FIVE

ALEXANDRIA COLONY COURT TUESDAY AND WEDNESDAY

'I'll put the bags in the car while you lock up,' Clive suggested as he carried the luggage into the kitchen and then down the back steps. It was quite dark by now, and he found it absolutely pointless working out the time, let alone what day of the week it actually was.

As the brown sedan turned off the highway and Michael took the exit for Alexandria Colony Court South, the rows of houses they passed began to look strangely familiar to the Englishman. When Dennis had driven him there all those years ago, Clive had been struck by what appeared to him to be a very pretty little suburban toy town of a place. There was row upon row of what were – by American standards – small, two-storeyed houses with neat, low hedges and well-trimmed front lawns all joined together. All the residences seemed to be individually designed from the outside, as well as from the inside, as he was later to discover. These surroundings were in such contrast to the sprawling Californian haciendas he'd got to know on the West Coast, let alone the tall Manhattan skyscrapers with which he'd become even much more familiar.

On that first visit to Columbus, Clive recalled that before getting out of Benjy, Dennis had proudly presented him with his own set of keys with a great flourish. There was a nameplate attached, with 'Clive Spoke' printed clearly on it, and it contained the address details of the house as well as its telephone number. Clive remembered being touched by such a kind gesture and wanted to show his appreciation by giving Dennis a peck on the cheek. However the ex-marine gently pushed Clive to one side and invited him to open the front door.

'Let's wait till we're inside, shall we?'

Now it was Michael who opened the front door to number 257 and ushered Clive into the sitting room, which appeared just as he remembered. Nothing much seemed to have changed at all and, not for the first time, Clive was struck by how cosy he found the house, although it was by no means small. He had always thought the main room tastefully decorated in its varying shades of grey, with that comfortable, large sofa still taking up the entire length of one wall, while a vast bookcase occupied the opposite side of the room, with all the record albums and stereo equipment still kept just where he remembered. The long dining table was placed parallel to the rows of bookshelves, while along the third wall was an open staircase leading up to the bedrooms and a large window, looking on to the street, completed the oblong-shaped room, in the middle of which stood an enormous coffee table laden with magazines and more books.

Then Clive noticed the drawing placed in a very prominent position in one of the alcoves next to the bookcase. Back in the seventies, he'd been surprised to discover that Dennis had been an artist's model in his spare time, and, once a week on his free morning, he would drive over to the Dennison University campus and pose in the nude for the life-drawing class. On that first day of Clive's visit back in '76, Dennis had told Clive about his modelling sideline and suggested he accompany him and watch the class. As they drove out to Dennison the following morning, Dennis told Clive that in some states it was still illegal for a male model to pose completely in the nude, and he revelled in the fact that elsewhere in the US he could be accused of breaking the law and locked up in jail.

The fine art department at this university, where Michael had been a student, was long established and it struck Clive that the building in which it was housed was located in a delightful rural campus setting. Although a smaller university than Ohio State, Clive soon found out that Dennison was large enough to harbour a very first-rate reputation in both the performing as well as the visual arts.

When they entered the room Dennis introduced his guest to the tutor in charge, then Clive went and sat down on the far side, so as to be as unobtrusive as possible. Several rostra were placed up against one of the walls, forming a dais, and in a carefully arranged semicircle around this podium were a series of chairs, easels and artists' desks, as well as some expectant students. Dennis disappeared from view momentarily and, in no time at all, re-emerged stripped and stark naked, carefully placing his clothes to one side. The lesson was to last a full three hours with a short break halfway through, enabling both model and class to rest and relax their concentration. By ten o'clock the semicircle was packed, and before Clive knew it, Dennis was off.

It was so gratifying for Clive to witness the transformation in his friend and watch Dennis utterly free from the inhibitions he might have demonstrated in Provincetown. The ex-marine showed no qualms about modelling in the nude and was now more than comfortable showing off his body to great advantage, and he was clearly in his element. He flexed his muscles and his torso positively rippled. He stretched, contracted and sat; he extended, knelt, crouched and stood, each pose occupying a given amount of time in which the students had to commit a likeness to paper.

Sometimes the tutor allowed them time for fine detail; at others, she made Dennis whip through a series of positions, barely giving him a moment to think up the next move. Although he obviously adored presenting himself in the nude and gloried in his manly beauty, he seemed, at moments, to display a genuine vulnerability, which also appeared to win over the class.

Despite the strength and power of his muscular physique, Clive felt that Dennis still possessed that same gentle quality that had been so attractive all those years ago back in Provincetown. Like so many extroverts, beneath his flamboyance there was a side to his nature that demonstrated that he could be very easily wounded and it was that chink in his armour that had endeared him to Clive when they had first met.

As Dennis's parts swung free, the performer in him revelled in the keen attention he was given by all who occupied that semicircle and Clive thought it was as though the very sound of the charcoal scratching on paper stirred his friend on to create bolder and more intricate poses. The passage of time had in no way diminished his muscle definition nor the splendour of his physique, and it was little wonder that the fine art department had kept the ex-marine so very busy, and Dennis told Clive that he was in such great demand that his bookings stretched well ahead into the following year, which seemed to please him no end.

The session finished with a series of quick-fire, sixty-second poses, barely giving any of the students enough time to commit his contortions to paper. Dennis appeared to speed up towards the end, like a runner towards the finishing line, and the class erupted into an almighty cheer as he suddenly jumped down from the platform that had served as his stage. He broke into a broad grin, bowed slightly apologetically, and seemed to step into his clothes with a good deal more embarrassment than when he had stripped them off. Little could anyone there at Dennison have possibly imagined that some eight years later that powerfully built human being would be reduced to a contorted and wizened little old man.

Dennis approached Clive where he was still seated at the back of the class, beaming as he carried one of the sketches.

'Look what I've just been given.'

He was holding a life-sized drawing: it was of his arse sketched out in orange chalk, and there, appearing on the horizon of his upper thigh, were a pair of distended testicles, which dropped down into the frame.

'Isn't it great?' said Dennis.

'You both are! And who did it?'

'That beautiful quiet boy with the glasses,' Dennis responded. 'He always sits at the end of the front row. I think his name is Edward.'

Now, on his second visit to Columbus, there in the alcove hung Edward's drawing, just as Clive had remembered it, showing Dennis off in all his glory and truly in his element. Clive had been dreading that it might still be there in the living room, and, on seeing the sketch again, he fought hard to control his feelings and not completely break down in front of Michael.

But the sight of that picture on the wall brought back such vivid memories of Dennis, so fit and strong, posing nude for the art students at Dennison, it just tipped Clive over the edge and he couldn't stop himself. With tears trickling down his cheeks, he began to sob like a baby. It was now his turn to feebly apologise for his outburst, causing Michael to retaliate by scolding him for even trying, and reminding Clive of their mutual pledge of trust.

With his voice still quivering, Clive said: 'I feel a lot better for that. I suppose walking in here, seeing that etching on the wall and knowing that Dennis isn't about any longer has finally hit me and I've been wanting to really let go ever since you picked me up at the airport. Now I feel I'm ready to hit the sack.' And with that, they both got to their feet, hugged each other yet again and Michael carried Clive's bags upstairs and placed them in the guest room.

'My old room,' Clive announced, trying to put on a brave face.

'With all that closet space for you to hang your clothes in,' Michael added in an attempt to lighten things up.

'Yes… funny, I just never could learn to travel light.' Clive seemed to have composed himself, 'Now, I'd like to take a shower before turning in, if that's all right.'

'Oh puh-lease, Clive, don't even ask. Just make yourself completely at home. Remember, *mi casa es tu casa*! Clean towels are on the bed and you know where the bathroom is. I hope you sleep well.' And with that, Michael was gone, leaving Clive alone to unpack.

So there Clive was, on his first night back in Columbus, Ohio after so many years' absence, unexpectedly sleeping in his old room at number 257, Alexandria Colony Court South. As he began to hang his clothes away, he was reminded of his first visit. He had brought Dennis a house present from New York, the original cast recording of *A Chorus Line*, which Clive had seen on Broadway and, as a theatrical agent, was extremely excited about. He'd insisted on playing it, but he had noticed that it seemed to make very little impression on Dennis, who impatiently ushered Clive upstairs and suggested that he take a shower. The ex-marine seemed always to insist his friend take a shower and Clive now reflected affectionately on how he thought Americans were obsessed with cleanliness, although he was also prepared to consider that Brits, himself included, didn't pay sufficient attention to personal hygiene, especially back in the seventies.

Clive felt that the compact bathroom hadn't changed either: it was well designed and very comfortable. The washstand still sported a small portable colour television set, which, on his first visit, Clive thought the height of decadence: so he now turned it on in an effort to keep himself awake – and to see whether it still worked. It felt good under the hot water, helping him relax, but, after a while, he finally allowed his jetlag to take over and was now more than ready for bed. Once all tucked up, Clive soon dozed off and fell into a very deep sleep. The next morning he was gently woken by Michael, who was sitting at the foot of the bed.

'Did you sleep OK?'

'Like a log! I always do when I'm away from home, and to tell you the truth I didn't get much sleep last night, so the time difference didn't give me a problem.', Clive replied as he took a good long stretch. 'Although it's very disconcerting waking up in this room after all these years.'

'I suppose it must be.'

'Added to which, my body clock is all over the place. What time is it Michael?'

'It's just after ten. I didn't want to let you sleep too long because Steve is coming over for an early lunch.'

Clive nodded as he got out of bed. 'Yes, I remember."

Then as Michael stood up to leave, he asked Clive whether he would like a cup of tea in bed.

'That's sweet of you,' came the prompt reply. 'But actually I'd kill for a coffee. Do you mind?'

'No of course not,' his host replied. 'I've made some for myself anyway.'

'I'm going to get straight under that shower and I'll be right down in a shake of a lamb's tail!'

'In the shake of a what? I dunno, you Brits with your quaint expressions. I'll fix you some ham and eggs.'

'Actually Michael, I'm really not feeling very hungry. Coffee and toast will do me just fine.'

'Sure thing,' Michael shouted back, already halfway down the stairs.

As Clive showered, he remembered that Dennis telling him that after that summer in Provincetown, he had finally come out and gone wild and had been completely frank about what he was up to. Dennis had become totally uninhibited and started whoring his way around Columbus and had built up quite a clientele, mostly closeted married men to start with, but as word got around the clubs, his popularity grew and so did his bank balance. He had become aware of how much he turned men on, what the nature of that attraction could lead to and, more importantly, how much his newly acquired clients were prepared to pay for his favours.

Dennis explained to Clive he'd managed to buy Benjy from his friend Gordon with his extra earnings, and that was also how he'd been able to supplement his schoolteacher's salary. It had not been easy for Michael to accept Dennis's other profession, and Clive later found out that it was Steve Leggard who apparently had helped salvage their relationship. Dennis had even mentioned Steve in one of his many letters to Clive, and had described how it was through his guidance and support that Steve had been able to convince Michael that Dennis really valued and loved his partner. After spending just a few days with his Dennis and Michael, their affection for each other had become obvious to Clive and there was absolutely no doubt in Clive's mind about how strong their relationship had become. Steve Leggard, using all his skills as a social worker, had been able to persuade Michael that sex for Dennis was like having a glass of wine and that he simply had to get used to his lover's consumption level and just look upon the whoring as a job, which finally, and with his friend's help, Michael was able to do.

Clive, putting all such memories aside, quickly showered, got dressed, and then went downstairs to join Michael in the kitchen. However, he found him on the phone.

'Won't be a minute, Clive – please help yourself to coffee,' whispered Michael, covering the receiver. 'Yes, Allen, I have an appointment with Doctor Norris on Friday morning.' Then he turned to Clive again: 'Milk's in the refrigerator ... No, Allen, that's very kind of you, but I have a very old friend of Dennis's over from England staying with me, and he's being a real help at the moment.'

Clive poured his coffee, added one lump of sugar, got the milk and then went and sat at the kitchen table opposite Michael.

'You bet! I'll call when I get back from the hospital. Bye, Allen, bye.' Then Michael turned to Clive. 'Sorry, but I've already had my cereal. Are you sure you don't want some eggs?'

'Really, toast's just fine,' insisted Clive. 'You go ahead. I like a man who eats a hearty breakfast.'

'I can't put away what Dennis used to eat. I suppose you could say that his appetite was enormous in more ways than one.'

Clive found it difficult to respond to that one, and sat silently sipping his coffee.

'That was Dennis's doctor, by the way,' Michael continued. 'Allen Levitt.'

'Yes, I remember now, he was that doctor you used to go to for regular check-ups. He treated Den for AIDS.'

'He's been most concerned about me too.'

'I'd really like to meet him.'

'That can be easily arranged. He's absolutely charming and so committed to his work. I know you'll like him, but I wanted you to meet Steve first.'

'Yes, of course. And I do remember Dennis mentioning Steve in one of his letters, but not Dr Levitt.'

'No, possibly not. As I told you, Allen only arrived in Columbus about twelve months ago.'

'And I do need to catch up with all that's been going on … I'm afraid I've been such a terribly bad correspondent of late.'

'Clive, don't be silly – I know how busy you are. Listen, Steve is one of my oldest and closest friends. He was sure helpful to me when I first met Den, and he continues to be such a rock, I just don't know what I'd do without him!'

'Friends are so important. Which reminds me – may I make a quick call to my PA in New York? Shirley's working with one of our clients, who's appearing on Broadway at the moment, and I believe she called you and told you my travel details.'

'Yes, I had a nice chat with her and she sounded real charming.

Clive, please just go ahead and use the phone as much as you want. Don't be shy.'

'Thank you. I'll get her to call me straight back. I promised I'd let her know I arrived safely.'

'Why don't you go upstairs and use the phone in my bedroom?'

'Thank you. You see, Shirley and I have become very close friends and I'm sure she'll want to know how things are with you, too.' Clive took his coffee with him, climbed the open staircase and, as he entered Dennis's old bedroom, he found himself thinking about Dr Levitt and the blood test he'd given Dennis. Then he double-checked the Spoke Associates' New York number and soon put a call through to Shirley.

'Good morning, Clive darling. I've been thinking about you. How's it all going? Can you talk?'

'Well, as a matter of fact I'm calling from an upstairs bedroom. Michael's in a bit of a state, which is hardly surprising. Shirl, he looks terrible.'

'Is he ill too?'

'He hasn't come clean about that yet although he was told by his doctor that because his partner had it, there was a strong likelihood that Dennis had passed it on to him.'

'And what is that Spoke intuition telling you?'

· 'I think he may have it, and I'm really finding that hard to handle.'

'Oh Clive darling, I'm so sorry. I guess you have to be strong for both your sakes. Is there anything I can do? Do you want me to fly down there?'

'I'm sure you've got enough to deal with in New York. How is Roberta behaving, by the way, and have you got her sorted?'

'Oh yes! Don't worry about her. I've found her a very nice apartment on the Upper West Side, convenient for rehearsals and near to St James's Theatre, for when the show opens. She's doing fine at the moment and behaving herself so far. Clive, give me your phone number in case we get cut off.'

'You remind me of Laurel Gotleib.'

'Who's she?'

'My old friend Laurel, who I met in New York. Those were exactly the words she used when I called her from Alexandria Colony Court South on my first visit here. By the way, that's where we're staying: in Dennis's old house. Michael thought we'd be more comfortable here, as there are two bedrooms.'

'I see. And what's the number there?'

'It's 738-1383: I'm not sure what the area code is. Could you call me back?'

And in no time at all, Shirley was quick to get back to Clive. 'By the way, your area code in Columbus is 614. So who is this Laurel Gotleib, then?'

Clive explained that he had first met Laurel in the sixties, during his student days, on his first trip to New York. Laurel had been a kind of den-mother to a whole set of gay men she'd introduced him to. She was a larger-than-life character with a heart of gold, and totally dependable. He always knew he could turn to her in an emergency and she certainly proved her worth on the day of the African violet incident on his first visit to Columbus. He told Shirley all about the morning he and Dennis were having breakfast in the garden, when Dennis had suddenly got up from the table, rushed to the other side of the patio and was clearly upset about something. His marine announced that the African violet was in full bloom, so Clive followed him over and started to admire the pretty little plant. That made Dennis turn on him in a fury, announcing that whenever it flowered it was an ill omen and always brought bad luck, and he listed a series of calamities that had coincided with its flowering, including the death of his friend Gordon, his mother's car crash, and him failing some exams.

Dennis always presented Clive with such a mixture of contradictions: here was a great strapping fellow of above-average intelligence, scared shitless by the flowering of an African violet. Clive couldn't understand how he could possibly believe in such superstitious nonsense, but Dennis truly saw the plant as a danger signal and their disagreement grew into a full-blown row. They both walked away from the plant at the same time, but Dennis turned towards him in such a way that Clive thought he was going to punch him. Clive's instinct was to get out of his reach: so he turned round quickly, ducked, and opened the sliding door back into the house. Dennis immediately followed him but seemed to falter as he crashed into a chair, lurched forward and fell to the floor, clutching at his forehead with his free hand.

Dennis's speech began to slur and Clive noticed that the right side of his friend's face had suddenly contracted. He remembered his first aid, and with all the strength he could muster, placed Dennis onto the stairs so that his head was higher than the rest of his body, enabling the blood to flow away from the brain. By now Dennis appeared to have lost consciousness, which panicked Clive even more, so he decided to call an ambulance. In London he would have dialled 999, but in Columbus he hadn't a clue what number to ring and realised he was losing valuable time, so he phoned Laurel in New York, who told him to call the operator and ask for the number of the local ambulance service.

'And so what happened. Did the ambulance come quickly?' asked Shirley.

'In no time at all two men arrived, looking more like policemen than medics. I explained that I was visiting and that it was the house owner who had been taken ill. After giving Dennis a quick examination, they started to give me the third degree and claimed that I wasn't telling them the truth about what had been going on, and implied we'd got into a fight.'

'But that's absurd – and besides, you wanted to get Dennis to a hospital, and quick.'

'Shirley, that's exactly what I told them, but they got all shirty with me and accused me of telling them that they weren't doing their job properly.'

'Which of course simply wasn't the case.'

They then noticed the nude etching of Dennis on the wall; the one from the weekly life drawing class he used to model for. That threw them into hysterical laughter and they started caterwauling, mincing about and accusing him and Dennis of being a pair of fairies.

'So what on earth did you do?'

'What could I do? I protested that Dennis could be dying, and pleaded with them to get him to a hospital. Then one of them said: "He don't need no hospital, sir. After what's been going on here, he deserves the jailhouse, more like... You both do!"'

'You must have been at your wits' end with Dennis lying there unconscious.'

'The more assertive I became, the more they poked fun at us and made jokes about what happens when two sissies get into a fight and slug each other.'

'That's appalling! So then what happened?'

'I pleaded with them to help me and they finally offered to move Dennis onto the sofa, sarcastically telling me that I could nurse him better there. They briefly examined Dennis one more time, gave me a jar of aspirin, told me to give him a couple when he came round and then they simply marched out.'

'The whole episode sounds unreal. What a couple of bigots.'

It certainly shattered any illusions Clive may have had back in the seventies about how gay-friendly Americans were in the provinces – and that was long before AIDS. He told Shirley that he soon came to his senses and finally found the Poledris' number in Dennis's personal telephone book and got through to Michael's parents. By the time Michael got back home, Dennis was looking a lot better and Michael told Clive that Dennis was prone to a mild form of epilepsy and that it wasn't the first time he'd had such an attack. To be on the safe side, Michael called a cab, woke Dennis up and took him to the hospital for a check-up. Then once they had left, Clive called Laurel back.

She told him that he should do what her dead mother would have advised – may she rest in peace: 'Honeybee, If you've had a bad shock, you should always take a piss!'

'Jewish mothers always know best,' agreed Shirley.

CHAPTER SIX

STEVE LEGGARD WEDNESDAY

'That will be Steve,' Michael yelled out. 'Clive, will you let him in, please?'

So, finally, there stood Michael's dear friend, and as his lips parted to speak, they revealed the most perfect set of pure-white porcelain teeth imaginable. Steve Leggard appeared to be in his late thirties, taller than Clive and thick set with a slightly greying full head of blond hair cut fairly close to his rather podgy tanned face. He wore a wonderful smile and his bright blue eyes greeted Clive most enthusiastically.

'Hi! You must be Clive. I'm so very glad to meet you.' And they shook hands rather formally as Clive welcomed Steve warmly into Dennis's house. 'I do hope you don't consider this an intrusion – this being your first day here and all – but I just couldn't wait to—'

'Not at all, it's a pleasure to meet you too, but I've rather lost track of what day of the week it really is and—'

'Actually, Clive, if you really want to know, it's Wednesday,' Michael yelled out from the kitchen.

'Whatever the damn day is, Michael,' Clive yelled back, 'I'm so very happy your friend Steve was able to come to lunch today. Then, turning back to the newly arrived guest, he added, 'I know what a support you've been to Michael and what a good friend you were to Dennis.'

With the preliminaries over, Clive took Steve's navy blue overcoat, and ushered him into where the chef was preparing lunch.

'Now, Steve darling, we're sipping our martinis.' And Michael went over to give his dear old friend a hug. 'Won't you join us?'

'Mmm! They look delicious. I'd love one.'

'I'm rather hoping it will help me wake up a bit,' joked Clive.

'I've never known a Manhattan fail,' and as he went to toast them, Steve came in quickly with: 'And here's mud in your eye!' delivered in a Bette Davis drawl, making the other two men giggle.

'Now, why don't you two get the hell out of my kitchen,' ordered Michael, 'and go into the parlour and get really acquainted.'

They did as bidden and obediently withdrew into the front room. The central heating was blazing away and Steve removed the jacket of his pale grey suit with a flourish, revealing his matching waistcoat, now leaving both men in their shirtsleeves. As they made themselves comfortable on the long sofa and sipped their martinis, Clive, who was used to advising his clients, couldn't help but think that if his new acquaintance were to lose a stone in weight, his love handles would vanish, and he would appear much more sexy.

Clive initiated the conversation. 'Michael tells me you're a social worker, but I don't know what that actually means you do here in the United States.'

'Well, I work for an agency that finds employment for people who are either physically or mentally impaired. There are about a dozen such organisations in Ohio State alone, and they're all privately run. Ours is called Columbus Cares.'

'Does that mean you receive no financial support from your government?'

'Absolutely right. We all have full non-profit-making, charitable status.'

'I see. So tell me more about your set-up.'

'Well,' Steve continued, 'folk with these sorts of difficulties get referred to us by medical teams, and then we try to find them the kind of employment that's appropriate to their situation.'

'So what kind of work can they do?'

'All sorts, really. It depends upon what our clients – as we call them – are actually capable of doing. I suppose it's mostly manual activities: it can vary from packaging articles to assembling very simple mechanical products. We run workshops and training sessions to assist them, supervised by our staff members, and we try to improve our clients' opportunities of employment.'

'I'm so desperately ignorant about this kind of important work,' Clive admitted.

'Oh, don't apologise, most people haven't got a clue about what our organisation gets up to.'

'It sounds like quite a big operation.'

'Yes, I suppose it is. I'm the assistant director and at present we have over three hundred people involved in our enterprise, including staff as well as clients.' After taking another sip of his martini, Steve added, 'My particular responsibility is to try to persuade local businessmen to provide employment opportunities for as many people as possible.'

'Sounds like a full-time job in itself.'

'I certainly think it is, but sometimes I feel I have a hard time convincing my boss.'

'What's he like?' Clive enquired.

'My boss? Oh I guess Bill's all right: middle-aged, married with three children and what I would call a liberal Republican. He doesn't know about my private life of course, and if he did, I should think I'd be out on my ass.'

Avoiding being drawn by that last remark, Clive asked, 'I suppose you have to work quite closely together?'

'As a matter of fact, I share the job with somebody else,' Steve volunteered. 'Jane Matthews functions more like Bill's personal assistant.'

'You know, Steve, I have a wonderful PA back in London, Shirley Morris. She's simply terrific and I'm so very lucky to have her on board, I can tell you.' Then changing tack, Clive asked, 'How long have you been in your current job?'

'I'll be going into my third year this September coming,' Steve proudly stated.

'Not very long, then?'

'No. I guess not. It just feels like it,' Steve smiled back.

Then, as Michael came in to tell them to sit at the table and that lunch was ready, he contributed to the banter: 'Clive, darling, Steve's a workaholic – he never stops! And you know, in his spare time, he's also a key player at our Men's Center.'

The meal started off with some delicious, comforting homemade vegetable soup and Clive told Steve that he'd been hearing all about the Men's Center. He had really taken a shine to Steve and his intuition had persuaded him that he was an honest fellow who could be trusted. The fact that Michael had found him such a dependable influence also informed that Spoke judgement, and Clive encouraged Steve to tell him more about Columbus Cares and what went on there.

'I love my job, but I wish I could be totally myself in the workplace and accepted as an openly gay man. I hear from Michael that you are in show business, and I guess you probably don't have the same problem.'

'You're mostly right. As a theatrical agent, being gay is not really a handicap. In actual fact, you might argue it's a positive advantage; although, as in all walks of life, you do encounter homophobic behaviour from time to time. But living in a capital city, there's always a degree of anonymity, which I find makes life easier.'

'I'm sure you're right there,' agreed Steve. 'I remember being out in New York, and there was definitely a lot more freedom there than here in Columbus.'

'That doesn't surprise me in the least. Only just today I was telling my PA about an awful time I had with some paramedics when I first visited this town. Michael, you remember that African violet episode?'

'Clive, I sure do.'

'Yes, here in the Midwest,' Steve added, 'it's not been so easy, and I've always had to lead a double existence at work and frankly that never used to bother me. But now, with this AIDS crisis, I'm finding bigotry is on the increase in Columbus, and it's becoming much more difficult to lead the kind of lifestyle that brought me out in the first place.'

Over the Chicken Maryland, which formed the next course, he elaborated further. He described how for the last twenty years, he felt that, along with other gay males in the state of Ohio, he had struggled for acceptance: the right to be equal and different at the same time. To live the kind of lifestyle that defines gay sexuality and to be an individual as well as part of the group which all gay men belonged to.

'In a way, we began to create a beautiful world; a world that finally made us happy, where we could live almost charmed lives, unencumbered by hostility and prejudice. Then this AIDS business comes along out of the blue and changes everything.' Steve continued, 'Some people think we're deliberately spreading disease and although we know that's far from the truth, we are having to deal with a good deal of hostility. Moreover, we're having to change our habits, and nowadays you dare not sleep with anyone you don't know, for fear of taking a risk, and you know what? You can't even be sure that your own partner is safe.'

'Perhaps the scale of anonymous sexual activity here in the States was bound to take its toll. Do you think we've all lost our way?' Clive asked.

This last remark caused the two Americans to chew on their food more slowly and they finally put down their forks. Clive quickly tried to salvage the situation with: 'Oh dear, now I'm beginning to sound like Jerry Falwell and his Moral Majority, and I honestly don't mean to. But wouldn't you both agree that so much promiscuous sexual behaviour did get a bit out of hand?'

And, still struggling to salvage his faux pas, he continued: 'I mean to say, I read an article in *Newsweek* – or was it *Time* magazine? I can't remember which – that stated that the director of public health in San Francisco ordered the closure of a dozen or so gay establishments: bathhouses, bookstores and the like, which he claimed were fostering disease and death.'

'Now national publicity like that does all of us in the gay community no damn good at all,' Steve responded.

Sensing the temperature of the discussion between Steve and Clive rising, Michael cleared away the dishes and interjected: 'I suppose we really should have taken more responsibility for ourselves. I mean to say, the combination of multiple partners and unprotected sex was bound to lead to the spread of all sorts of sexual diseases. But who could have anticipated this plague that's hit us now?' he called out over his shoulder as he headed for the kitchen.

'Steve, do you think it's a plague too?'

'Oh. I think it's worse than that Clive, much worse.' And then he whispered: 'I think it's murder!'

It was the kind of near-hysterical remark that Clive had come to expect in the States, but hearing it from Steve somewhat surprised him; he began to see Mr Leggard in a different light, and so he urged him to elaborate.

'I'm prepared to go so far as to say that I have collected enough evidence to persuade me that there is a strong possibility that the spread of AIDS amongst us could have been motivated by powerful forces in authority. And you've got to remember that those gay rights activists in San Francisco, protesting against the closures you mentioned earlier, claimed that such action had been taken for political reasons rather than for medical concerns.'

Clive remembered what his dear friend Susan Carlsberg had told him while he was in New York a year earlier, and that prompted him to say: 'Next you're going to tell me that your government are also directly involved.'

Then in hushed tones Steve added: 'Clive, I'd really rather not talk about this any more tonight, if you don't mind, for reasons I'll explain some other time. Look, here's my card – give me a bell. Why don't you come down to my office tomorrow afternoon and see what goes on at Columbus Cares? There we can talk this thing through a little more, and maybe have dinner afterwards and get Michael to join us. You know there are some very good restaurants downtown, and I'm particularly fond of Le Gai Paris. Say, Michael told me you were half French.'

'*Oui monsieur. Ma mère était française.*'

'*Et voilà les fraises,*' announced Michael with a flourish as he arrived with the dessert.

'Michael, I didn't know you spoke French.'

'Really Clive, I haven't told you all my little secrets – there's quite a bit more you don't know about me.'

'What I do know for certain is that you're a jolly good cook. And to top it all, it's such a great treat to eat strawberries this early in the year. Back home in Blighty we don't normally have them till June.'

'We don't either. Michael has had them flown in specially from Florida in honour of your visit,' Steve joked.

Over coffee and brandy, Clive tried to steer the conversation back to the remarks Steve had made about the American government, but Mr Leggard wasn't having any of it. 'Look, I really think I got a bit carried away with my conspiracy theory just now and Michael's excellent brandy won't help me do justice to my own arguments. And Clive, as charming as you may appear to be, for all I know you could be a secret agent.'

Clive took the hint, and rather than spoil what had been a

delicious luncheon and delightful first meeting, decided to let his new Columbus acquaintance off the hook and turn on that Spoke charm, which he was becoming well known for amongst his new American pals.

'Listen chaps, the only agent I am is a theatrical one, and there's no secret about that.' Which received an amused response from his two Columbus buddies.

So, with lunch over, their guest took his leave of them, first reminding Clive that he was looking forward to him visiting his office at Columbus Cares the following day. Helping Michael clear the table, Clive began to question his host about the earlier discussion he'd had with Steve, admitting that he found Steve's ideas quite fantastic and wondered whether his best friend had ever mentioned his so-called conspiracy theory to him before.

'No, not really,' came Michael's reply.

'Well, Steve said that he thought the spread of AIDS could have been motivated by governmental forces and suggested that there was some sort of plot to wipe out the entire male gay population in your country.'

'Oh really! That's Steve for you. But it wouldn't be the first time in this century that extermination has been tried out – genocides are always planned. Do you suppose those Jews in Poland had any idea of what was going on in Treblinka? They had become victims, were identified because of differences that made them unpopular, and people got jealous of them too.'

'That's perfectly true. But, Michael, this is 1984, for goodness sake. I know bigotry exists all over the world, but there's no war going on now and surely your government wouldn't be crazy enough to wipe out an entire section of its own people?'

'Sometimes I wonder about this great democratic country of mine. Things still get covered up, and certain interests have to be protected. Injustices have become endemic here in the States and you don't have to look far beyond what happened to the Kennedys for evidence of what I'm talking about. You do know that the FBI files were later to reveal that several CIA operatives were mixed up with those two murders?'

'Yes, I've read up quite a lot about the Kennedys, but please go on.'

'You can't convince me that the murder of one of the potentially greatest presidents of the United States of America can still remain such a mystery. All that hogwash about one bullet ricocheting when there were actually three bullets fired. And why was it so easy for Jack Ruby to kill Lee Harvey Oswald? It's just one big cover-up after another, leaving so many questions unanswered and evidence that never came to light. It's all bullshit!'

Michael was now getting quite agitated. Clive tried to appease him, but the next thing he mentioned gave further impetus to his host's argument. Clive had just read a very convincing book, *In God's Name*, which alleged that Pope John Paul I had been poisoned in his own bed by some cardinals in the Vatican.

'That's precisely what I'm getting at, and of course it doesn't just happen here in the USA. It's the sort of thing that goes on all over the world in this so-called Western democratic society of ours, and is kept covered up by all the people with money, power and influence.'

'You and Steve are obviously not alone in your opinions, and I have to admit that a very dear friend in New York has also expressed similar views.' Then Clive added: 'What does that doctor friend of yours think?'

'Oh, Allen's rather enigmatic. He claims he's too busy treating his patients and doesn't want to get involved in politics. In fact, he's really quite private and appears to lead a rather solitary existence, which is surprising when you think how eligible he is. It's always difficult to get anything out of him except when you get him on the subject of health.'

'Really? He sounds rather intriguing.'

'He's that all right, and he's a wonderful human being.'

'I can't wait to be introduced to Allen, now I've met Steve. Listen Michael, I'm sorry to go on about the rather bold assertions Steve made about your government, but I find them, how can I say—'

'Clive, believe me, they aren't just Steve's opinions. There was even stuff that Dennis was trying to tell me just before he passed away. He led me to believe that he might have been onto something too.'

'What do you mean?'

'Well, at the time, he was so very ill and was struggling to get his words out. I had to urge him to save his energy and so it was never really clear what he was trying to tell me. And anyway, whatever he may have got hold of, got hold of him in the end.'

'You don't mean to tell me that Dennis was also involved in this conspiracy theory of Steve's too?'

'I think I'm rambling – it must be the brandy speaking. All I can say is that following the results of the blood test Allen Levitt gave him, I was so very distressed to find out the nature of the illness that Den had contracted, even my own reality became somewhat distorted and it was hard for me to keep my cool … Look, Clive, can we drop all this for now?'

The Englishman clearly saw that his line of questioning was going nowhere and, furthermore, it was upsetting his friend. So, much to Michael's relief, Clive extricated himself by announcing that jetlag had kicked in and that he needed to lie down for a while and take a nap, which is what he told Michael he liked to call his siesta.

As he climbed the open staircase, he just couldn't get Steve's remarks out of his head, so he decided he would phone his new acquaintance after he'd had his rest, and take him up on his invitation to meet up downtown the following day at Columbus Cares. He really wanted to find out more about Steve's conspiracy theory.

After his siesta, Clive rejoined Michael and told him that he'd arranged to meet up with Steve the next day at his office, but led Michael to believe it was on the pretext of finding out more about the workshops that went on there rather than reveal his true intention. Michael felt that they should try to take things easy that afternoon and have an early night, but he did broach the subject of a visit to the cemetery where Dennis was buried for the next day. Clive said he had hoped Michael would suggest that they went, since he was keen to go and pay his final respects and thought that might help to bring greater closure for him.

So on Thursday morning they woke bright and early, had a light breakfast, then occupied themselves with clearing out the attic, which Michael claimed badly needed attending to. After lunch, Michael offered to drive Clive over to Columbus Cares for his rendezvous with Steve, and arranged to collect him at four-thirty so that they could go to the cemetery together.

CHAPTER SEVEN

THE FRED MACADAM SAGA THURSDAY

'Steve, it's so very kind of you to invite me here to Columbus Cares.'

'Clive, don't be silly, it's really a great pleasure. I so much enjoyed meeting you yesterday, and I just know we are going to become real good friends. Now I thought my tour could start with a visit to the factory space.'

'To be honest, and I hope you won't think me rude, but I'm much more curious to learn more about what you started to tell me while we were having lunch yesterday. Of course I am very interested in what goes on here, but I just can't get over what you were saying to me while Michael was in the kitchen ... You remember – all that amazing stuff about how you thought that your government was involved in a plot to rid the United States of its gay male community. So I've got lots of questions to ask you.'

'I see ... then fire away!'

'Well, I first want to start with Dennis.'

Clive's remark seemed to throw Steve off his guard for a moment, but he quickly covered up and tried to dismiss the question with: 'Oh, you know what Den was like.'

Clive's reaction was quite intense: 'Yes I certainly do, he's part of my history. That man meant more to me than anyone I have ever known, before or since our affair on Cape Cod. It may be nothing at all, but actually it was also something Michael had started to tell me last night as we were turning in that made me think that maybe Dennis had picked up some incriminating material before he died, and somehow it seemed to link in with your conspiracy theory.'

'As a matter of fact, when he came to the Men's Center, Dennis did share some rather extraordinary information with me.'

'Oh, really! Like what exactly?'

'He called it his wipe-out theory.'

'His what! You're kidding – surely Dennis was far too intelligent to get mixed up in some stupid gay avengers soap opera.'

'This is no cloak-and-dagger story. Thousands of us are dying and if Dennis was right, and I now believe he was, we're talking about a carefully calculated plot to get rid of a lot of us here in the United States, and on a massive scale.'

This last remark only confirmed the rumours Clive had picked up on while in New York the previous year, and so he urged Steve to tell him how Dennis had got so involved in his so-called 'wipe-out theory' in the first place.

'Look Clive, I just don't know where to begin with all this, and if you're meeting Michael shortly, and going to Dove Park with him, then we need to find another time and place to get together and talk this thing through. Why don't you get Michael to drop you off at my place later today? I feel I can talk more freely in the privacy of my own home than I can here, and then I'll tell you everything I know.'

Clive went along with that suggestion, which helped ease the tension between his new acquaintance and himself. He knew full well that Michael was visiting his folks that evening, and told Steve that he thought that he and Michael could probably benefit from a break from one another after their proposed trip to the cemetery that afternoon. Steve completely understood how Clive was feeling and so he agreed to go along with the idea that they meet up later that evening. He announced that he was more than happy to start his tour of the premises: they would begin in the practice rooms, have some coffee in the cafeteria and then Steve would set about showing Clive around the rest of the establishment. Later on, and punctual as ever, Michael turned up on time and was waiting for Clive outside at four-thirty as arranged.

Clive hated cemeteries at the best of times, since he thought there was never a good moment to visit a graveside, but he knew it was his duty to accompany Michael and, besides, he hoped it would make Dennis's death a fact and help bring a degree of finality, if not solace, to his friend's passing. So the two mourners set off on their pilgrimage to Dove Park while it was still light. They headed out of the city in a southerly direction and once they had branched off the motorway, they drove through what appeared to be quite ordinary parkland. Clive thought it looked like a large estate, with row upon row of meticulously planted evergreen trees stretching far off into the distance. Eventually the wooded glade thinned out and they found themselves driving along a broad, tree-lined avenue, on either side of which were acres of grassland, speckled sporadically with tiny marbled mounds set far apart from each other, but dotted all over the sprawling lawns.

Clive couldn't help being overwhelmed by the scale of Dove Park, mirroring the vastness of the country its occupants had once peopled. It was in such stark contrast to the compactness of the smaller European walled cities of the dead with which he was so much more familiar. Clive reflected that back home the deceased were kept locked up and sometimes stored one on top of the other, whereas here in the States they were positively encouraged to roam freely all over the wide-open spaces. Once parked alongside a grass verge, they left the brown sedan and approached a small marble headstone set way off from the roadside, each clutching a small bunch of flowers. As the grave came into view, it had an unexpectedly numbing effect on Clive as opposed to the rush of emotion he had anticipated.

The fact that Dennis's remains were buried somewhere under a modest stone slab offered him small consolation, though clearly he recognised that it all meant quite a lot to Michael.

The simple inscription read:

DENNIS MONTROSE
(1941–1984)
Lying in the mud, but looking up at the stars

However, when he took in what was written on the headstone, Clive became deeply moved, and he smiled with a mixture of joy and tears as he read the wording. Michael told him that Dennis had chosen the quotation himself and Clive realised, perhaps for the first time, that his lifeguard had been much more theatrical than he had ever thought. Michael explained that Dennis had been reading up on old movie stars and that just before he had gone back into hospital for the last time, he had found an autobiography about Ida Lupino and the quote came from her book.

It is difficult to say how long the two men remained there, kneeling by the graveside and gazing at that stone slab, both in their separate and private worlds of remembrance, uselessly willing Dennis back to life again and both mutually sharing the need to be there. At times, they silently vented their emotions, at other moments they erupted into roaring anger and their uninhibited cries echoed loudly around the cemetery.

After having placed their flowers on the grave, they bade farewell to their dear friend, got back into the car and drove back along the tree-lined avenue. The two mourners were obviously exhausted by what they had experienced, and silenced by their act of commemoration, breathing a sigh of relief as they left the blaring silence of Dove Park behind them. That block of stone had solidly confirmed that their friend was gone for ever, but perhaps no more emphatically than returning to his house in Alexandria Colony Court to find it so empty without him.

The two didn't stay long in Dennis's house, since Michael had arranged to visit his folks and Clive was meeting up with Steve at his home. Michael dropped Clive off there and after they had exchanged the briefest of goodbyes, Clive couldn't but feel more than a little guilty about leaving his friend alone in his car in such a solemn mood. However, he was more determined than ever to get to the bottom of what Dennis had found out and truly believed that only Steve held the key to solving that mystery.

So, deposited outside yet another Columbus residence, and despite the fading light, Clive realised how very spacious and comfortable the local Ohio architecture appeared to be. He noticed that Steve's place was one of those semi-detached ranch-style wooden houses with a steep, sloping roof and elaborate front porch. His host came to the front door and Clive was greeted in a most friendly manner. Steve, who had changed out of the suit he wore for work, was now in a pair of jeans, a T-shirt and a cardigan, and seemed a good deal more relaxed on home ground. The gin and tonics flowed but Steve was clearly sensitive to the effect Dove Park had had on his new English buddy and admitted that he also found a visit to the cemetery a draining experience. He heaved himself out of an ample armchair and then proceeded to top Clive up and offer him some delicious hors d'oeuvres. Clive thanked Steve for inviting him over to Columbus Cares earlier that day, and commented on how impressed he was by the entire operation.

Steve was evidently proud of what his team had been able to achieve, and pleased that Clive had been able to find the time to visit. He was well aware that Clive had come to talk about the subject that had been broached earlier on that day, so after a while, when they had both relaxed, he felt that the moment was right for Clive to be enlightened about what their late friend had got up to.

'Clive, apart from teaching, you do know about Dennis's other profession?'

'You mean, did I know he was on the game? Yes, of course I did. He told me all about it, and was pleased as punch that his earnings had helped buy Benjy and allowed him to put a deposit down on his house. But I gather Michael found Den's sideline difficult at times.'

'Oh, he learnt to live with it – eventually, but I have to tell you that at the start of their relationship, their rows got so intense that Dennis announced he was going to spend the summer with his folks, who had moved out west to Sacramento.'

'I bet he didn't spend much time with them. Steve, these hors d' oeuvres are simply delicious, by the way.'

'Oh, thank you … and yes, you're sure as hell right. He soon hightailed it down to Los Angeles, where he got involved with a very fast crowd and hawked his ass around clubs, discos and the Strip, of course. He was doing all right, but then he met Fred Macadam and his whole world was turned upside down.'

This was a name Clive had not heard before and his slightly puzzled look caused Steve to offer more of an explanation. Clearly the Macadam case had not made it into the British newspapers, but from what Steve related, it had caused quite a stir on his side of the pond. Fred Macadam had been a jobbing actor in New York, but he became disillusioned with the Broadway scene and, like so many before him, decided he would try his luck in Hollywood. However, although he was a talented, well built and good looking guy, his acting career didn't appear to take off there either and so, Steve explained, Fred put his talents to other uses.

Within no time at all, he acquired quite a following, but not of the kind he had aspired to as an actor and, by the early seventies, he had started to organise private sex parties for a circle of rich gay Californian men who could not be open about their sexuality. Fred used to take orders in advance, could supply on demand and, since his clientele didn't want to be seen cruising the downtown

Los Angeles fleshpots, what had begun as a sideline soon turned into a lucrative business. In no time at all, he'd bought an old hotel in which he set up a high-class male brothel, one of the first of its kind in the state of California.

This was a period of Dennis's life Clive knew relatively little about, and Steve really relished filling him in on the lifeguard's Californian escapades. Although Fred had lots of young men on his books, Dennis soon became one of his most popular sex operators, and Steve went on to explain that the brothel regulars came from far and wide, and one of them had taken more than just a shine to him. This was hardly surprising, since the client in question was only turned on by marines and bodybuilders, and Dennis fulfilled those requirements twofold. What's more, the guy was no ordinary meal ticket either, since not only was he not hurting for money, he was also a respected member of the Senate, and so you could say Dennis had hit the jackpot.

When Clive pressed Steve to reveal the identity of the senator, he began to prevaricate somewhat, and said that he would prefer to refer to him as Jim, for reasons which would become a lot clearer when he got to the end of the Macadam saga. Clive remembered that on his first visit to Columbus, Dennis had mentioned a chap called Jim who was a senator, and that he was one of his 'regulars', so Clive was keen to hear more about the man.

Steve set about revealing that a well-known Los Angeles investigative magazine had planted an undercover reporter in the brothel, and that subsequently it ran an explosive series of articles, naming names and exposing Fred Macadam's sex business. The police finally raided the joint, closed it down, and Fred was accused of employing underage young men, for which crime he was finally sent to jail. Steve suggested that because Jim probably had contacts in high places, he had managed to keep his own name out of the press, since it would have been devastating for the senator and his family if he'd been shopped. He also told Clive that, as luck would have it, Dennis had decided to move back to Columbus by then, and despite all that had happened, both men managed to escape controversy and had both weathered the storm.

'So how long did their liaison last?' asked Clive.

'They kept in touch just up until Jim died, about twelve months ago.'

'Don't tell me this Jim had AIDS too?'

'No. Jim was murdered.'

'Now you're not going to tell me that was because he stopped paying his brothel bills?'

'Clive, this is serious stuff. I know for a fact that according to the FBI criminal records division, Senator Jim was leading a very complicated kind of existence. Few things aroused J. Edgar Hoover's wrath as much as sexual misconduct and, unbeknown to Jim, Dennis told me that there existed a file against his senator friend. At the time, Dennis didn't explain how he had acquired so much information about Jim, but it was clear from what he did tell me that his Senator friend liked to live on the edge, and although married with four children – to whom, by the way, he was devoted – his domestic situation did not prevent him from dabbling.'

'A true bisexual. You know, when I first met Dennis, that's what I thought he was.'

'Really? Now that doesn't surprise me for one moment. Anyway, to get back to Jim, before he became a senator, he'd been a football star at Amherst College in Massachusetts; but instead of turning pro, he went into politics with a capital P. If he'd had any boyfriends in his team, Jim must have kept them well hidden and besides, because he was such a good-looking all-American jock, no one ever suspected him of being a faggot.'

That word jarred and reminded Clive of how angry its use had made Dennis feel.

'Maybe he was just a late starter,' Clive suggested.

'Probably. We've all been to bed with those, and thankfully too, as I recall. There's nothing like introducing a straight to the joys of gay sex. They usually want it bad, to make up for all that lost time – and who can blame them? And, if my memory serves me right, they usually like to take it and want to be fucked into the next decade.'

Clive thought that Steve was beginning to show quite another side to his character. He had begun to wonder whether it was the endless refilling of the glasses that revealed Steve's true personality or whether his Spoke judgement was simply beginning to find Mr Leggard rather common. What was clear however, was that as the evening wore on, he thought that his companion was becoming much less guarded and slightly irreverent.

'Why exactly do you think Dennis came back to Columbus, if he was doing so well in California?' asked Clive.

'Maybe he got ass-ache. No, really, I don't know. Maybe he just had enough.'

'I can quite understand that. Or perhaps he wanted to live a more normal existence with Michael.'

'Clive, you know it may indeed have been to get back with Michael again, but Den never told me exactly what made him come back here, although I have to admit that it was just as well he returned before that magazine scandal erupted.'

'So when was this? I mean, what year?'

'Let me see, I think he graduated in '69, did a year's teaching probation and then went out West for about eighteen months. I think he moved back to Columbus over Christmas '72 or was it '73? … I can't quite remember.'

'And so he took up again with Michael?'

'Yes. As I said, they'd met one another before Den went out to California. Michael had been studying fine art at Dennison and Den used to model for those life-drawing classes there and that's where they first met.'

'Yes of course. And, by the way, you know I went to watch him pose for one of his weekly sessions when I visited Columbus the last time I was here? He was such a natural and I shall never forget the superb performance he gave.'

'Well, naturally all of that had to stop when he got sick. His health deteriorated so quickly, he started to lose weight and became so weak that he could barely walk, let alone model.'

'It must have been agony for him. Witnessing that body he'd taken such good care of waste away, without him being able to do anything about it. You know, I still just can't believe this could have happened to our big, strong Dennis.'

'Don't worry. Neither could he.'

They both then seemed to observe a minute's silence. Steve broke the pause in their conversation: 'I say, I need another, don't you?'

This time Clive volunteered to bring the gin over to where they were sitting, poured two good measures, adding the tonic, and left the glasses on the table close by: 'Please go on.'

'Now where was I?'

'Dennis returned to Columbus and took up with Michael once more,' Clive prompted.

'Right. But then after about six months, Jim contacted him again and invited him out to Washington DC and this time, he wouldn't take no for an answer.'

'Didn't Michael mind?'

'Of course he minded, but he couldn't give Dennis up. Besides, he knew what was going on in Columbus right under his very nose. Dennis had his regular clientele here you know, and the extra dough came in handy for both of them.'

'I suppose Michael simply turned a blind eye.'

'He knew the score and, let's face it, Dennis always came back to him. Anyway, Michael wasn't totally innocent either. He was very popular too, you know. He didn't do it for money, of course, but he often cruised the biology faculty tea room and, being a good-looking young man, he did very well there, or so I gather.'

'Yes, I'm sure. Anyway, so Dennis took up with Senator Jim

again and … did their relationship last long?'

'Curiously no, not at the time. I don't know exactly what occurred, if indeed anything in particular did actually happen. I think Jim must have just got tired of him and so he found someone younger and closer to hand. After all, DC is quite a way from here and so, by employing a local, he saved on airfares and his new trick would have always been on tap. According to Dennis, Jim was a very attractive, bright and powerful man, and would have had no difficulty in finding a replacement and impressing some young stud in Washington. As far as I know, I don't believe that Jim and his new boyfriend were ever found out there, but I believe this new relationship had something to do with what happened later.'

'But you still haven't told me why he was murdered nor why he had a history with the FBI's criminal records division.'

'Yes, you're right, and this is where I do get a little confused about dates. But I think it was the spring of '79 when Den told me he had heard from Jim again.'

'After not having heard from him for some time?'

'Exactly. This time Jim had invited Dennis to join him on a skiing holiday in Colorado. Aspen, of all places! Now I don't know how much you know about American ski resorts, but honestly you couldn't pick a more rednecked part of the woods if you tried.'

Clive remembered Aspen well, and realised that his visit must have coincided with the time Dennis had joined the senator there.

'Maybe that's the reason why this Jim chose it. Hardly the kind of location for their sort of assignation,' Clive said, deciding to conceal the fact that he had gone there himself to meet up with Dennis.

'Anyway, the choice of resort made no difference to our Den,' Steve continued, 'and so off he trotted with his ski boots intact. He was never one to turn down a free trip, especially if it meant a couple of hundred bucks fuck money thrown in, and all expenses paid.'

As the evening wore on, the more Steve revealed his uncharitable colours, and, not unsurprisingly, the less Clive warmed to him;

although he also had to admit to himself that there was bound to be a certain amount of truth in what he was hearing. He decided to put Steve's unfortunate turns of phrase partially down to alcohol while, at the same time, he was aware that his Spoke nose was more than capable of catching a cold. He really felt Steve was being disrespectful to speak of the dead in quite such a forthright manner, even though he recognised that it was probably an accurate description of the way Dennis operated. At any rate, Clive was determined to keep his Aspen rendezvous a secret from Steve for the time being, until he felt he could trust him more. He realised that he simply needed to persevere with his host if he was to acquire the information about Jim which he now so desperately wanted. The more so because his visit in '76 had made him realise how much senator had come to mean to Dennis.

'Den found Jim a very changed man,' Steve continued.

'You mean he'd come out and was liberated?'

'No. Quite the reverse. He was twitchy and nervous and told Den that several attempts had been made on his life. You know, the FBI was perfectly capable of creating a climate of discord and mistrust for anyone they were on to, and clearly they had Jim under surveillance. He had become really scared, apparently needed to talk to someone he could rely on, and that's why he invited Den to join him in Aspen.'

'So this time he needed Dennis more for counsel than pleasure.'

'Den didn't quite go that far. But what he did tell me was that Jim was travelling under an assumed name and had taken an extended leave of absence, attributed to overwork, ill health and exhaustion. He'd even changed his appearance and went to great lengths to disguise himself: he'd shaved his head, wore narrow-rimmed hippie-style glasses, dirty old jeans and ex-army clothes. Dennis told me he scarcely recognised his suave senator when they met up again at the airport in Aspen.'

'How do you know so much detail?'

Steve continued to explain that when Dennis turned up at the Men's Center in such a disturbed state and in need of counselling, he was on duty that morning and interviewed him.

'I was a volunteer there, and the day Den wandered in with his story, he got me. It was quite obvious that he didn't want to offload any of his findings onto Michael.'

'So that's how you two met. Of course, Michael told me you're a volunteer there. But you know, I simply thought you were one of his tricks, like the rest of us,' Clive said to lighten things up a bit.

'You're right of course. We had met in the mid seventies. For sure, I did it with him when I could afford him. He was a tremendous fuck and he knew it. He had such amazing stamina, it's little wonder he made so much money out of it.'

Once again Steve revealed his unattractively bitchy side, had strayed slightly off the subject, and left Clive impatient to bring the discussion back to what he had learnt from Dennis that morning at the Men's Center. It emerged that Jim had confided in Dennis and told him that the person he'd become involved with was a young marine stationed in DC, called Hank Watson. There they had both been very discreet, led double lives, and were certain that they had kept their relationship a secret.

Then one day the young marine came to Jim with an unbelievable story. It appeared that because he had been posted to the White House, Hank had access to classified information, and had uncovered some top-secret material that had really alarmed him. He informed Jim that he had discovered a memo warning that the gay male community was becoming too powerful, some even achieving high office. This greatly worried the prejudiced majority of straight American men who ran the country. They believed that homosexuals could be an easy blackmail target potentially leaking state secrets and presenting a considerable threat to national security. It was apparent that there was a plan to curb the rise of the gay rights movement in America. Steve made it clear that this was serious and not just some kind of new legislation or social reform bill backed by the Moral Majority.

'No – Dennis told me that Jim's marine claimed he'd found out something very disturbing. You see, Clive, at the FBI headquarters in Washington some official in charge of the Immigration and naturalisation service had issued a top-security document addressing the possible elimination of the entire male gay population of the United States of America and Jim's marine had stumbled upon it.

'At first Jim thought the discovery preposterous, but Hank must have been insistent, and finally produced a copy of some written evidence, which persuaded the senator that there could be some truth in the young man's claim. Then, as a senator, he was able to pull a few strings and started to make some discreet enquiries of his own. He gained access to the security document himself, and was therefore finally able to corroborate the marine's claim. So, you see, by the time Jim met up with Dennis in Colorado, he had unravelled the entire show.'

'Wow! No wonder Jim needed to confide in somebody he trusted, and I suppose Dennis was the obvious candidate.' Clive was now more convinced than ever that Dennis had asked him to join him in Colorado for similar reasons.

'Absolutely. Dennis also told me that he believed that the FBI must have intervened and that was why Jim was finally outed, although at the time, he was unable to prove who had shopped him. It was around this time that a smear campaign started to discredit Jim, and he realised that his political career was hanging in the balance. Indeed he was not the first politician or movie star to receive such treatment from Hoover's men. Look at what they did to Jane Fonda, for heaven's sake, just because she became so involved with the Black Panther movement and publicly supported them. Jim was in an even more vulnerable situation, since he had found out far too much. He was being publicly accused of being homosexual and because of what had become a powerful anti-gay lobby, he was one of the many who were posing a threat to society, even though at that point the real reason for his victimisation had not yet been fully revealed.

'Overnight, this successful senator had his reputation destroyed, was having his home telephone monitored and he felt that his family's safety was possibly also at risk. Jim had become yet one more casualty in the powerful hands of the FBI and the intolerant system in place at the time, and he truly believed that they were out to get him, and of course he was right! Clive, you know that by the end of the seventies, cover-ups and injustices against folk who had become problematic to the nation had become endemic here all over the United States.'

As Clive listened on, he became convinced that his invitation to visit Dennis in Aspen must have also been a cry for help and that his friend had needed someone to talk to and a person he could trust. Clive thought he must have planned to tell him what his senator friend had discovered that evening but then had changed his mind at the last minute. Dennis must have obviously decided not to implicate his English buddy by revealing what he had discovered from Jim, since divulging so much incriminating information would have also placed Clive in a potentially dangerous situation.

'Dennis believed that this was more than just some move to get the fairies out of power,' Steve continued. 'He wasn't only alarmed by what was happening to Jim, he began to realise the magnitude of what was essentially an insidious campaign to eradicate a minority group who, as well as becoming a political source of embarrassment for our government, had also become an economic threat.'

'Steve, why does economics have to come into it? Surely what we're talking about is prejudice. I'm sorry to say this, but why do you Americans always have to bring money into the argument?'

'For one very good reason, and for once I have to disagree with you. Let's examine what I mean by an economic threat, and look at some of the financial implications of what I'm talking about.

Have you ever stopped to think about how many guys have become wealthy as a result of this so-called gay liberation?'

'To be honest, I don't suppose I have.'

'Think about how many chains of gay bathhouses, bars and discos have grown up all over the United States in the last twenty years, with hotels and restaurants all catering for an exclusively homosexual clientele. Not to mention the porn industry with its cinemas and bookshops, and the ever-increasing demand for home videos? Just think about it!'

'You have to understand that it's not like this back home, countered Clive. 'But from what you're telling me I can see that some people are making a great deal of money here in the USA out of exploiting the gay community.'

'Exploitation or not, what we're talking about is big bucks. A lot of us gays have been growing fat off the profits. And I just don't mean the porn stars or the Mafia.'

'So what you're implying is that a lot of you American gay businessmen have become very wealthy as a result of all this commerce ... I suppose I can see that now, but, sorry to sound so naive, I still don't see what that has to do with murder.'

'I'll get to that in a minute. But don't you see that guys who once found themselves socially unacceptable when poor, soon found that their money, however it was acquired, empowered them and made them feel more than welcome when it was a question of helping to back certain political causes.

'So, what you're trying to tell me is that the economic threat caused by the power of gay wealth is what has driven some of your politicians in high places to launch this audacious plot, by way of the FBI.'

'Yes that – combined with a good deal of prejudice and jealousy. What do I have to say that will convince you? You mustn't underestimate the power of some of these so-called gay corporations. Here in America, money talks.'

'And money silences. Is that it?'

'Now you've got it. For example, have you any idea how much money is needed to launch a presidential campaign over here? '

'I don't suppose I have.'

'We're talking in terms of billions of dollars, and when such sums are involved, people are none too fussed about where that money comes from. We gay men have become a potentially powerful and rich minority group, which, when organised, could begin to back its own political nominees. After all, way back in the sixties, anyone who had dared to suggest that there could be a black candidate running for the White House would have been lynched.'

'And a gay one hung, drawn and quartered!' Clive smiled. 'I think I know what you mean.'

'Well, all right, you've persuaded me,' Clive admitted. 'I concede that there is an economic threat and people in high places are getting nervous about the importance of the "pink dollar" and its potential to back a gay president. But how on earth did they intend to go about wiping us out? Jim and his marine must have discovered something else. And why was the senator bumped off?'

'Jim's marine friend had also claimed he'd discovered something much more sinister than a memo. He had also uncovered that down in Tucson, Arizona there was a germicide warfare centre involved in virus research. I'm really sorry, but I can't go into that right now … it' s a whole other story and it will have to wait till tomorrow. You see, you must excuse me, but I have to prepare an important paper I need to give at Columbus Cares in the morning.'

Clive made no attempt to hide his frustration, but since he clearly saw that Steve was not prepared to go any further that evening, he suggested he call a cab to take him back to the Colony, which his host was more than happy to arrange. Besides, he'd already uncovered a great deal of very fascinating information and there was much to absorb. What he'd previously thought of as rumour, as his friend Susan had once implied, he now believed had turned into fact and he needed to get his head around all the information he had acquired and make some clear notes. He decided he would list all the facts that Steve had told him and then adapt them in much the same way as he did when reading a movie script.

Once back home at 257, he set about drawing up a sort of storyboard listing the names of all the characters involved and mapping out the apparent chronological series of events. This pictorial approach would help him to clarify some of the facts and details that Steve had revealed, and create a visual guide to the conspiracy theory as he understood it thus far. Neither had he forgotten that there was also new information about Arizona, which he had not been successful in acquiring. It had been a long and eventful day and he decided not to wait up for Michael. With his account of events clearly drawn up and illustrated, he was exhausted, and he turned in before midnight.

CHAPTER EIGHT

SENATOR JIM FRIDAY

The next morning, Clive woke much earlier than the previous day, his jetlag clearly still giving him a problem. Michael was already up and moving around downstairs, so Clive decided to join him, and as he walked into the kitchen, the electric kettle was immediately switched on.

'I hope I didn't disturb you when I got home late from my folks?' Michael enquired.

Clive admitted that he must have been fast asleep and didn't hear his host come in. He confessed that he had consumed rather a skinful at Steve's the previous night and so had made straight for his bed when he got home.

'Does that mean you two were buzzed? Clive, you do make me laugh with all those quaint expressions of yours, you know. I'm so glad you two hit it off … Look, I'm just about to make some coffee. Would you like some?'

'I'd love some. How were your parents, by the way?'

'They're just great and thanks for asking. I told them you were here in Columbus and they are really looking forward to meeting you. I've invited them over for dinner next Monday night.'

'Michael, that's wonderful. I look forward to meeting them too. What are they like?'

'Well, I think they're terrific. My mom and dad were so understanding when I came out to them just before I went to art school and then, when I introduced them to Dennis, they totally accepted him and welcomed him into our family.'

Both friends seemed to float off into their own worlds for a while and it was the sound of the boiling kettle that brought them back to reality. In an attempt to change the subject Michael remarked: 'Say, that's a terrific sweater you're wearing. It must be English. You've got such great clothes.'

'In fact it's Scottish, from the Isle of Arran. And you know what? … It's yours.'

'Clive, I said I liked it. Not that I wanted it.'

'I've got loads of sweaters and besides, you must always accept a gift with grace. One of the first lessons I learnt from Mr Montrose.' And Clive pulled his jersey off over his head and put it round Michael's shoulders.

'Well, that's very generous of you.' And as he put it on, Michael turned to Clive: 'You know I always feel so drained when I visit the cemetery and I really want to thank you for coming with me yesterday.'

'Please don't thank me. I wanted to go to and isit Dennis anyway.'

'Funny to talk about him like that: almost as though he's still with us.'

'And I suppose in a way, he still is, although I have to admit this house does seem pretty empty without him, doesn't it?'

'It sure does, and I'm not certain I would have stayed here on my own. Not that I'm frightened or anything. Just saddened because he's not here and that makes things so final for me. Which reminds me, I really ought to start sorting through Den's clothes.'

'Why don't you? And, by the way, that sweater looks great on you. Do you mind if I put a quick call through to my PA? I said I'd ring her.'

'Clive, please stop being so polite about using the phone … you go right ahead and, by the way, thank you again for my new Scottish addition.'

'It's a pleasure and honestly, I will get used to the open-house rules here, I promise. You see, I suppose in England we use the telephone more sparingly. I'll make my call and get Shirley to ring me straight back, then fix some lunch for us. I noticed you've got half a cooked chicken and some salad in the fridge.'

'In the what? Oh you mean in the icebox: there you go again. That would be great and, just to remind you, after lunch I have to go to the Columbus General Hospital where I'm due for my check-up later today.'

'I'd like to come with you. If you don't mind, that is.'

'Don't be silly, I was hoping you'd say that. Besides, the more company I can get at the moment, the better. Especially when said company is English and so very charming.'

Clive thought that Michael seemed less tense than the previous day and decided it was now appropriate to ask some of the more practical questions relating to Dennis's estate and belongings. The Englishman realised that he had become far too preoccupied with the Fred Macadam saga and had neglected to focus on Michael's current state of affairs and, in particular, on his financial situation. He decided he would change tack after lunch and endeavour to find out about the practical details relating to Dennis's will. In the meantime, he put a quick call through to Shirley, who phoned him straight back.

'Clive darling, how's it all going?'

He explained that he had a great deal to tell Shirley but was about to prepare lunch, and that he had offered to accompany Michael to his check-up at the local hospital.

Shirley replied that he was not to worry, she understood and would call back the following day around 11 a.m. his time

'Yes please. I want to fill you in on my latest discovery. It seems that Dennis had become mixed up in a lot of pretty alarming stuff.'

'Like what?'

'I can't talk now and anyway, by tomorrow, I hope I will have got to the bottom of it all.'

'Gosh, it all sounds very mysterious. Just mind you don't get into any trouble yourself!'

'Yes, Mummy dearest.'

With lunch over, Clive and Michael were back in the car again and on their way to the hospital. As they pulled away from number 257, Clive became aware that there was no sign of Benjy parked outside in the street, and so he felt the time was right to take the plunge and ask Michael some of the many questions he'd been avoiding.

'Michael I can't remember, but did Dennis have a garage here?'

'No – why do you ask?'

'I just wondered why I hadn't seen Benjy. It's only just occurred to me that I hadn't seen his pride and joy.'

'Oh, we had to sell Benjy. Dennis had to get rid of the car to help pay for all the medical bills.'

'What a terrible shame. I suppose there's no National Health equivalent over here, is there? And unless you have private medical insurance…'

'Believe me, extended medical care works out damn expensive in the United States, so there was no alternative. And Clive, you do realise that in this country, insurance companies have the right to unlimited access to your medical records and unless you've had an AIDS test anonymously, you can be classified as uninsurable.'

After a long pause, Clive asked, 'What will happen to the house?'

'I'm really not sure yet.'

'I hope you won't be offended by what I'm about to say,' said Clive gently, 'but if you need anything, you only have to ask. Spoke

Associates is doing really rather well at the moment, and I'd be more than happy to—'

'That's so very kind of you Clive, but honestly, financially I'm fine.'

'I'm relieved about that. What with medical bills and the funeral expenses, I just felt I had to ask. I hope you don't mind.'

Michael responded that he didn't mind in the least and said that as far as he was concerned, Clive was like family to him now. The mention of the word 'family' prompted him to tell Clive that the Montroses had offered to pay for the funeral, but since he and Dennis had made out their wills in each other's favour, he already had the money in place and didn't need to ask them to contribute. He further confessed that Dennis didn't have much to do with his folks once they had moved out to California and that he knew that Dennis had come out to them when he had gone to Sacramento for that last visit. The Montroses had found that very hard to handle, which he thought possibly also accounted for why Dennis had become estranged from them.

'You know … I guess I'm so very lucky with my mom and dad,' Michael continued. 'They've always been so completely understanding and accepting: and, by the way, they're really looking forward to meeting you on Monday. Dennis was like a son-in-law to them, and they were such a support to me when he got sick. My dad makes sure I don't go without, and that's why I'm so undecided about whether to sell Den's house or rent it out.'

Hearing this information was a huge relief for Clive, who had felt quite uncomfortable asking Michael about the more personal details concerning the instructions Dennis had left behind. Clive assured Michael that, if he were in his shoes, he wouldn't rush into making major decisions about the sale of number 257 for the time being. Michael found his words reassuring, but there were issues that did need addressing and he really had to get down to the business of sorting through all of Dennis's effects, but he also confessed that he was finding the task somewhat onerous. He insisted that Clive take a memento back to England with him and asked if there was anything in particular that he wanted. Clive thought for a moment, and then answered that he'd like one of the drawings in the front room. Michael responded that he was more than welcome to any of them, but wondered which one in particular, since there were so many to choose from.

'You know, the orange one … the one of Den's arse.'

Finally they arrived at the hospital, parked, and once in the waiting room Michael opened up to Clive.

'I feel so fortunate to have landed such an understanding specialist and that is all due to Dr Allen Leavitt. When Dennis became ill, Allen referred him to Dr Norris and now I'm his patient too. I feel lucky to be in such safe hands when there are rumours flying around about how some doctors are withholding treatment from some AIDS patients. I've heard even worse tales of hospital staff actually refusing to touch anyone they suspect may have the disease.

'That's scandalous', responded Clive. 'How can they abandon people like that and treat them so unfairly. I wonder whether the Hippocratic Oath that doctors back home had to swear helped avoid such appalling practice in Britain?'

'I'm convinced that the Moral Majority had infiltrated the medical profession; those guys believe that homosexuality is as evil as legalised abortion or socialism. You know Clive, there is a particular religious group that is releasing pamphlets quoting the Old Testament, and the book of Leviticus in particular. Those dangerous religious fanatics believed that sexual relations between males was a sin and that such unlawful sexual practices should be punishable by death. In fact, I've even tried to discuss it with Allen Levitt, who I believe I told you is Jewish.'

'Really,' Clive responded, 'and what did Allen say?'

'I'm afraid I made him feel most uncomfortable and he confessed to being very conflicted by his faith, which he knew considered homosexuality to be a detestable sin.'

Michael maintained that it wasn't just the Orthodox Jewish community who believed that homosexuals were contributing to the deterioration of the moral fibre of the nation: there were many other conservative groups who felt similarly. All in all, these sentiments seemed to fit in with the discussion Clive had had earlier with Steve and gave added credence to any drastic plans that his new friend thought the FBI might be proposing.

Michael's specialist was punctual for his appointment, but his patient seemed to be gone for quite some time, and while Clive waited, he started to thumb through a number of leaflets that Michael had given him to read. They were published by the self-help organisation set up to advise gay men on health issues in the Columbus catchment area. However, he found his concentration lacking, and he was far too distracted to sit there reading, being only too aware of the pressure he knew Michael to be under. Clive had come round to thinking that it was high time he got himself checked out too. After all, Michael had told him that AIDS can lie dormant, and Clive was now alarmed by the fact that the last time he met up with Dennis, in Aspen, they'd had unprotected sex.

Earlier on, when they drove over to the hospital, Michael told Clive that he, and so many of his friends, had altered their lifestyles and revised their attitudes toward casual relationships and sexual activity. They had developed a much more moral sense of responsibility towards protecting their gay brothers and strove to achieve a means of surviving, which was something Dennis had clearly been denied.

Eventually, Michael emerged and, as he came walking towards Clive, he appeared a little less tense. He apologised for having kept Clive waiting such a long time, but added that he was pleased that he'd been given such a thoroughly good going-over.

As they drove away from the hospital, Clive skirted the question he really wanted to pose, but eventually brought himself to enquire, 'By the way, do you have to keep coming back for these tests on a regular basis?'

'God only knows … until they tell me the worst, I suppose. You know, Clive, I am prepared for it. Of course I don't want to die, but I have had enough time to think what I would feel if the worst should happen and I find out that I'm just one of the many thousands who have contracted this damn thing. I just have to keep telling myself that AIDS is not a punishment: it's sheer bad luck. And I have to keep damn well reminding myself that I'm dealing with something that's bigger than me … bigger than all of us. And what's more, I can tell ya, if I'm gonna go, I'm gonna go with dignity.' And as he released the handbrake, he added: 'After all, I'm not ashamed of being gay.'

He now seemed to be getting angry and so Clive asked him if his doctor had upset him in any way. Michael explained that, on the contrary, it had been one of the lab technicians who had really distressed him when he had deliberately waited for Dr Norris to be out of the room. The guy had intentionally chosen that moment to tell a colleague about a child who had recently died following a blood transfusion that had been traced back to a man who had AIDS. The technician went on to add within earshot: 'Homosexuals, whether healthy or not, should be segregated and not be allowed to donate blood. They're a menace to society and should be got rid of!'

'That's terrible – no wonder you're so upset. But surely the donor didn't give his blood knowing it was contaminated?'

'Clive, that's not the point. I wouldn't have thought so for one minute. But you see, it has obviously maddened some of the health workers and I dread to think what the parents of the little girl must be going through, let alone all the other children in the school that she attended. It's just like Dennis warned us: he said there would be a witch-hunt and that we would be treated like scapegoats.'

'Please try not to upset yourself,' said Clive. 'That's precisely the kind of ignorance that sets out to undermine the kindness and understanding we are receiving from so many other people throughout the world. We do have to try to keep calm and hold on to our self-respect.'

'I'm sorry, but it was so frustrating. That guy had the audacity to say that we were unclean and I had to just lie there, with all those needles in me, and take all that shit: I couldn't even answer back with all those pipes in my mouth. That bastard wouldn't have dared say such things if Dr Norris had been there in the room at the time. Outsiders we may be but some people are treating us like lepers'

That last remark silenced Clive as they drove back to Dennis's house, but clearly Michael now had a lot more to get off his chest and Clive was more than prepared to listen to his friend's outpourings.

'I made a stand nearly twenty years ago, when I came out at art college, Michael said. 'I really enjoyed sex. I liked it a lot and had as many men as I could handle long before I met Dennis. Sure, we were a sort of couple, and we loved each other. But, Clive, neither of us was monogamous, nor did we live like some of those terrible suburban married gays you meet. We never deliberately tried to corrupt or split people up: that wasn't our scene either, and we certainly had no intention of killing people. We just wanted to enjoy the sexual freedom that existed then amongst us gay men, either separately or together.'

'Yes, I remember the first time I met you.'

'You mean when we lured you into a threesome? Well, looking back on it now, I'm not sure I'm too proud about what happened that afternoon.'

'Don't be silly. You and Dennis just wanted us to be one big happy family. And although I was a bit of a prude, I was finally able to indulge in a greater degree of sexual freedom. Thanks to Dennis, my Provincetown experience had certainly given me more confidence in the bedroom department, and I know that when I returned to England, I was a very changed man and felt much more relaxed about my sex life. I also now acknowledge that I still had a way to go when I first visited Columbus, which must have been only too apparent on that afternoon. Anyway, that was then; and now we're in the eighties, we have AIDS to contend with and we are all so much more careful, and we jolly well have to be.'

'Yes, of course we do. But when you have to deal with people like that bigot at the hospital, I lose heart and get so depressed. I feel that the finger of contempt is being pointed at me and it leads me to wonder whether anything is worth fighting for any more. The tip of the iceberg has just smashed through our pleasure cruiser and if that deadly virus doesn't get us, public hatred will, and social ostracism will banish us from the rest of society with the kind of loathing we haven't witnessed since the rise of fascism back in the thirties.'

Clive realised there was no point disagreeing; in fact, he knew there was a great deal of sense in what his friend believed. He was sympathetic to what Michael had been saying about the Jews in Nazi-occupied Europe: the wealth of some and perceived difference in lifestyle had led them to be persecuted in much the same way that gays were being ostracised now. Clive also pointed out that many gay men had also ended up in the concentration camps. However, the Englishman declared that time was a great healer and that even in Europe, the Germans had been forgiven for what had happened in the Second World War and amends had been made.

When the two got back to the Colony, Clive persuaded Michael he should have a lie-down, take a sedative, and try to relax after the pressure of what had been an exhausting visit to the hospital. As Clive poured himself a scotch and examined the storyboard he had drawn up so far, he began to wonder whether the plan that Jim had uncovered was working sooner and with greater effect than was perhaps ever anticipated. He needed to really get to the bottom of the so-called conspiracy, and knew that he hadn't heard the full story from Steve, since Mr Leggard had said as much the previous evening. So, with Michael now out like a light, Clive decided to invite Steve round to number 257. Clive was more determined than ever to find out what the senator had discovered in Arizona and why he'd been done away with.

'Steve, you must think I'm a terrible nosy parker, but I do want to learn as much as I can about what Dennis had stumbled upon, and how he had discovered that the FBI – or whoever – were planning the spread of AIDS here in the States. I'm beginning to get my head around some of what you told me when we last met, but I have to admit there are still a few missing pieces to the jigsaw.'

'Clive, I know how much Dennis meant to you, and I'm more than happy to tell you everything he told me. Mmm ... this martini is going down real well. Thank you.'

'Michael has been giving me lessons. Oh, and by the way, he was so exhausted after all those tests at the hospital, I made him lie down and rest. Poor Michael said that lying there with all those needles in him made him feel like a pincushion. And talking of which, I hate needles, don't you?'

'Funny you should say that. I realise I never got around to telling you about what was going on down in Arizona. You see, needles were involved in the laboratory experiments being carried out near Tucson, and Jim's marine finally shared all this classified information, which he had gathered down south with his senator friend.'

Steve told Clive that what he was about to reveal some highly confidential and very incriminating material. He explained that when Dennis went into hospital for the final time, he had told him that Jim, in his capacity as senator, had managed to get himself attached to a team of government officials making a rudimentary inspection of an experimental germicide plant not far from Tucson. At this top-security site down in Arizona, The Central Intelligence Agency had developed Operation Mukultra; a programme to research the use of biological and chemical materials and Jim was able to collect just enough information to make him believe that his young marine friend had definitely been on to something.

Clive admitted that it was all beginning to sound like some sort of B-movie.

Steve became quite adamant, and insisted that he wouldn't personally call germ warfare B-movie material, and he also believed that Jim didn't either. He explained that when Jim finally returned to Washington, he told Dennis that the information he had discovered for himself in Arizona seemed to tally with what his marine buddy, Hank Watson, had confidentially reported to him back in DC. As a result of all these shenanigans, Jim had told Dennis that it was decided that it would be a lot safer for him and his paramour not to see each other any more. As a result of this, Hank decided to go on compassionate leave and got himself stationed out in Kentucky so that he could be closer to his mother, who was conveniently ailing at the time. The more Jim uncovered, the more he became aware of the seriousness of what the FBI were up to and, once his friend had left Washington, he began to feel extremely isolated and vulnerable.

Then, about two months later, Jim was informed that Hank had been killed in a car crash. On the face of it, it seemed like an ordinary accident which could have happened to anybody, but Jim was not convinced and believed that too many question marks still remained unanswered.

'So they got rid of Jim's marine too.'

'It would appear so. Then shortly afterwards – and this is where maybe it does begin to sound like a bit of a mystery thriller – Jim told Dennis that he had started to receive a series of threatening and anonymous telephone calls in the middle of the night.'

'Jesus, you're joking!' Steve's last remarks helped explain why Dennis had been so troubled in Aspen and why he had invited Clive out there.

'It was the straw that broke the camel's back, I suppose,' Steve continued, 'and it certainly scared the shit out of Jim. He just panicked, and once in possession of all that information, he didn't know what the fuck to do with it. There was no one in Washington he trusted and he felt he couldn't go to the police, let alone the press. He certainly didn't want to endanger the safety of his wife and kids back in Illinois, but he was desperate to talk to someone.'

'So he got in touch with Dennis again.'

'And that's why, when they met up in Colorado, Den thought he was behaving like someone on the run, and in a way, I suppose he was, and I certainly know that Jim's visit to Arizona had alarmed him enormously. Jim told Dennis that he was anxious about the phone calls he was getting, and after his marine's demise, he was terrified by the death threats he himself was now receiving. So Jim finally decided to step down as senator and go into hiding, and who could blame him?'

'That doesn't surprise me in the least. And I suppose that's why, when Dennis walked into the Men's Center that day, it's little wonder you found him in such a terrible state: he must have been terribly concerned about what might happen to Jim.'

'Absolutely spot on. I can tell you, I was convinced that Den had been drinking or something. I thought I was listening to the ravings of someone who was high as a kite. Then, when he came back to see me the following morning, I changed my mind. He had calmed down a good deal and sounded plausible and was highly articulate. As our trust grew, he told me all that he knew and I began to believe in the plot as well. Then,' Steve uttered in very hushed tones, 'in January 1980, something very untoward happened, which convinced me utterly that his were not the ravings of an hysterical queen. Den and I were really shocked to read in a national newspaper that shortly after Christmas, Jim had been found dead on the ski slopes in Aspen, Colorado.

It dawned on Clive that Jim's death must have occurred the year after he and Dennis had met up there. 'Den must have been devastated.'

'And terrified also. He didn't believe for one moment that it had been an accident, and so he began to fear for his own life. After all, Senator Jim had told Dennis everything he had found out about in Colorado, thereby incriminating Den too.'

'Now you're not going to tell me the FBI tried to bump Dennis off too?'

'Unfortunately, something much more deadly got hold of our Den. But the supreme irony was that the last person alive – apart from me, that is – who knew everything that Jim had found out about goes and gets AIDS himself. You see, just before Den went into hospital for the last time, he told me that Jim had found out that the germicide plant in Tucson had been carrying out experiments and had reproduced a swine virus that could attack the helper cells in the bloodstream and that, if administered, could in time reduce their number radically. In short, those damn scientists had succeeded in manufacturing a virus that could eventually cause AIDS.'

Now the missing pieces of the jigsaw suddenly dropped into place for Clive. The novel viral agent that Jim and his marine had found out about was in all probability the cause of this outbreak of what the doctors now referred to as Acquired Immune Deficiency Syndrome. Although Clive realised that Dennis's death was one of some 6,000 cases openly reported in the USA, he couldn't help but think that his demise was all too convenient for the FBI. However, he decided to curb such thoughts and steer their conversation away from Dennis for the time being.

'How long did you say it took the virus to take effect?'

'I didn't say, Clive, but I think it can lie inactive in the system for some time before any symptoms appear. And that was an important factor. Those guys experimenting in Tucson were able to isolate a virus which they would then introduce into a highly promiscuous group and, moreover, it could lie dormant and eventually spread undetected.'

'I suppose the sixties and seventies offered them a golden opportunity.'

'Yes, I would agree with you. But in our defence, I would also say that our promiscuity was a reaction to all the repression following the war years.'

'Oh really? What do you mean?'

'Well, back in the forties and under the pressure of warfare, men in all the armed services had the opportunity to develop the sort of close relationships with each other that they didn't even recognise as being gay.'

'Oh, I see now,' Clive replied. 'I suppose I'd never thought about it like that.'

'Anyway, as you were saying earlier, by the seventies there was one hell of a lot of indiscriminate gay sexual activity going on here in the United States. You know as well as I do that by now, in the eighties, some amongst us might have sexual contact with as many as over three hundred men in one year alone. So if one of us already had AIDS, we could have passed it on to hundreds of others. That's how efficient the virus was.'

Clive thought for a moment, and then added: 'You might say that those scientists had found the perfect vehicle for total destruction. A sort of human time bomb, difficult to identify and harder still to deactivate once it had been set up.'

'And, another thing, Clive. It's almost impossible to monitor the spread of the virus, due to the fact that gays often had so many casual encounters that it's hard to trace things back. It struck right at our Achilles heel, and at first began to work in a slow and deadly way up until now, when it has gathered such enormous momentum.'

'Now I'm beginning to understand how it has managed to spread so easily. But how on earth did they plant the virus in the first place?'

'You know, when Dennis came to me with what I thought was such a tall story, I began to think of possible ways myself: that is, before he told me everything.'

'What do you mean?'

'It seems quite ridiculous now that I know,' Steve continued, 'but at the time I thought it was some special chemical substance that could be secreted in the steam rooms of all those bathhouses and saunas we used to go to. Do you remember that all-too-familiar smell that hit you whenever you entered those confined little rooms? I even asked a friend of mine who was a biochemist if it was possible to spread the virus in that way.'

'And was it?'

'He thought it a very dramatic idea, but totally unscientific. No: those Tucson guys were no amateurs. They really knew what they were doing.'

'And now you're telling me that Jim and his marine had found out how they were doing it?'

'That's why they had to be eliminated, and I guess Dennis was also in danger: although, he went along and contracted the damn thing himself.'

'You know, somewhere at the back of mind is a feeling that they did get Dennis.'

'I'm not so sure about that one. He certainly died of AIDS, but I'm not sure he was bumped off by that swine virus'

'Yes of course he did. But Steve, you still haven't told me how the virus was spread.'

'No, indeed I haven't. I'm going to ask you to take your mind back to when you came into the USA on a student visa. Do you remember the exact procedure they put you through on entering the States for any degree of permanency?'

'Yes, as a matter of fact I do. But I don't see how that has anything to do with the spread of AIDS ... Another martini?'

'You don't even have to ask.'

As Clive fixed the drinks, he remembered the endless forms he had had to fill out in order to get a student visa; of the interview that followed at the American Embassy in Grosvenor Square in London and, of course, that vigorous medical examination they gave him, and that was certainly something he had never been able to forget.

'Clive, cast your mind back. Do you remember a blood test?'

'Now you come to mention it, I'm afraid I do. The chap in front of me passed out when they took a blood sample, and as I said earlier on, I hate needles, but, fortunately for me, that morning I was fine.'

'So they put a needle in your arm, and extracted a sample of your blood. Is that correct?'

'Yes. But it was no different from any other blood test I'd ever had.'

'That's exactly my point.' Steve was now adamant. 'A simple pinprick, and it was over.'

'Yes, I suppose so.'

'And what would you say if I told you that as well as taking a sample of your blood, the doctor was more than capable of injecting you with a virus?'

Although Clive was no scientist, he recognised the logic behind Steve's theory: that a contaminated needle could inject a virus at the same time as it was taking a blood sample. He decided that, he would phone and ask his doctor in Hammersmith whether such a procedure was possible.

Steve went on to explain that it was the Caribbean resort of Haiti that had been targeted to launch the lethal vaccinations and since it had long been a fashionable gay holiday paradise, it was known that privileged American bachelors would arrive in their droves and shower dollars on the local young men in exchange for their favours. There was a lot of unemployment on the island, so business was brisk, and some of the wealthier Americans were also on the lookout for permanent houseboys they could take home with them. A visa was requested and the normal procedures for obtaining one were adopted.

'Those poor unsuspecting Haitian boys who had found work in the USA,' Steve continued, 'applied for a permit and were subject to the usual formalities. While giving a blood sample in order to gain official entry into the United States, they were also being injected with a deadly virus. Of course, they would come in contact with their American sponsors in more ways than one, and slowly but surely they would help spread what they had been infected with, without having any idea that they were responsible for causing the ensuing calamity.'

'But Steve, blood tests are pretty routine. I mean, didn't Dennis have one when he visited Dr Levitt at the STD clinic here in Columbus?'

'Yes, I believe he did.'

Then Clive asked. 'Is it possible that's how Dennis contracted AIDS?'

'Now you're really putting me on the spot, Clive. If that were to be the case, it would suggest that Allen is also involved with all this.'

'And do you think he might be?'

'Allen's a very charming, attractive, young gay doctor.'

'Steve, my dear friend, you're avoiding my question.'

'Since coming to Columbus, Allen has been very active in our gay community and is completely committed to the Men's Center. He's done so much to help prevent the spread of AIDS that I'm just finding it hard to believe he would want to cause it.'

'Yes, Michael has told me how much help and support he has provided. But, you see, I haven't met him yet, so it's somewhat premature for me to make judgements about someone I don't even know. Tell me – is he really the angel of mercy everyone says he is?'

'He certainly appears to be, but please don't repeat a word of what I'm about to say about him to Michael.' Then, lowering his voice, Steve continued. 'You see, now you come to mention it, just lately I've felt uneasy about Allen ... I can admit to you that I find there is something about him that doesn't ring true for me – it's just that I can't quite put my finger on it.'

'And yet Michael seems to have formed such a very trusting

relationship with him.'

'Yes, I know, and after Dennis passed away, they've become very close. And that's why you mustn't repeat what I've just said to you. But you know, all things considered, and despite my doubts, I really am finding it hard to believe that he could have been responsible for injecting Dennis with that deadly virus.'

'I really have to meet him,' admitted Clive.

'And I'm sure you will.'

'But Steve, with all this information, don't you also feel at risk yourself?'

'Yes, of course I do. But you are the very first person I've shared all this with and I suppose that's because you're a foreigner. I've no intention of telling anyone here in the USA. It's all hearsay and anecdote: I have no actual proof of Den's wipe-out theory. And besides, Jim, that marine of his and our Dennis are now all dead.'

So at last Clive believed he had got to the bottom of it all. He was now convinced that his friend Susan Carlsberg's rumour wasn't so far-fetched after all and his storyboard was finally complete. Contamination through infected needles, which could spread a deadly virus extremely efficiently.

A virus that won't necessarily affect most of the population and that can be contained and nurtured in a minority group that rarely goes outside its own ghetto.

A virus that can be spread through sexual contact.

A virus that, once implanted, can lie dormant.

A virus that, once it takes hold, reduces the body's ability to fight disease.

A virus that can not only destroy a subculture physically, but that can also cause a breakdown of morale and massive loss of confidence.

A virus that can ultimately lead to hatred and ostracism.

A virus that can exterminate an entire minority group.

MURDER!

CHAPTER NINE

DR ALLEN LEVITT SATURDAY

'Shirley darling, it's Saturday already and my week is almost up. You see, with all that's been going on here, I do feel I need a little more time here in Columbus.'

'Well, that's not a problem. I can change your reservations if you have to stay on a bit longer.'

'It's just that I've found out the most unbelievable information.'

Clive then proceeded to relate his findings so far. He told Shirley all about the Fred Macadam saga and Dennis's involvement with the mysterious senator known as Jim. He then went on to describe what Steve had told him about the classified information uncovered at the White House, and really relished sharing the bit about Jim uncovering the existence of an experimental germicide plant near Tucson and how the senator became convinced that the scientists working down there had created a virus which, once administered by injection, could lead to the spread of AIDS.

Clive explained that Jim had shared all his information with Dennis, including the blood-test theory and how the entire operation was believed to have been instigated in Haiti. Shirley just sat glued to the phone and lapped up the minutest detail, fascinated by every moment and finally admitted that it would all make a great film script.

'Darling, this is serious stuff and it's certainly not B-movie material. I'm scared, not just for me, but for these Columbus boys too!' said Clive. 'If what Steve told me turns out to be true, then they could both be in danger because of what they know, and now that I've become involved, so could I!'

'Clive, darling, I didn't mean to sound flippant, but don't you think you're overreacting? I do realise you are anxious: I can hear it in your voice. Of course, I haven't taken it all in yet, but do you have any real proof of this so-called conspiracy theory?' And before she gave Clive the chance to answer, she offered to come out to Columbus the following week so that she could talk everything through with him and try to be of some assistance.

'To be honest, that might not be such a bad idea,' said Clive. 'But darling, do you think you could fly out as early as tomorrow night? I realise that's very short notice and doesn't give you much of a weekend off, but if you think you can leave Roberta for a few days, I really would appreciate your support here as soon as possible.'

Shirley recognised the agitation in Clive's voice, and knew her boss well enough to realise that he definitely needed her help. So she calmly assured him that she'd be happy to fly out and that she'd get onto it right away. In the meantime she would also cancel his reservation back to London.

'There are still a few parts of this jigsaw that I haven't pieced together yet. I need to meet the man who gave Dennis his blood test; this Dr Allen Levitt sounds as though he could be involved in all this, and if he is, I'm beginning to believe he could be an undercover agent working for the FBI.'

'Now Clive, you're not serious!'

'Well, I've yet to meet him, but I've got a sneaking suspicion that he might be a major player and mixed up in it all. Listen, darling, I'll tell Michael that you have Spoke business to discuss with me and that you and I have important work to do here and consequently he'll understand that I need to stay with you in a hotel for a few days. So could you also book us a couple of rooms?'

'You bet. Now just you keep out of trouble and take great good care of yourself. Especially when you meet up with that ... Dr Levitt, did you say his name was?'

Clive told Michael that Shirley needed to come out to Columbus with some contracts they had to go over together. He apologised profusely, and said that he would have to move into a hotel for a couple of nights so that he and Shirley could get their work done. He also admitted that he felt somewhat overwhelmed by all the medical information he had gleaned in the last few days and was beginning to wonder whether he should try to see someone at the hospital himself and have an AIDS test. Michael felt that was easily arranged but pointed out that Dr Norris was a specialist, a research urologist, and he therefore felt that his friend Dr Allen Levitt would be a better person for Clive to see.

'Actually Michael, I meant Dr Levitt,' said Clive. 'Now that I've heard so much about this doctor friend of yours, I would really like to meet him. He sounds absolutely the kind of medic who could help me get to grips with all this AIDS information I've been learning about. Do you think he'd see me?'

'I'm sure he'll see you. And besides, I think you'll like him, he's very attractive.'

'And ... does he have a lover? Oh! I'm only joking.'

'Funny you should ask, but I've never seen him out with anyone and, try as we might, we could never lure Allen into bed, but of course we only got to know him just before this AIDS scare hit us. He's also quite religious and maybe he only dates Jewish boys, and I believe there are not too many of those in Columbus. Say, why don't I call him right now?'

With that, Michael went and dialled Allen's number and immediately got through to him. He assured Allen that everything went fine at the hospital and that he had no new developments to report about the state of his own health. He said that his very dear friend Clive Spoke was over from the UK, staying with him, and that Clive had expressed the need to talk to a doctor about AIDS while he was still in the United States and maybe have a test.

Allen said he was thinking of calling round to see Michael that evening anyway on his way to giving his weekly talk at the Men's Center, and that his English friend was more than welcome to attend if he felt that it might be helpful.

'Allen's coming round this evening and you can meet him then. He wondered if you'd like to go to the weekly AIDS meeting he hosts tonight?'

Clive nodded back.

'Great! Allen, Clive would love to go. See you at six-thirty, then? Bye … yes … bye.' And he hung up.

'That's all fixed, then. He'll drop round on his way to his usual Saturday-night meeting, you two can get acquainted and then go with him to the Center. I can meet up with you afterwards, and we can have dinner later.'

'Sounds like an excellent idea. Steve told me about the Men's Center, but tell me, how did it start?'

Michael couldn't quite remember the exact date when it was set up, but he believed that it was certainly some time before Dennis became sick. He told Clive that it was established by a group of men in the local gay community to offer advice and provide a place for people to congregate and have social evenings that were not an excuse for finding a quick pick-up. Then he added that with the outbreak of AIDS, its purpose became more and more relevant, and when Den went into hospital, some of his friends rallied round and formed a self-help group based there. At first they created a rota system for visiting Dennis, which gave Michael a much-needed break. Although Michael was by his partner's side most of the time, he told Clive that it wasn't easy for either of them and the more Dennis had to distract him while he was just lying there, the better it was for all concerned. Then, when other AIDS patients were admitted to the hospital, the support group grew bigger and was also enormously helpful to all the families involved. Michael explained that they had now formed a fundraising organisation, to help with the crippling medical bills. The Columbus AIDS Now Trust Fund had been officially established to offer financial assistance, and the current premises which had been acquired, operated the entire shebang.

'Wow, that's really impressive.'

'There have been twenty-two cases reported here in Columbus, at the last count, so you can imagine how much assistance is now needed. But to get back to Allen, I'm sure you two will get on, and since you're staying on for those meetings with your PA, you could ask him to make you an appointment for an AIDS test at his clinic next week.'

'Michael, that's a super idea. But why shouldn't we get on?'

'Well, you have rather indicated that Steve Leggard is something of a handful.' And, without waiting for a response from Clive, he continued: 'Now, if you don't mind, I'm feeling a little washed out, so I think I'll take one of those little "naps" you're always talking about.'

'You go right ahead. I've got all those publications you gave me to read when we went to the hospital. I must confess, I just wasn't in the mood then. But now I know your friend the learned doctor is coming round, I need to study them and be prepared to ask the right sort of questions and not waste his time. And, by the way, you don't happen to have the leaflet published by that religious group you mentioned earlier on, do you?'

When the buzzer to number 257 went, Michael was still resting, so Clive went to let the doctor in. He really didn't know what to expect though he had heard that Allen was really rather good-looking, but his eyes nearly popped out of his head when he opened the front door. There stood a tall, elegantly dressed man in his early thirties, wearing a smartly cut Italian-style double-breasted suit in navy blue, with a white shirt and discreet red-and-blue striped tie. His thick, dark hair was combed back off his forehead, and on either side of a slightly aquiline nose were the largest pair of blue-grey eyes. Clive tried to cover up the delightful surprise he was given by quickly ushering Allen into the house and introducing himself and saying rather apologetically:

'I say, Michael's having a nap, but I can quickly go and call him.'

'No. Please don't do that on my account. I'm sure he probably needs his rest.'

'As a matter of fact, we have had quite a hectic few days. What with all the packing up to do here, our visit to Dove Park the day before yesterday, which was rather draining, and then the hospital today. Now I seem to have forgotten my manners. What can I offer you to drink, Dr Levitt?'

'Oh, please call me Allen. And coffee's fine. I won't have a drink, thank you Clive, not before the meeting: I need to be able to think straight. So tell me, when did you arrive in Columbus?'

'I think it was Tuesday. But, you know with jetlag, it's so easy to lose track of the days and we have had rather a lot to do.'

'Yes, it sounds as though Michael has been taking on a little too much for his own good.'

'And what with putting me up as well. That's why we moved in here, by the way, where there's more than one bedroom. And honestly, Allen, I am trying to help Michael with all the packing up he has to do here.'

'I'm sure you are, but you really must try to stop him from overdoing things. Whether he realises it or not, he is still suffering from delayed shock and I'm sure you'll understand when I tell you that it will take him quite some time to get over the sort of thing he's just been through.'

'Of course, you're absolutely right. I suppose I ought to try to get him to slow down a bit.'

'Get who to slow down a bit?' Michael emerged around the bend in the stairwell. 'Is Uncle Allen telling you I'm being a naughty patient?' And he went straight over to Allen and gave him a huge hug.

'No, of course not. Would I say that behind your back? You're damn right I would. Listen Michael, just try to deal with one stressful event a day, and not three!'

'Well, with Clive staying here and keeping me company, I feel I really can cope. And what's more, I've been trying to stay off the booze.'

'That's something, I suppose. You know I have your best interests at heart, and I know you don't mind me checking up on you, which is what Dennis would have wanted.'

The briefest of silences followed, which Allen broke. He asked Clive how long he had known Michael and where he was from in the UK. The Englishman responded with a potted history of how he had met his Columbus boys and described his glittering career as a theatrical agent in London. While Michael made some coffee in the kitchen, Clive seized the opportunity to explain to Allen that his few days in Columbus had made him realise how ill-informed he was about AIDS, although he admitted that on his last visit to New York he had become aware of its existence. Consequently, Michael had suggested that they meet so that Clive could go home with a much better picture of the latest medical developments in the USA.

'I'm more than happy to answer any questions you might have, Clive. I believe everyone should be kept up to date about AIDS in order to safeguard their own health as well as take responsibility for others'. But that's why I suggested that you come along to the talk-in at the Men's Center tonight. Our weekly meetings are designed to put people in the picture. I want to try to help everyone cope with this terrible illness, share information about the research that's going on, and prevent the kind of alarm and hysteria that comes from listening to far-fetched rumours.'

When Michael brought the coffee into the lounge, Allen asked him if he minded if Clive went along to the meeting.

'Of course not. Besides, Clive must need a break: we've been spending far too much time together; he must be sick to death of me.'

'Don't be ridiculous, Michael. I came back to Columbus specially to be with you. But this meeting does sound like the kind of session which will help me get my head round all this AIDS business. '

'Then you shall go to the ball!' joked Michael. 'Seriously though, you go right along. Why don't we all meet up for dinner afterwards somewhere downtown? I'll book a table at Le Gai Paris.'

'Sounds great. Let's meet at my clinic at nine o'clock. It's close by the Center and that will give me enough time to check my message service after the meeting and make sure there are no emergencies to deal with.

Then Allen suddenly looked at his watch. 'I really think we better get going, Clive.'

He added something to his coffee before quickly gulping it down, then explained that he had to get there a little before time to make sure that everything was set up and ready.

'Yes, of course. I'm ready. I just have to get my mac.'

'Your what?' Michael asked.

'Oh! My raincoat. Mac is short for mackintosh. We may all speak English, Allen, but you Americans speak an entirely different language. See you later, Michael.'

With that said, Clive was escorted to a black Cadillac saloon, which was parked outside Dennis's house. Although he thought himself mature enough not to be overimpressed by such a luxurious vehicle, he had to admit that he hadn't ridden in such a posh car for quite some time. He had also noticed the rather expensive gold

Jaeger-LeCoultre Reverso that Allen sported on his wrist. However, as his New York millionaire friends the Carlsbergs had told him so frequently, there was a lot of new money around in the US of A, and Clive simply assumed that Allen came from a wealthy background.

On the drive downtown, Allen explained that the STD clinic he ran was attached to the Columbus General Hospital, but set back in its own grounds, and added that he had largely pioneered the work being undertaken there. The Men's Center had asked him whether he could do more educational work within the gay community, to which he'd agreed and so he had decided to set up weekly AIDS information sessions on a Saturday night and be their facilitator. He also told Clive that although he had not officially come out to the hospital personnel manager, he had never denied his own homosexuality when challenged. He had made it quite clear that he had a personal as well as professional interest in assisting the local gay community, and was determined to try to prevent the spread of AIDS in the Columbus catchment area.

Although such honesty might be considered detrimental to his career prospects, he maintained that he was totally committed to the gay cause and that now, with the AIDS scare, it was more important than ever to stand up and be counted and help in any way possible. As a medic, he was in a privileged position to make a uniquely important contribution to society, which left Clive thinking that, to all intents and purposes, his new acquaintance was a very impressive young man.

However that Spoke nose of Clive's picked up on something else. Certainly Allen Levitt was handsome and, clearly, gifted, but slightly too keen to stress how dedicated and unselfish he was for Clive's taste. So as they drove through town, Clive felt his sympathy with Allen wane. Although later on, at the meeting, Clive was soon to discover that Allen's charm and good looks seemed to have an almost mesmerising effect on most of the young men with whom he came into contact.

'I've been in Columbus for less than a year, but I really feel at home here: it's really quite laid back you know.'

'Tell me, what drew you to work in such a small town, when I imagine you could have chosen a more prestigious hospital. Do you have family here?'

'No, as a matter of fact I don't. I grew up in New York but there's less pressure here. My parents lived in Manhattan where I was born but sadly my dad passed away when I was three and mum remarried so I was raised by my stepfather who I must admit I didn't get on with.'

At which point Clive's questioning became somewhat more personal, until he finally came out with it and plucked up the courage to ask him if he had a lover in Columbus. At first Allen tried to brush off Clive's line of enquiry, but when pushed further he responded:

'You see Clive, we were quite observant at home and homosexuality was frowned upon by my mother. I guess although I've moved away from all that now, I can't escape my roots and my upbringing does make me feel more than a little uncomfortable about my orientation.'

Clearly Clive's prying into the more private aspects of Allen's life had touched a raw nerve and he realised that despite the young doctor's apparent confidence regarding professional matters, Allen was much less forthcoming about his personal life, which was clearly rather complex.

Clive decided to drop his line of questioning and simply accepted he'd been possibly too forthright. He reminded himself that back home he had always believed that personal privacy should be respected at all times and he had endeavoured to make that clear, especially on the work front at Spoke Associates. Back at the office, he revealed little about himself and, similarly, he knew only too well that despite their closeness, Clive had never dreamt of prying into Shirley's past and consequently knew relatively little about her pre-Spoke days either.

So, as they drove along, Clive was able to restrain his curiosity about what made Allen tick, and the physical attraction he had initially felt for the young man began to wane. Finally, the professional in him asserted itself: Clive decided to change tack completely and bring his line of questioning back to the meeting he was about to attend. Allen, now on more comfortable ground, said he was determined to be as supportive as possible and allay all misconceptions that might confuse and distress anyone in his audience. He admitted it was no easy task to pitch his talk at the right sort of level, and made it clear to Clive that he welcomed all members of the Columbus community, including the families and friends of patients, and wanted to create a warm and friendly atmosphere.

Clive admitted that he was very sympathetic to Allen's concern about his people skills, and pointed out that he knew how important it was to be firm while also being able to put folk at their ease, especially when it came to dealing with thespians. Allen welcomed Clive's confidence and went on to describe how hard it was not to sound too condescending nor underestimate the intelligence of his audience. Clive, adroitness personified, responded that although they'd just met, he felt sure that Allen was more than capable of pulling the event off with great aplomb.

CHAPTER TEN

THE TALK-IN SATURDAY

When they finally reached the Men's Center, Allen directed Clive towards a room set out with rows of chairs lined neatly in front of a projector screen, to the side of which was a small desk and a slightly more imposing chair. Five or six men were already waiting and they appeared to be acquainted, since they were heavily in conversation. Clive took his place in the back row and watched on as the room gradually filled up. A little after half-past seven, Allen made a sudden, quiet entrance, and an immediate hush fell on those assembled.

'Gentlemen. Firstly let me apologise for keeping you all waiting, and welcome you to this week's AIDS talk-in. Let me say how very pleased I am to see so many of you here tonight, and how much I appreciate your attending. However, I would also like to stress that these meetings are open to all members of our Columbus community and I would be so happy to see more families and friends here. So do please spread the word and let's try not to make the Men's Center in any way exclusive.

'This isn't a formal lecture, but it will contain a certain amount of medical detail, as those of you who have been here before have come to expect. So please go ahead and feel free to interrupt me at any point during my talk with questions. However, before I begin, I want to be frank with all of you and, in order to avoid any mixed messages, tell you that I am also a gay man.'

At this point the entire room seemed to adjust its seating with what Clive thought was an almost tangible sign of approval. Allen assured his congregation that any questions answered would be in complete confidence and apologised for the fact that his statistics might already be somewhat out of date.

Then, reading from his notes, Allen went into some historical background concerning the discovery of the disease. He explained that in the United States, AIDS had come to the attention of the general public only a few years ago when the first official report appeared in 1981 and was issued by the Center for Disease Control in Atlanta, Georgia. He also revealed that in New York, back in '79, there had been an outbreak of an unknown disease, unclassified at the time, which had caused some deaths, but he pointed out that it was only later that it had been identified as AIDS. Professional colleagues, whether they be immunologists, haematologists, virologists or pathologists, had applied themselves to dealing with what had now become a crisis. Current research specialists were attempting to discover the cause of the outbreak and ultimately find a cure. However, he regretted to have to inform the gathering that so far none of his colleagues had reported any kind of breakthrough.

'AIDS stands for Acquired Immune Deficiency Syndrome, which is a condition that causes a complete or partial breakdown of the body's natural ability to fight off an illness. We still haven't been able to find a procedure that can put right the body's immune machinery and restore its defence mechanism once AIDS has been contracted. And I'm sorry to have to tell you that anyone diagnosed with the disease will have a difficult time surviving once this illness takes hold.'

This last remark caused a strong reaction amongst those gathered, not least from Clive, who now felt more determined than ever to have an AIDS test.

'However, it is also true to say that life expectancy varies, and current research does indicate that some cases live longer than others, which some of us believe is due to the more positive attitude taken by some of the patients dealing with the illness. But let me be clear ... the number of people being diagnosed with AIDS in the US is developing at an alarming rate and almost doubles every six months. It is estimated that by 1985 we will have some twenty thousand cases to deal with and this is expected to increase twofold every six months.'

One of the youngest men attending that evening immediately shot his hand into the air and Allen quickly responded with: 'Yes, go ahead.'

'You say that there's no cure as yet. But does that mean that there is no treatment being administered at all?'

'Good question. As far as I know, some patients have been given certain drugs that seem to attack the opportunistic infections, but getting at the agent that actually causes AIDS itself is the problem. Perhaps we're just not looking in the right places, or maybe our research equipment isn't advanced enough. However, I do know that some colleagues are hopeful that the drug Interleukin 2, which can stimulate the development of new helper cells in the immune system, may be a breakthrough. But the fact remains that trial tests on humans require at least two more years to complete and even then there is no guarantee that any conclusive deductions will be made.'

At which point he took a sip of water, and then continued to point out that current research also indicated that the figures had levelled off somewhat recently and he thought that the de-escalation was probably due to a greater sense of responsibility amongst the gay community as a whole. Nevertheless, he stressed that the most important fact was that nearly three-quarters of US AIDS patients up to that point had been gay men under the age of sixty, and he regretted to inform the gathering that there had already been eleven deaths reported in Columbus, as some of them were already aware.

Despite the slightly alarming nature of these facts and statistics, Allen wanted to stress how important it was for all of them not to panic. Although he admitted that it was legitimate to be concerned, he also insisted that it was important not to overreact and, despite the fact that there was an immense amount of research still to be carried out and many questions continued to remain unanswered, he assured them that what doctors did know for certain was that they were dealing with a disease that could not be spread casually. In other words, he maintained that it was absolutely not possible to catch AIDS from drinking from a glass, using a towel or sitting on a toilet seat used by any AIDS patient. He also added that it had not been proved that it could be passed on by coughing and spitting, although he also confirmed that it could be transmitted from the exchange of saliva.

At which point there was another reshuffling of chairs and Allen sensed that his last comment made many of his audience feel uneasy, which caused him to pause for a moment. This halt in the proceedings encouraged another question.

'Excuse me, sir,' asked a young man, 'but how much research is actually being undertaken? I mean, is there enough money being put into all this?'

'I thought that this question might be asked, so I've brought some statistics to read out. It says here, and I quote: "In 1983 our government invested some forty-eight million dollars into AIDS research." Now, that sum represents twenty-four thousand dollars towards each of the two thousand cases reported at that time. In addition to this, several cities and state councils have also funded research. For example, New York and San Francisco did, and I know for a fact that the California State Legislature voted to give nearly three million dollars for research. In New York, The AIDS Medical Foundation has been established with funds donated privately, and similar gay health-action groups have been set up in other cities with big gay communities such as Los Angeles, Chicago and Philadelphia. Here in Columbus, I am pleased to report that a group of us recently started the Columbus AIDS-Now Trust Fund, which has also been privately sponsored.'

The same young man stood up again: 'Dr Levitt, I would like to make a small donation to that fund. I recently inherited some money from my grandfather, and I would like to pass some of it on.'

'That's great and I'll be more than happy to provide an address where money can be sent here in Columbus, to our new local Trust Fund.'

This last statement produced an encouraging round of applause from all those gathered. Then Allen told his audience that he wanted to address the symptoms commonly found in AIDS patients. Before doing so, he stressed how important it was for them not to internalise what they were about to hear and see. It was very important that they didn't start to imagine they had everything he was about to describe and although it was legitimate to be concerned about one's health, it was also imperative to understand that AIDS was not the only cause of immune deficiencies. If by any chance anyone there believed that they really did have any of the symptoms he was about to list, he would be glad to arrange an appointment for them with a professionally qualified person at the STD clinic attached to the Columbus General Hospital where he worked.

Allen then went on to address the following symptoms, which he explained were not in any particular order of importance.

'Lymphadenopathy: the medical term describing swollen glands. It can develop in the neck, armpits or groin and it can be painful in some cases, and not in others. If the condition lasts for more than two weeks, I would strongly advise that you see a doctor.

'White spots: persistent white spots or unusual blemishes in the mouth.

'Night sweats: occurring intermittently over a period of at least several weeks, and leaving the body wringing wet.

'Weight loss: not through diet, but rather a sudden and unexpected loss of weight, greater than ten pounds in less than two months.

'Fever: which lasts for more than ten days, with the body reaching a temperature well above ninety degrees.

'Dry cough: not from smoking, but a condition accompanied by shortness of breath and has lasted too long to be described as a classic lung infection.

'Diarrhoea: that has no obvious cause and seems to persist for a long period of time.

'Kaposi's sarcoma: pink or purple flat or raised blotches or bumps that occur on or under the skin, usually inside the mouth, nose, eyelids or rectum. At first, they may look like bruises that don't fade and they are usually harder than the skin that surrounds them, however, they are not to be confused with moles or birth marks.

'Now I'd like to show some slides which give examples of patients with swollen glands of the throat … under the armpit … and, lastly, in the groin.'

Allowing time for these three slides to make their impression, he continued: 'When the lymph glands are swollen, it is a sure indication that all is not well, and were this to be so, I would suggest that you should almost certainly make an appointment to visit your doctor.'

He then showed two slides of the feet of a patient suffering from Kaposi's sarcoma. The instep of one foot was covered in purple blotches, forming raised scabs on the surface of the foot. The other slide was a shot taken from above, looking down onto the toes. Here again there was a mass of circular blemishes, dark pink in colour, forming clusters all over the upper section of the foot. Allen explained that both slides showed how this form of skin cancer had attacked a patient's foot because of reduced immune defences. However, he went on to argue that there was still much disagreement as to whether the cancer predated the immune breakdown or not.

For some time now, Clive had been worrying about a dark blotch on his left foot and seeing these slides made him more convinced than ever that he needed a proper examination to reassure himself that he was OK.

Allen informed the group that many people with AIDS are susceptible to infections, which a healthy immune system usually attacks and deals with. Opportunistic infections may be caused by germs such as a bacterium, a virus, a Sporozoa or, and less commonly, yeast or a fungus. As the name implies, these infections seize the opportunity to gain hold when an immunological malfunction occurs. He ended the slide show on a more positive note with a series of stills showing that healthy people with a good T-cell count ratio in their system were able to avoid catching the kind of infections that can attack the body of someone with AIDS.

Then a short stocky South American-looking guy raised his hand and Allen invited him to ask his question.

'Is there any truth in the rumour that poppers have something to do with transmitting AIDS?'

'I'm glad you asked. Amyl and butyl nitrites used as stimulants during the sexual activities of many AIDS patients were thought, at one point, to be a contributory factor. These recreational drugs – and I need hardly have to mention them by name to you guys, but I will: Thrust, Locker Room and Hardware – were examined thoroughly. A report brought out in '82 produced inconclusive evidence, as it was found that a certain percentage of patients had never used any of them. However, it can also be argued that, as stimulants, they do encourage a good deal of sexual activity and promiscuity.

'No one yet knows what actually causes the breakdown of our immunity, which can lead to AIDS, although there are two theories put forward by our research scientists, which I can only express in medical terms, so you must all bear with me. The first theory is that it is a novel viral agent, or an old one in a new guise, which attacks the defence cells of the immune system.'

This last remark caused Clive to wonder whether this so-called 'novel viral agent' was the one being produced down in Arizona.

'The second is that multiple factors may be responsible, including a combination of the body's reaction to the constant reactivation of cytomegalovirus, a member of the herpes family, and some research has even indicated that semen itself has been shown to be immune-suppressive.

'Which brings me to examine the sexual implications of these theories. As you are all well aware, the vagina is designed to receive semen and process it. The rectum, on the other hand, is not equipped with the same deactivators. It is designed to extract water from faeces, and will readily absorb semen when present, through its walls. Cytomegalovirus, or CMV for short, is often secreted in saliva, semen and urine, and if found in the rectum, can very easily be absorbed into the body. Sex with a partner who has CMV in his semen could lead to an irreversible breakdown of the immune system, which can cause AIDS. If this conclusion is correct, it is most important to avoid contact with CMV carriers, and wise to reduce the number of different partners you have sex with. The more men you sleep around with, the more you are putting yourself and others at risk.'

The next question came from the other side of the room.

'Even if you do stick with the same guy all the time, could you clarify ... Oh! I don't quite know how to say this...'

'Please go on, I want to be of help.' And Allen's persuasive smile seemed to encourage the young man to continue.

'Thank you. I mean, could you say what sort of sex is recommended. Like, is being fucked by your lover now allowed – provided he's clear, that is?'

'Look, to put it bluntly, getting fucked by your lover, if he comes up your arse, and even if he is wearing a condom, is a huge risk factor. But then, we all know that you can catch gonorrhoea that way too. The greater the number of alien body fluids you allow into your blood and lymph system, the greater the danger you're going to be exposed to. So, I do believe that the passive partner is at greater risk, and until more is known, it is surely advisable to act as though viruses like CMV and even sperm itself, for that matter, are causative agents and are dangerous.'

'I guess that means that blow jobs are out too?' asked the same guy.

'Correct. And here I would go further and say that swallowing piss and rimming should not be practised under any circumstances. Both carry such high health hazards anyway, and very often lead to contracting other sexually transmitted diseases.'

Allen didn't want to blind his audience with science, so simply explained that viruses themselves were baffling and complex, and said out that in the three years of research already undertaken, no one agent had been identified as being common to all patients suffering from this disease. Together with many of his colleagues, he also found it difficult to explain the cause behind the considerable spread of the syndrome in the United States and confirmed that the latest medical opinion was beginning to believe that AIDS could be caused by a new, and as yet unidentified agent or germ.

Once again Clive wondered whether Dr Allen Levitt was referring to the virus Senator Jim had been convinced was being developed near Tucson.

Allen went on to mention that yet another hypothesis, but one supported by only some researchers, was that the hepatitis B virus, known as HBV, may also be a cause of AIDS. In some of the case studies undertaken in the United States, almost half of all the gay men examined were seen to be carrying antibodies against hepatitis B, indicating that at some point they had been exposed to HBV, and were consequently vulnerable to the possibility of catching AIDS.

Allen was absolutely adamant that, given the complexity of the situation, what was certain was that there could be a long incubation period prior to the illness developing, and it was therefore essential that everyone at risk should take the greatest possible care to protect their immune system. With that smile of his, which Clive was now finding irritating, Allen gently stressed the importance of sleep, of maintaining a healthy diet, and of giving due care and attention to personal hygiene in order to avoid any infection. He added that a hundred years ago, sexually transmitted diseases such as syphilis and gonorrhoea were classified as deadly. With research and the discovery of antibiotics, progress was made and cures were found and he was hopeful that, in time, they would find a remedy for this new disease. Then, in conclusion, he informed the gathering that the one thing that was certain and all research agreed upon, was that the transmission of AIDS is almost certainly sexual.

'The fewer people you sleep around with, the smaller the risk you take. Here in America, we sure do have a lot to tempt us, with all the bars, bathhouses, saunas and cinemas exclusively created for us to indulge our pleasures and live out our fantasies. It is also true that in many of our states, sex between consenting underage males is still an offence, and it is clear that in many towns it is not easy to live an openly gay existence. I understand why, in such circumstances, it has often been necessary to seek out anonymous sexual encounters in a variety of locations, and temptation has been great everywhere.

'But gentlemen, now really is the time to curb it. Whatever the reason for so much promiscuity, whether it be to cover up any doubts we may have about how attractive we are, to help us feel less insecure about our masculinity, or whether it's down to simply how randy we may be getting, it's all got to stop!'

There appeared to be a sudden mood change in the room, as though each man there was sharing the same thoughts. Those years of enjoying the delights of sex between consenting males had passed, and what even the most closeted of men thought liberating in the sixties and seventies was, in one lecture, taken away from them and established as taboo. The honeymoon of liberal gay sexual freedom in the eighties was now over, and it was time for a stricter and more conservative approach to life. It was the end of an era that might never return.

Allen broke the heavy atmosphere that had descended on the room: 'We all have to be highly selective when finding the person we're going to have sex with. Don't be shy about asking the guy you've chosen all sorts of personal questions relating to his sexual habits before you decide to go to bed together. Even check him out. I mean it: literally give his body a thorough inspection and encourage him to do the same to you, even if it does give both of you an instant droop. So what? What's in a fuck, when it's a matter of life and death? You should both share a mutual interest in staying alive. And now I would like to read out a quote from a pamphlet published recently in New York by Gay Health: "Sex doesn't make you sick, diseases do. Gay sex doesn't make you sick, gay men who are sick do."

'There may not be conclusive proof that promiscuity is a major factor, but research has indicated time and time again that many gay men with AIDS have been more promiscuous than healthy gay men. Surely it's foolish not to take heed of such findings and go on leading a life that involves multiple partners, whatever we may think the sacrifice. It's in the interests of good health and of the gay community as a whole to curb all such desires. If you cannot cope with a monogamous relationship and have to indulge in group sex, then develop your own closed circle of fuck-buddies with guys who you know are free from infection and who only have sex within the group. Don't get fucked without a rubber and remember that good hygiene is most essential at all times; washing before and after sex. Lastly, I have to admit that I always recommend masturbation: it can be great fun and is risk-free.' And with that, he sat down.

Allen's last remark was accompanied by a huge round of applause and quite a good deal of laughter, which was badly needed after the serious nature of his talk. There was yet another noticeable readjustment of chairs and he again invited questions from the floor. With what Clive thought was an immense display of charm, Allen urged the men to be as open and frank with him as he had been with them. He assured them that they could ask him absolutely anything they wanted and express themselves naturally and in laymen's speak, without attempting highfalutin' medical expressions.

After a series of nervous coughs and throat-clearings, one of the older guys in the room asked : 'Are you saying that sex is now completely out, unless your partner swears on the Bible that he has been totally faithful?'

'No. I'm not saying that. However, what I am saying and really want to stress is that until we know more, you have to be sure about who you're sleeping around with. Any kind of sexual contact with someone you don't know and have casually picked up may put you at risk. To be crude about it, do you think a fuck is more important than your own life?'

Then a rather well-dressed elderly gentleman rose slowly and asked: 'Sir, can you tell us about the self-help group that they run here at the Men's Center?'

'I sure can. It first started as a social centre for gay men to meet in a venue which was free from the kind of pressure you would find in a gay bar or disco. Then when a friend of mine, Dennis Montrose, became the first AIDS patient in Columbus and was hospitalised, a small number of his friends rallied round and formed a support group to help him, as well as his partner.'

That mention of Dennis by name had a sudden impact: whatever the cause of AIDS might be, it was now certain that Dennis was one of the first of the eleven Columbus fatalities and Clive now found it difficult to concentrate on the next question.

'What sort of help does the group actually provide?' asked a man sitting next to Clive.

'All kinds really; it depends what's needed. We provide meals twice a week, giving people the chance to gather for lunch. We've created a safe space for gay men to meet and socialise, along with friends and extended family. Some parents need advice in coming to terms with the fact that their son is gay and they need to understand the whys and wherefores of what has happened to their child. Sometimes it's simply a question of visiting a terminally ill patient in hospital and you can well imagine that it's not easy when they just lie there knowing they're gonna die. Sometimes it's offering practical and emotional support to the patient's partner. So, as you can see, a great deal of help is needed and if you would like to be a volunteer and be put on our mailing list, please leave your details with me before you go. The more hands on deck, the better.'

Allen then insisted that there was one other way that the meeting could help, which was even more important: it was to assist the medical research being carried out there in Columbus. By filling in one of the questionnaires which he passed around the room and answering the questions as truthfully as each man possibly could, they would be able to provide the local medics with invaluable information. Without the correct data, the epidemiological knowledge about homosexual health patterns in Ohio state, which his colleagues were keen to gather, would never be conclusive. He assured the gathering that the forms he was giving out were confidential, and that he and his colleagues would be most grateful if each man there took one away with them, filled it in and either delivered it to his office at the Columbus General Hospital, or returned it at next week's meeting. He also added that it contained the address of the local Trust Fund.

'Well, if there are no more questions, I would just like to bring this evening's meeting to a close with a few parting words. Use common sense: eat right, exercise, reduce stress, avoid exposing yourselves to infection, and surround yourself with those who love and nurture you. This disease is epidemic in America today, but we can get through this difficult time if we live healthier and more disciplined lives. We may be paying for all those years of sexual liberation, but if the only price to pay is a little abstinence and self-control, then what price is fasting, I ask you? Lastly I'd like to thank you all most warmly for coming along this evening. We hold these sessions here every Saturday and at the same time. So do tell your friends and help spread the word throughout this town of ours. Let's all work towards making our gay community a healthier one and let's all aid Columbus by making Columbus AIDS-free!'

Allen's sudden departure from the room echoed the swift entrance he had made at the start of the evening. He had ended his talk-in on a rousing note, leaving his audience feeling positive and strong, and they showed their appreciation in the customary and enthusiastic manner. However the assembled gathering failed to disappear anywhere nearly as quickly as their guest speaker had vanished. Many of the guys seemed to want to linger on and needed to chat to each other about the information they had just gleaned.

Some men expressed their appreciation of Allen's optimistic energy and despite many of the depressing facts he had put before them, agreed that they felt inspired by his positivity. Judging from the buzz of lively conversation, Clive felt that Dr Levitt had an almost hypnotic effect on his audience and appeared to have most certainly won the respect and admiration of his congregation. But after a while, and without his dynamic and positive presence to fire the gathering, a more subdued atmosphere began to take hold in the room, with some of the men becoming morose and negative. Before long, a noticeable feeling of melancholy had descended on those remaining, slow to take hold at first, but nonetheless highly contagious.

One chap said he felt like going out and getting totally shit-faced.

Another agreed to join him, admitting that the only way he could face the loneliness he felt was to go and get drunk. Then, as they were leaving, a tall man barred their way and severely reprimanded them for being so irresponsible. He told them that by getting tanked, they wouldn't be in total control, and he warned them that they might pick someone up for sex, someone they'd never met before, and that would lead them to regret the potentially dangerous outcome of their actions.

'Listen you two,' said an African-American, 'after what we've heard tonight, we can't move backwards.'

'He's right,' agreed the tall man. 'We're back to square one if we get drunk and go round screwing the nearest dude that comes along.'

'Brother, I don't wanna give up sex, but my life is more important to me. Call me selfish, if you like, but I dunno...'

'I'm with you a hundred per cent.'

And so the chat went on, until all the stragglers got back to a much more positive frame of mind, drawing strength from each other, and becoming resolute in their determination to face up to the future with optimism and hope. Finally the room cleared, and although Clive felt he had watched the meeting from the sidelines, he had also been inspired by the talk-in and couldn't wait to tell Allen about the positive turnaround he had witnessed amongst those men who had stayed behind, and how much he personally had learnt about AIDS that night.

However, there still remained some puzzling issues. They weren't so much of a scientific nature, since Clive accepted that much research still had to be done and Allen had been very clear about listing the details of the medical condition as it was currently understood. However, he was still baffled by why there were almost double the number of cases of AIDS in America amongst gay males than had been reported throughout the rest of the world. And although Steve Leggard had also mentioned cases in Africa as well as Europe, Allen had not explained the cause of such a startling discrepancy between the significantly larger number of patients in the United States and those found elsewhere. Were American gay men really more promiscuous than other gays around the world or, in fact, was it the case that their promiscuity had been targeted by something much more sinister?

Clive also began to analyse Allen's approach to the evening, which although unquestionably impressive, was, to his way of thinking, a little too over-rehearsed. Allen's furrowed brow and immense concentration made Clive wonder whether Dr Levitt had used self-hypnosis to get him through his talk, and that made him remember that he had slipped something into that cup of coffee he'd had earlier that evening. Amphetamine was known to energise performance and he may very well have taken some.

In addition to this, Clive believed that there was something more than professional about his delivery, suggesting that it might have been manufactured and rehearsed by outsiders, and there was also that cheesy grin. Clive started to think about the research that he knew was being carried out at the Pavlov Institute in Moscow, where they had developed a technique that could penetrate the subconscious mind. He had read that in Russia, it had been discovered that a person, when programmed for three days, could be made to memorise imaginary action. Then there was also something else that struck him: Dr Levitt's strange twitch of the mouth.

Clive was reminded that wonderful cult film by John Frankenheimer, *The Manchurian Candidate*, based on the book by Richard Condon, and it slowly dawned on him that Allen's presentation that night reminded him of Lawrence Harvey's immaculate performance as Raymond Shaw. Harvey played an American soldier who had been hypnotically brainwashed by the North Koreans in order to assist them in the assassination of a presidential nominee. He also remembered that, in that famous film, no candidate could be hypnotised to act against their own moral character.

So, finally, he asked himself: Is that what was happening here in Columbus, Ohio?

Could it be that Dr Levitt was a modern-day Manchurian Candidate? And had he been recruited to come to Columbus to bump Dennis off? Was it possible that not only had Allen been willingly brainwashed, he had been positively dry-cleaned? Clive remembered that in the film, those who had voluntarily enlisted as Candidates could be programmed to do almost anything. If Allen was an undercover agent with such a specific agenda, Clive thought that he must surely harbour a very deep grudge against homosexuals and that only such a degree of hatred could have led him to become voluntarily caught up in such a dangerous mission, which had caused so such suffering.

He also felt it couldn't be Allen's religious convictions alone that might have made him behave in such a destructive manner, and then he remembered what Dr Levitt had said about his upbringing, which caused him to wonder whether Allen might have been sexually abused as a child by his stepfather.

On the other hand, Clive also had to admit that Allen's well-briefed talk had been extremely helpful and even included information about a new and mutating virus, as yet unidentified, which Allen suggested might indeed be responsible for the outbreak. Could that be what was being manufactured, and was it so absurd to think that some scientists down near Tucson, Arizona, had cloned the swine virus and invented a new one? Clive was getting quite carried away with all these musings, when Allen poked his head round the door and jokingly called out: 'Next'!

'Left alone in here, I did feel for a moment as though I was in a doctor's waiting-room,' laughed Clive, in an attempt to clear his head of his musings.

'Michael's just left a message on my answering service in my office across the street to say he's running a little late and will meet us at the restaurant in about fifteen. I hope you like French food?'

'Yes, of course I do, and I do hope he's all right.'

'He sounded fine to me, said something about needing to take a shower after rummaging around in the attic. You know Clive, you must try not to smother him too much. He's got to learn to stand on his own two feet now and live without Dennis, as we all do.'

That touched a raw nerve: 'Yes, of course, Allen, you're absolutely right. I do sometimes get very protective and overreact. But now I'm not reacting nearly enough.' Then, setting aside all thoughts about *The Manchurian Candidate*, Clive's own thespian skills took over: 'Forgive me, but I must be losing my manners. Your talk-in was superb. You made us all feel terrifically positive, which, considering the enormity of the problem we all face, was most impressive. You explained so much and so very clearly, and at the same time gave us all such tremendous hope.'

'Thank you, and it's very kind of you to say so. You know, I'm so close to it all, I find it difficult to be objective.'

'Well, judging from the discussion in the room after you had left, I would say it was a very successful evening.'

'I'm so glad to know that. I must admit, I have been encouraged by some of the feedback we've received so far.'

'Honestly, Allen, there was a good deal of positive talk going on amongst those guys after you left, and a jolly good atmosphere.'

'That's very good to hear. Now I think we should get to that restaurant, don't you? I can't dine on compliments alone … I'm starving.'

Then, just as they were leaving, Allen said: 'By the way, if you want to have a screening and blood test while you're here in Columbus, I can arrange it. I'm on duty all next week and I call the shots.'

'That's most kind of you, Allen. Maybe a screening but – call me a sissy – perhaps not the shots. I can't stand needles.'

CHAPTER ELEVEN

LE GAI PARIS SATURDAY

As they drove away from the Men's Center, Allen pointed out where his clinic was located so that Clive would know where to go for his check-up the following week. He said that he was glad that Clive had been able to attend the talk-in, and delighted that the meeting had helped explain away some of his queries. Clive responded in an equally positive vein, although he also admitted that there were still a few points he'd like to have clarified – that was, if Allen wasn't too exhausted.

'After all, I know it's after hours, and I'm sure you've had enough questioning for one evening; however, there's just—'

'Look, Clive, you don't know me very well yet, but I have to tell you I love the work I do. So if you have anything you need to ask, please don't hesitate. Go straight ahead – that's what I'm here for.'

Clive thanked Dr Levitt for being so understanding, and said that although he now acknowledged that AIDS was part of a world epidemic, with outbreaks in Africa, Haiti and Europe, he still remained puzzled by why the USA had now become its epicentre. More importantly, what disturbed him even more was the fact that it had hit the male gay community in the United States with such a terrible vengeance and that he was saddened to have lost so many of his friends.

Allen responded by confirming that it was indeed part of a worldwide epidemic and added that current research indicated that the spread of a viral infection often produces a number of epicentres. He quoted the outbreak of influenza in Europe back in 1918 as an example of what he was describing.

Clive said he wondered whether the current outbreak of AIDS only became known abroad after it had first developed in America. Allen replied that, on the contrary, many of his colleagues were sure that it had been going on for some time in Africa, particularly in the Congo. It had now been established that AIDS had existed in Africa for years, and amongst a largely heterosexual population, but he added that it had been more or less undiagnosed at the time. On the other hand, he agreed with Clive that it was also probable that the severe outbreak in the USA drew the rest of the world's attention to it. Allen thought that the States was leading the field in scientific research and had therefore been able to alert other countries around the world about the spread of AIDS. However, although a certain amount of progress had been made, what still concerned him as a doctor was the need to find out more about the root cause behind the disease.

'But do you think that like Africa, the same could be said about Haiti?' asked Clive. 'That it was indigenous to that island? And that, as has been rumoured, it was passed on by the poor local boys who had sex with those affluent gay New Yorkers who came in their droves to the island in search of their services?'

Allen replied, 'I'm a medical man and my background is in science. I'm not the least bit interested in rumour.'

'No, of course you're not. But please forgive me, I'm just trying to understand why there is such a huge discrepancy between the number of cases reported here, and the lower number of casualties throughout the rest of the world.'

'I'm sorry, but I really can't give you an answer, nor, as far as I know, can any of my colleagues. What we do know for certain is that it is sexually spread, and we gay men in the States are known for our promiscuity. It may be that when we discover what causes the breakdown in the immune system, we'll find out why it took on with such a strong hold over here amongst us gays.'

Despite Allen's response, Clive was becoming more persistent: 'But you do surely admit that it is curious. Isn't it odd that it has developed at such an alarming rate over here and that it has had such a particularly devastating effect on gay men?'

'Sure, it's odd. And very alarming. A disease doesn't usually strike at such an easily identifiable group of people. It's one of the reasons why it has been of such considerable epidemiological interest to those of us in the medical profession. It's very rare that we get the opportunity to study the emergence of a newly discovered disease at such close hand, then chart its development with considerable accuracy, and over a relatively short passage of time.'

'Of course I can see why the medical profession is so interested in the spread of this damn thing, but I believe that there may be other interested parties involved.'

'Really! And who are you getting at?'

Clive's next question didn't appear to trouble Allen in the least. 'How well did you know Dennis Montrose?'

Dr Levitt smiled back at the Englishman. 'I treated Dennis when I first arrived in Columbus, and he and Michael used to come to the STD clinic for regular check-ups. Eventually I got to know them real well, especially during the last six months of Dennis' life, when he became extremely ill.'

'How much did he tell you about himself?'

'Really quite a bit. We used to have long visits together, specially after he was admitted into hospital.'

'And was he completely frank with you?'

'Why don't you stop being so English and diplomatic? Come on, stop beating about the bush – come straight out with it. Shoot!'

'Well, we all knew Dennis was on the game and led a busy sex life, but did he ever mention to you what a close friend of his had discovered while on an official governmental visit near Tucson, Arizona?'

'Now I can see what you're driving at. What Dennis used to call his "wipe-out theory". Is that what you mean?'

It was now clear that Allen knew all about Dennis's conspiracy theory but sounded rather sceptical about it. However, having brought the subject this far, Clive was unable to stop himself from further questioning, especially if his suspicions about Allen's possible involvement in Dennis's demise were to be confirmed. Then he rather lost his cool by bluntly pointing out that he felt that Dr Levitt didn't believe a word of what Dennis had discovered.

'Look Clive, I'll say to you what I said to Dennis when he was alive. At times like these, it's very easy to get all paranoid and think that the entire world is out to get us. Of course, we have become the focus of a great deal of attention, but we have to keep our cool right now. We'll just blow it if we start spreading all these far-fetched rumours.'

Clive just persisted. 'So you don't believe any of it is true? And yet, you have to admit that so many of the things that Dennis predicted have come to pass.'

'Like what, for example?'

'Oh dear, I had prepared a list of things I wanted to discuss with you, and now they've all completely gone out of my head.'

Then, with that alarming grin of his, Allen turned to Clive: 'Look, I want to help, honestly I do. Let's try and remember together, shall we?'

'OK. Sorry if I was getting emotional. I just hate the idea that this gay plague has killed one of my dearest friends.'

'As do I. I'm a doctor, for fuck's sake!'

Now, for the first time that evening, Allen was beginning to lose his cool as well, which made Clive adopt a much more level-headed way of arguing. He rationally pointed out that some gays had lost their jobs because it was believed that the disease was contagious and that as carriers, they could infect other work colleagues. Of course now, after Allen's talk, he was aware that, medically speaking, it was impossible to pass on the disease socially, but he stressed that he realised how very ignorant the general public was. Allen agreed with Clive absolutely, and thought that any sort of discrimination was totally unjust, which led Clive to tell him about what had happened to Michael while he was having his check-up at the hospital the previous day.

'One of the technicians had waited for the doctor to be out of the room and then announced that gay men were the slime of the earth and needed to be put down for spreading AIDS.'

'Clive, I fully agree that there does appear to be a growing campaign against us. I hear similar things all the time and I also know that recently in Washington DC, there was a terrible gaffe that also caused a bit of a scandal.'

Clive immediately thought he was going to get the germicide theory corroborated. Instead, Allen told him that a federal government agency had inadvertently released a pile of confidential information, the result of which was that certain men in the public eye had been openly named as practising homosexuals. Once they were on an official state register like that, it produced a devastating effect on their careers, especially in the states where homosexuality was still illegal.

Clive pointed out that sex between consenting male adults had been illegal in his country up until 1967 and he agreed that they were not living in easy times. He mentioned that in the UK, journalists often got hold of confidential information which was splashed all over the newspapers, but admitted that, to his knowledge, there was no group like the Moral Majority to deal with, at least, as far as he was aware.

'Well you're lucky there. It's true, we do have right-wing activists who campaign against us and I have to admit that this AIDS scare has added impetus to their cause. I suppose that's to be expected.'

'And is it to be expected that we should be treated like scapegoats, with landlords evicting their gay tenants because they're so afraid of catching what they refer to as "the gay plague"?' asked Clive.

'It's sheer ignorance, ' said Allen.

'And is it sheer ignorance that caused a residents' association in Tulsa, Texas to have the local swimming pool drained out and disinfected, because they claimed that some gays had used the pool and other bathers could become contaminated?'

'It's appalling, I know. I'm ashamed of my ignorant fellow countrymen, and their total unawareness of the facts. Having said that, you do know how fanatical Americans are about cleanliness?'

'I certainly do,' Clive responded, 'and what's more, I'm beginning to learn how fanatical some Texans are about gays. You're surely not going to tell me that the Alert Citizens of Texas Brigade in Dallas were merely acting out of ignorance when they recently demanded that their state legislature restore the Sodomy Law, which had been declared unconstitutional by a federal court years ago?'

'Clive, I'm not saying that there aren't bigots here in the United States. We all know that. But that's no reason to believe in Dennis's theory: that there was a calculated plan to eliminate the entire gay male population of America and possibly Europe also.'

Clive suggested that they leave Europe out of the discussion for the moment, since as far as he knew, gay political power had in no way become an obvious threat in the House of Commons. But he did point out that in America, the power of the pink dollar and the importance of the gay vote were, as far as he knew, highly significant when it came to electing councillors and senators. Who knew how vital it might be for funding a presidential campaign? He knew that in certain large cities, like San Francisco, New York and

Los Angeles, the gay community represented a substantial voting bloc when it came to elections, and that in those cities up to 40 per cent of the electorate could be gay.

'You've certainly done your homework.'

Clive pushed on: 'So you would agree that when it comes to election time, the gay vote is an important one to win over. Politicians must be aware of the need to promote issues that are of concern amongst their gay constituents and, in return, the power and generosity of the gay electorate can surely make or break a candidate.'

'Clive, all that is absolutely true. And just like the black vote, the gay vote has certainly become an important factor in winning seats on the council in quite a few towns, as well as gaining ground in congressional elections in many of our states.'

'In some towns, many of the elected officials are openly gay. I know for a fact that in West Hollywood, where at least fifty per cent of the electorate is gay, they have been able to elect a majority of gay members onto the city council.'

'Yes, I believe you're right.'

'Allen, don't you think that such a strong vote could be a severe handicap for right-wing politicians?'

'Not all gays vote Democrat, you know.'

Clive smiled and confessed that he was aware of that, but that he'd been led to believe that the majority did. He'd also been told that along with gay voting power also goes gay spending power and, with bathhouses, bars and restaurants closing down, the value of the pink dollar was diminishing. Clive maintained that because the disease was eliminating so many gay men, it was, at the same time, reducing gay wealth and influence, and consequently undermining the strength of the gay vote. The gay community in the States had come so near to achieving respect, acceptance and power by the end of the seventies, but it was now slowly being severely undermined and eroded in one way or another. Then, to be even more provocative, Clive added that he'd even heard that some right-wing religious groups were also getting involved.

'I come from a Jewish background, so I understand what you're saying. But do you really believe that the American government is behind all this?'

Then without fully realising the consequences of what he was about to say, Clive admitted that he believed Dennis's story.

'Clive, I spent a lot of time with Dennis. I know how much he suffered, and I had to watch my patient die. I sat with him and listened to the delirious ravings of a sick man. At times he talked wildly, at other times he was totally lucid. It is true that he believed that there was a CIA chemical warfare division in Arizona that had managed to isolate an extremely rare swine-fever virus, which had existed in Africa and which was considered, at the time, to be spread by monkeys to humans. He thought that this reinvented virus was being manufactured and used to cause the breakdown of the immune system, which has been responsible for this AIDS epidemic. Now that's what Dennis was on about, isn't it?'

'Well, yes ... in a nutshell!'

'And he had absolutely no proof.'

'But his senator friend did,' countered Clive.

Then in a very nonchalant manner Allen changed tack: 'How did you find out about all this? I know it couldn't have been from Michael, because Dennis told me that he'd agreed to keep the whole thing from him, and I certainly believe that! So did Den write to you and tell you himself?'

Now it was Allen's turn to make Clive feel uncomfortable, since he had let Dr Levitt know how much he had learnt. Clive realised that he'd been hoist by his own petard and had placed himself in a certain amount of potential danger. Would he be the next to get bumped off? he wondered.

'No. As a matter of fact, we weren't in communication for several years.'

'So how come you know so much about Dennis's theory?'

'It was Steve: Steve Leggard who told me.'

'Oh, him. I might have guessed as much. You surely don't believe what that old woman has to say? He's so neurotic, he probably thinks that the Martians are responsible.'

'He was one of Dennis's closest friends.'

'Sure. I know. He's also a volunteer at the Men's Center, and comes to my clinic for regular scanning, though I can't think why. He claims he hasn't done it with anybody for years, which I believe. He's so uptight about sex, I can't understand why he continues to make appointments to see me.'

Clive was mortified that, having informed on Steve, he had just placed Michael's best friend in a highly dangerous situation. Consequently, he felt he had to try and backtrack and focus Allen's attention away from Steve, and back to himself. 'So you think I should put this wipe-out theory of Den's just down to a lot of hysterical gossip?'

'I just think this Arizona business is rather far-fetched, that's all, and there's no hard evidence to back up Den's theory. You know, Clive, we have to be very careful not to stir up a hornets' nest right now. Things are looking bad enough for the gay community here in Columbus, and we don't want to inflame what is already a delicate situation with false accusations of treason.'

'And what if these are not false allegations? Was it treason to uncover the Watergate affair? If it hadn't been for the determination of those two brave journalists, that scandal would never have come to the attention of the American public either.'

And then without thinking that he might be putting himself in the greatest danger of all, Clive added that was exactly what he was thinking of doing. He said that he thought that his PA, Shirley Morris would know the right journalist to go to with Dennis's story; someone who'd be prepared to put him or herself on the line.

'I think that's a very bad idea, Clive. A very bad idea indeed!

Think of the trouble you might cause. The best thing you can do right now is to make sure that Dennis's name is kept clean and remain absolutely quiet about the rumours you've heard. And you'd be helping the Columbus gay community much more by doing nothing at the moment … Absolutely nothing.'

Then, trying to extricate himself from the hole he seemed to have dug himself into, Clive admitted that perhaps Allen was right and he should just drop it all. He apologised profusely but said that he didn't feel he was on top of his emotions at the moment and perhaps losing Dennis had caused him to lose the plot completely.

'And that's totally understandable,' Allen admitted. 'But we have to be rational about all this. For heaven's sake, I'm trying to protect the gay community and urge them to take medical precautions. That's different from suggesting that they get themselves involved in subversive politics.'

'I understand where you're coming from,' said Clive. 'But the more I learn about what's going on over here, the more I fear for what will happen in Europe, and in my own country in particular. And without appearing to sound too paranoid, I'm frightened that AIDS will have an equally devastating effect on the entire gay community over there, if not physically then politically and, ultimately, psychologically. I now know for certain that it doesn't just afflict the body; it can equally destroy the spirit. It just seems too coincidental that it's affecting mainly gays – and who really cares if a few Haitian lads fall by the wayside?'

'Clive, you're a very intelligent man and, without wishing to sound patronising or too condescending, I simply think we must do all we can to prevent the spread of this damn thing and that this should be our priority at the moment.'

Clive thought that was rich coming from the very man whom he now suspected of having injected Dennis with the deadly disease in the first place.

'Let's face it, as I've heard you say many times: we may speak the same language, but we don't go about things in the same way, now do we?' Allen remarked.

'That's perfectly true,' said Clive. 'And you know what? I should stop poking my nose into other people's business. You see there's still a great deal I don't understand about this wonderful country of yours, even though I've been coming here, on and off, for the last twenty years.'

'And I hope we'll see you over here for the next twenty years.'

'I'll drink to that.'

'Speaking of alcohol, now I could do with that drink you offered me earlier on.'

'You and me both,' said Clive, 'and I think we should go and eat, don't you?'

The two men had been so engrossed in their heated debate, Clive only then realised that they'd been in the restaurant car park for some time. He hoped he'd managed to ease the tension between them, and had successfully assured Allen that he would put Dennis' wipe-out theory out of his mind completely. He now needed to camouflage any suspicious feelings he still had about the good doctor and hoped he had succeeded in so doing.

'Dear me,' Clive admitted, 'I got so carried away, I forgot all about dinner.'

'I hope you're still hungry?'

'Ravenous.'

'Great. The food is very good here. Listen, I'm not unsympathetic to what you've been saying, really I'm not. Let's continue our discussion when you come and see me next week for your check-up. Try to make it late morning, so we can have lunch afterwards.'

'I'd like that very much indeed. Let's not talk about this business over dinner tonight in front of Michael, if that's all right with you?'

'Whatever you say, Clive.'

The restaurant was relatively small by American standards, charmingly decorated, and had a distinctly French atmosphere, with lots of red-checked tablecloths, posters of various Parisian landmarks on the walls, and there were French songs playing in the background. Allen seemed to know some of the waiters and he was warmly greeted by the maître d' who, with a distinct French accent, asked them what he could offer them both to drink as he began to usher them over to their cosy, candlelit corner table. As they meandered their way through the restaurant, Allen said hello to a number of people and exchanged the odd quick joke. Then at one table, he was stopped by four gentlemen, shook hands with them, and briefly introduced Clive. It soon became abundantly clear to Clive that they had entered a gay establishment and the fact that there wasn't a single woman in the place did not surprise the Brit in the least. So, having caused quite a stir as they wended their way, making several stops en route, they finally arrived at their corner destination to find Michael already ensconced and waiting, seemingly amused by their grand entrance.

'Well, here you are at last!' Michael left his friends standing as he continued. 'Honestly … I'm only onto my third Manhattan … I just couldn't wait any longer. Oh, do please sit down! Anyway, what have you two guys been up to? Tell me Clive, has Uncle Allen just been giving you a private examination?'

'No, that's arranged for next Tuesday,' Allen replied apologetically, seeming not to get Michael's joke.

'Now, don't be so cheeky!' exclaimed Clive. 'I'm so very sorry we're late, but actually it's all my fault. You see I was the one doing the cross-examining, since there were just a few questions I needed to put to Allen after his talk, which was terrific, by the way, and tremendously well attended. It was so awfully useful and it has really helped me get my head around a lot of this AIDS stuff. *Mea culpa* … so please forgive us.'

Michael responded that he was glad it had helped. 'And there you go again with your quaint expressions. Anyway,' he continued, 'I'm only joking. And this is my first by the way.' And Michael raised his glass and took a sip of his martini.

'Michael, I did get the message you left for me on my answering service at the clinic and I figured that as you were going to be late, there was no need for us to rush.'

'I've really only just got here myself. There was so much to sort through in the attic, I completely lost track of the hour. And by the time I had cleaned myself up, I realised that I was running late. Then, Allen, just after I'd put a call through to you at the clinic, I got Steve on the phone, which further delayed me. He sounded very agitated and, well ... I know this is supposed to be a strictly off-duty evening for you, but he said he was feeling real sick and I was wondering...'

'You know what a hypochondriac Steve is. It's probably nothing that a few dozen more vitamin pills won't cure.'

'Honestly, he sounded very distressed and not at all like his usual jolly self.'

'Oh, really? Then I'm sorry. I didn't mean to be unkind just then.'

'He thinks he's got it!'

'AIDS, you mean? That's extremely unlikely. You know Steve better than I do. He swears he hasn't been with anyone for ages, and he's always telling me that he's terrified of having sex and catching something.'

'But you said earlier on tonight,' Clive interrupted, 'that it can lie dormant for years.'

'It's perfectly true that I did say the incubation period can be several years in some cases. In fact, without wanting to sound too alarmist, that's why I suggested you come in and have a check-up yourself next week, while you're still here in Columbus.'

'Allen, I'm so grateful to you for organising that for Clive,' said Michael. 'But although I realise that tomorrow's Sunday, I just wonder if you could possibly spare the time to call in on Steve. We'd all be very grateful, wouldn't we, Clive? He says his glands are swollen and he's got night sweats. I suppose it could just be a chill...'

'And I suppose I'm being unreasonable. Of course I'll see him tomorrow and take a blood test.'

Would that be the end of Steve too? Clive began to wonder, and he started to feel guilty because he'd incriminated Steve. So, in an attempt to cover up his true feelings of distrust for Allen, and using all his thespian skills, he embarked on the performance of a lifetime: 'Poor Allen, you really do seem to have your work cut out, don't you? What with me bombarding you with endless questions when you're supposedly off-duty…'

Michael chimed in: 'And me asking you to be an angel of mercy on your day off…'

Allen simply smiled back at the two of them, straightened his tie, raised the martini that one of the waiters had placed in front of him and with that awful sardonic grin of his replied: 'Now listen, you two guys. You very well know that's what I'm here for!'

CHAPTER TWELVE

SHIRLEY AT THE SHERATON SUNDAY

Shirley's flight from New York arrived on time on Sunday evening, and Clive was there to meet her at the airport as arranged. As she walked towards him, wearing a striking Jean Muir outfit in dark purple, and as usual, with her Auntie Flo's mink jacket draped around her shoulders, Clive realised how much he had missed his dear friend and the extent to which he relied on her support and trust. Although his love affair with America was by no means over, the events of the last week had made him feel rather homesick and somewhat isolated, and the sight of Shirley in the airport arrivals hall made him cheer up enormously.

With affectionate greetings accomplished, they took a cab into town and Shirley directed the driver to the Columbus Sheraton, where she'd reserved two rooms. Over dinner Clive brought her up to speed with everything he'd found out in the course of the last few days. He took her into his confidence completely, and confessed that he was now more convinced than ever that, because Dennis knew too much, he had to be got rid of and had been a target of the FBI.

Then, with dinner over, Clive suggested that they returned to the privacy his room, where he felt he could go into greater detail, so long as Shirley wasn't feeling too exhausted.

'Don't be ridiculous, you don't get jetlag just coming from New York, and besides, I want to learn more. You surely don't really believe that they bumped Dennis off?'

'I didn't to start with, but now I think there's a strong possibility that they did!'

'Oh my goodness! I thought he died of AIDS … Now, come on darling, what's that Spoke intuition telling you?'

'It's this blood-test business. You see, I think the two things are connected and although I know that Dennis had been to the STD clinic months before he contracted AIDS and that he—'

'Sorry,' Shirley interrupted, 'but just remind me, what does STD stand for?'

'Sexually transmitted diseases: it's what back home we call the VD clinic.'

'Yes, of course it is. But,' Shirley persisted, 'what has this STD clinic actually got to do with contracting AIDS?'

'Well, I think it may have a lot to do with it.'

Shirley claimed that she still didn't quite understand what Clive was driving at. She thought that medically speaking, as far as she was aware, one sexually transmitted condition didn't automatically lead to another. 'Am I right – or what?'

'Yes Shirley, that's possibly so … But in Dennis' case, I believe it may all be interconnected. You see I've got a horrible feeling that a certain Dr Allen Levitt may be mixed up with all this and he's the chap who runs the STD clinic attached to the hospital here in Columbus. It was this doctor who treated Dennis for a mild bout of syphilis last year and gave Den a blood test for AIDS shortly before he contracted it.'

'Oh, I see. Now, you've told me about meeting Steve Leggard, but when we last spoke, you were just about to be introduced to Dr Levitt. So tell me, how did he strike you?'

'Although I think he's very charming and clever, there's just something about him that I'm beginning not to trust.'

'And he runs the STD clinic?'

'Correct. He's in charge there, and apparently, according to Michael, earlier this year, Dennis had gone along to see him for night sweats, and then shortly afterwards developed full-blown AIDS.'

'And so you really believe this doctor has something to do with it all?'

'Well now I'm truly beginning to think so... I could do with a nightcap, how about you? Let me order two whiskies...'

'That's a very good idea. So, tell me more about this doctor.'

Clive called room service, ordered their drinks and then told Shirley that he thought Allen was a very cool operator. He described Allen's performance the previous evening at the Men's Center, and explained about the self-help group set there. Shirley seemed most impressed and observed that the local gay community sounded extremely well organised in Columbus.

'Yes it certainly is,' Clive continued, 'and you know, there have already been twenty-two cases here in this town, and so they've had to get their act together. I'm also sorry to say that there have been eleven fatalities reported thus far, and consequently there's a lot being done to educate and offer advice and help in Columbus, and Dr Allen Levitt has been highly instrumental in organising much of what's going on.'

Shirley thought that he certainly sounded impressive, and wondered why the doctor made Clive feel so uneasy. 'So tell me Clive, what was his talk actually about?'

The whiskies arrived and Clive set about describing the weekly AIDS talk-in he'd gone along to. All in all, Clive felt that Dr Levitt made his audience feel relaxed and was able to persuade the guys sitting there that they could interrupt at any time and question him as he went along, which they did.

'Wow! He sounds brilliant,' Shirley enthused.

'Oh, I think he's brilliant all right,' came Clive's quick response.

'And is he very handsome too?'

'Yes, Shirley … unfortunately.'

'Now Clive, don't tell me that Cupid has struck?'

'Well, as a matter of fact, to start with I did feel the prick of a little dart. But you know how much I detest needles.'

'Yes, I remember what trouble you caused when you passed out the last time I took you to your dentist.'

Bringing the conversation back to Allen, Clive added that from what he was able to uncover about the doctor's private life, he felt it all sounded quite complicated. Although he was an openly gay man, Clive informed Shirley that Dr Levitt appeared to have certain religious convictions, and being Jewish, he was somewhat guilt-ridden and seemed to find it difficult to get involved with a guy.

Shirley had a number of Jewish friends and said that she could totally understand where Allen was coming from.

'But despite his declared honesty,' Clive continued, 'there's just something about him I simply don't trust. His talk last night seemed to be far too manufactured, as though he'd been professionally briefed and rehearsed. Do you remember that wonderful film *The Manchurian Candidate* and the leading character, Raymond Shaw?'

'Of course I do. The Oppenheimer film hit of 1962. Lawrence Harvey was terrific in the role.'

'Well Shirley, I got the impression that Dr Levitt's performance was just too perfect. I almost felt he'd been programmed like that character in the film. And then there was that unrelenting sardonic smile of his, like the Cheshire Cat.'

Shirley admitted that the smile did sound a bit disarming, but suggested that Clive was being somewhat unreasonable. She felt it only natural that the doctor should be on top of his subject matter, since if anyone was going to stand up and speak in front of any group of people, they would need to be well prepared. Then she reminded Clive about how much work he'd had to put into the talk he gave to the RADA graduates last year.

'Come on, Clive, surely it's not surprising that he was well rehearsed?'

'I'd like to think you were right,' admitted Clive. 'But I just feel there's something fishy about him: it was like he went into autopilot. He oozes far too much charm and sophistication and he just makes me think he's a bit of a fake.'

'You mean like one of our clients, who shall remain nameless, and who we never quite think is being truthful in the part he's playing?'

'Exactly. Do you remember that awful *King Lear* we went to? Well, Allen Levitt's performance was similar; somehow not quite believable. Added to which there was that strange twitch of the mouth, which also reminded me of the one Lawrence Harvey's character developed after he'd been hypnotised and programmed.'

'Now that is scary ... So that Spoke nose of yours really does smell a rat?'

'Precisely. His smooth delivery and selfless need to constantly be of help somehow just doesn't convince me. I mean, when I asked him why he chose to practice in Columbus of all places, he went all strange on me.'

'Maybe he's got family connections here, or a lover?'

Clive freely admitted that he'd thought of that and asked him, but Allen had said not. Clive said he simply couldn't imagine why an ambitious, good-looking and talented young gay doctor would want to end up in Columbus, Ohio, of all places, when surely he could have had the choice of more challenging postings in New York, San Francisco or LA?

'Clive darling, surely it's not a crime to want to settle in Columbus? Your friend Dennis did.'

'But Den was born here. Allen also drives a Cadillac and wears a very expensive gold watch.'

'Maybe he's on the game too.'

'Now you're being naughty.'

'And you're sounding a little too unreasonable. It is possible that his folks are rich and he's inherited his wealth. I mean to say, didn't you tell me that Susan Carlsberg's father was a banker and that's how she got her millions?'

'You're certainly right there. And talking of Susan, you remember what she told me last year when I was in New York?'

'Yes, I do … But going back to this doctor: do you really believe he's not on the level?'

'Yes, I'm truly beginning to think so. There's just something that niggles me about the timing of his appearance in this town. He arrives out of the blue, was responsible for treating Dennis at the STD clinic and then gives Den a blood test just before he catches AIDS. Talking it through with you just now has made me feel that it's more than pure coincidence. I know for a fact that it is possible to inject the virus at the same time as taking a blood sample. I put a call through to my doctor back in London and checked that was possible.'

After a slight pause, Clive asked Shirley whether she remembered what he'd said on the phone the previous Saturday about Dennis's connection with the senator, Jim.

'Yes, but what has that got to do with Dr Levitt injecting Dennis with a lethal virus?'

'Remember I told you that Jim had found out about a swine virus being developed in a chemical warfare centre near Tucson, Arizona?'

Shirley nodded.

'But did I tell you the most alarming bit? Shortly afterwards, the marine goes and dies in a car crash and then Jim himself is found dead on a ski slope in Aspen, Colorado in what Steve Leggard – who is to be trusted – says were rather suspicious circumstances.

'Steve maintains that Jim and his marine could have been placed on the FBI's Security Index list: Priority Three. Priority Three is only reserved for individuals who are potentially dangerous to US security, and are under active investigation. So I believe that Dennis was on that list as well and was also a target who had to be eliminated.'

'Wow! This is all sounding very plausible,' agreed Shirley.

'I believe,' Clive continued, 'that when I went to Aspen, Dennis wanted to share all this information with me, but he changed his mind at the last minute. When he got back to Columbus, he told Steve everything he'd found out from Jim – who, by the way, had gone into hiding in Colorado under an assumed name. Now, if Den had to be got rid of as well, who was better qualified to accomplish such a mission than a brainwashed doctor, posted to Columbus and easily able to administer a lethal injection under the guise of innocently offering a blood test?'

'This is all beginning to make total sense.'

'Shirley, I'm really glad about that! Later on, I also discovered from Allen Levitt that when Dennis was in hospital dying, he told Allen everything about his wipe-out theory. That must have confirmed Den's involvement and possibly helped Allen justify his actions. As a result of what I've discovered, I've decided to make an appointment to see him at his STD clinic on Tuesday morning and have a check-up myself.'

'You're not serious, are you?'

'Shirley, my Spoke instinct isn't worth a penny unless I have some hard evidence to back up my reasoning. I'm hoping I will find some incriminating evidence at Allen's surgery which will prove me right. Even the good doctor admitted to me that there was no proof positive which could verify Den's conspiracy theory. Of course not. All the protagonists are dead – that is, apart from Allen.'

'I suppose you're right,' admitted Shirley. 'Amazing as it all sounds, it is beginning to add up … although, as I said before, it really does sound like some sort of a movie script.'

'You know what Shirley, you're not too far off there, and that's why I've prepared a storyboard. Even if there's not a shred of truth in any of this, and it's simply been a case of my imagination running riot, I think it all might provide Spoke Associates with a brilliant idea for a feature film. We could call it *The Rainbow Conspiracy*!

'And we could commission Anthony Silver to write the screenplay.'

'But, Shirl ... seriously now. You know me really well. Do you think I've lost the plot? ... Am I losing my marbles?'

'Clive darling, I certainly don't think you're going crazy. But you've just told me one hell of a story and there is rather a lot for me to take in.'

'You better believe it.'

'You know what? I'm going to get my notebook out.

'Good idea! But what am I going to do with all this information? Do you think I should take my story to the press?'

'Well, not tonight, Clive darling. I think you ought to get some rest: you badly need your eight hours. I know what you're like without them. I've brought some sleeping pills with me and I think you should take one ... here!'

'I don't normally, but I think tonight I'm going to make an exception. Thank you.'

Shirley got up to go to her room, but Clive clearly wasn't ready for her to leave just yet and as he hugged her, he confessed: 'I'm just not sure about this one. Perhaps I shouldn't go poking my nose into what is ultimately none of my business. I mean the ramifications might be enormous. What if it's all true and there really is a wipe-out conspiracy? For all I know, my own life could now be at stake and I'm just not sure I've got the courage to see this through to a satisfactory conclusion. For the first time in a long while, I feel utterly out of my comfort zone and I'm so very glad you suggested that you came out here to Columbus.'

'Well, now I am too.'

'I just don't know what to do for the best.'

Shirley had never seen Clive quite like this before and wondered whether he should make his information public. 'I could give my friend Sylvia O'Connor a ring tomorrow: she works on the *New York Times*.'

'Or there are those Washington lads who spilt the beans on Nixon and the Watergate scandal,' Clive suggested.

'But not tonight, Josephine. We both need to sleep on this one and start afresh in the morning. We really do need to talk this thing through over breakfast when we've both had a good night's sleep.'

'Darling Shirley, as always, you are so wise. Thank you so much for coming out to Columbus.'

'You are more than welcome, you know that.'

'What more can I say?'

And with that, Shirley hugged Clive goodnight and blew him a kiss from the door.

In fact she was the one who was in need of the sleeping pills. Clive's words kept going round and around in her head as she lay in bed, unable to get to sleep until all the facts as she remembered them were clearly listed in her notebook. For her, this wipe-out theory was the most challenging production that Spoke Associates had undertaken in years. And besides, this was no film script or West End play: it was for real. However, although she had not yet met any of Clive's Columbus players, Shirley was aware that if this Dr Allen Levitt really was a serial killer, Clive, as well as Michael and Steve, were probably also in deep water and now she might be too.

She suddenly sat up, quite wide awake, and came to the realisation that they both should get out of town as soon as possible. She decided that over breakfast the next day, she would firmly suggest that they leave Columbus straight away that morning, before Clive had the opportunity to get himself further involved.

With that resolve, she reached for a sleeping pill, turned out the light, tucked herself up in bed, and hoped that she would wake up refreshed the following morning with enough energy to persuade her boss to leave town immediately.

CHAPTER THIRTEEN

THE DINNER PARTY MONDAY

Over breakfast the next day, Shirley plucked up the courage to advise Clive that in her opinion they both needed to get out of town right there and then. She warned him that should Allen Levitt be an undercover agent, as they both now thought, he was obviously a very dangerous man and Clive's life was almost certainly in danger. If Allen had killed Dennis because he knew too much, whether Dennis realised it or not, she thought that Clive had put himself in a similar perilous situation and she firmly added that she most certainly had no intention of witnessing her boss's demise in Columbus.

Clive listened patiently to everything Shirley had to say, but when he finally responded, he stubbornly argued his corner. He maintained that he couldn't just turn his back on all that he'd discovered in Columbus and simply walk away. He also told Shirley that he felt a duty towards Dennis, and really needed to get to the bottom of what his late friend had unravelled, even if it meant there could be deadly consequences. He declared that he fully recognised that his life could be at risk but pointed out that he wasn't alone and that Steve and Michael were in a similar situation.

'I've never said this to you before, but do you really trust Michael?' Shirley bluntly asked. 'You did tell me he had become very close to Allen.'

'Yes that's true, but Allen has been very helpful to him since Dennis passed away and … I really don't feel…'

'Well, without actually having met him, I just felt I needed to know what you felt, that's all. And what about Steve?'

'I think he's all right.'

'You sound a bit doubtful about him too.'

'No. Not really.'

'Come on Clive, what is that Spoke nose telling you? You don't think Steve could be in cahoots with Allen?'

'Not for a moment. He's just a bit heavy going, that's all. You'll see when you meet him.'

'Yes. I can't wait.'

'Now listen here, Shirley, I do value your advice as you well know, but, in this instance, I'm not sure you're right. I really do need to find out the truth about Allen and this conspiracy business and therefore I hope you'll understand when I say that I'm simply just not ready to leave Columbus until I've got to the bottom of all this … OK?'

Clive rarely adopted such a tone of voice with Shirley and she certainly knew her boss well enough by now to realise that he wouldn't have spoken to her quite like that unless he was under a good deal of pressure. Also, she'd worked with him long enough to know that once he had reached a decision about anything, it was always hard to get him to change his mind, and with something as serious as the current crisis, she knew it was going to be almost impossible to get him to budge. Consequently, she decided to adopt a much more conciliatory tone and said that she was now persuaded why he needed to remain in Columbus and assured Clive that she would stay on too, and do everything in her power to protect and assist him in any way she could.

Clive was clearly relieved, and the two Brits set about devising a modus operandi. They knew full well that whatever had to be done, it was imperative that their mission be accomplished within the next twenty-four hours. Clive instructed Shirley to go ahead and organise their travel arrangements back to New York with connecting flights on to London. He then called Allen's clinic and made an appointment for early the following morning, explaining that he had an urgent meeting to get back to in London, and had to catch an afternoon flight, apologising for not being able to join him for lunch as had been suggested. He certainly didn't mention that Shirley would accompany him to the surgery.

With breakfast now over, they returned to Clive's room, ordered more coffee and then, after making other necessary phone calls, continued to develop their plan of action. Clive pointed out that he needed to have his check-up interrupted and get Allen called away from the room where the examination was being conducted. He thought that would be the moment when Shirley would play her major role in the scenario and act as a decoy. Shirley loved the idea and suggested that she simulated a fainting fit, which would hopefully cause so much fuss in the surgery that it would eventually disrupt any procedure taking place in Allen's office. Being diabetic, she had sometimes allowed her blood-sugar level to drop and had even been known to pass out, making her feel more than confident about pretending to faint. Clive thought her suggestion a great idea and commented that it would leave him alone in Allen's room and free to look for the crucial evidence they needed to obtain. The obvious target of his search would be to find any incriminating needles that he believed might be contaminated and if he could lay his hands on anything that looked like a toxin, that would be an added bonus.

They agreed that in the event of not finding any proof of Allen's involvement, the worst that could happen is that they came away from the clinic empty-handed, leaving Allen above suspicion and, more importantly, none the wiser. For their part, they would then be prepared to drop the entire ploy and return to London the next day, having at least followed Clive's instincts. What might have existed in Arizona, or had or had not happened in Columbus, would remain an unsolved mystery. Should that be the case, Clive assured Shirley that he would consider Dr Levitt beyond reproach and forget all about Dennis's wipe-out theory, or maybe, all joking apart, be tempted to turn the entire saga into a movie.

While they were in the midst of their deliberations, Michael called, reminding Clive of the dinner party that he was giving that night and just confirming that his English friends would be there. He told them that Steve and Allen were also invited and he stressed how much his folks were looking forward to meeting everybody. Clive and Shirley graciously confirmed that they would most certainly be there and offered to bring wine and a dessert. Shirley realised that this get-together was going to provide her with an ideal opportunity to meet all Clive's Columbus players in the flesh, and put faces to their names: with the exception of Dennis, of course. She would then be able to make up her own mind about Allen Levitt and decide whether any of the others were to be trusted or not.

Steve also phoned and insisted on collecting them from their hotel and driving them over to Michael's house. He maintained he was feeling so much better, and although he'd avoided Dr Levitt's kind offer to visit him on Sunday, he assured Clive that he wasn't at death's door and really didn't need to be examined by Allen.

'I'm so glad to hear you're feeling a lot better,' said Clive. 'Why don't you call for us at about six. I want to introduce you to Shirley, and over a cocktail or two you can both get better acquainted before we go over to Michael's. Shirley's nodding. She obviously thinks it's a good idea too.'

Steve thought that would be swell, adding that now he was feeling on the mend, he really was up to meeting up for cocktails. He confirmed that thank goodness his glands had gone down and declared that he was definitely in the mood to party.

Clive decided to take his camera with him that evening, since this time he wanted to have a photographic record of his stay in Columbus. He took the lift down to the lobby and waited for Steve by the hotel reception desk. His new friend arrived on time and greeted him most warmly. However, Clive couldn't help thinking that Steve did in fact look somewhat under the weather, was rather subdued and wasn't his normal jolly self. As they made their way through the hotel, Clive decided to skirt health issues and explained that Shirley was still powdering her nose and would meet them in the bar.

'You know what women are like.'

'I sure do … and I'm really looking forward to meeting this one. You've mentioned your PA quite a lot.'

When Shirley finally arrived it was obvious that she had forgone her siesta in favour of a visit to the hotel hairdresser's. She had decided to go for a chignon that evening and wore a gorgeous off-the-shoulder cocktail dress in midnight blue and a pair of sapphire and diamond pendant earrings, which had belonged to her Auntie Flo. As she made her stunning entrance and swept her way towards the bar on a pair of gorgeous black high heels, she caused many heads to turn and stare in admiration, and as she approached her escorts, both men immediately rose to their feet. Steve was the first to greet her; bowing, he took her hand, placed a polite kiss on her extended right wrist, and she responded by dropping him a very deep curtsey.

'Shirley, it's such a great honour to meet you and may I say you look absolutely stunning.'

'Why thank you, kind sir! And I'm delighted to meet you too,' she flirted.

'Now guys, photo opportunity,' declared Clive. 'Smile … and look at the camera!'

Clive was obviously so proud of his dear friend, who clearly had great style and possessed such a wonderful wardrobe and he wanted to put on record how stunning Shirley looked that night. He drew immense satisfaction from the attention she had already been paid, but of course it didn't occur to him that she could have walked straight out of one of those Gainsborough films which, unbeknown to him, her Auntie Flo had so regularly appeared in. Added to which, there was no doubt that Shirley certainly sported the same good looks as her mother's sister.

'Shirley, you look amazing. What more can I say?' Clive finally commented.

'Well, for starters, I think you could ask me if I cared for a Manhattan?'

This prompted Clive to go into his frequently used patter. 'Oh. Please forgive me, Madame. I seem to have mislaid my manners. Waiter! Waiter! Please bring a Manhattan for the lady.'

'Certainly, sir. Right away, sir,' came the immediate response from the bell boy, who had also been stopped in his tracks by Shirley's impressive entrance, and on his return, Clive asked the young man to snap all three of them and they compliantly raised their glasses and looked towards the camera.

Miss Morris had come to the rescue once again and her arrival had alleviated any hint of awkwardness either men had been experiencing earlier on; and now both chaps were smiling and feeling a lot more relaxed. As was her wont, she took total command of her first meeting with Steve and as she sipped her martini and took in her new acquaintance's smartly suited appearance, she was struck by Clive's genuine ability to give such an accurate sketch of him, since he looked just as he'd described. Because of this flair, when Shirley was finally introduced to the two other major players in Clive's Columbus set later that evening, she also felt she already knew all of them.

After the second cocktail, Shirley rose to her feet: 'Now

gentlemen, if you'll forgive me, I need to fix my face, and Mr Spoke, I just need to confirm our travel arrangements back to New York for tomorrow. Is that OK?'

'Certainly, Miss Morris,' Clive chuckled.

With that, the two gentlemen stood to attention and Shirley sailed through the bar, yet again turning many heads as she steered a steady course back through the hotel lobby. Once she reached the door to her room, she paused, took a deep breath, swept through, kicked off her high heels, tossed herself down on her bed, cocktail dress and all, and bounced back.

There was no doubt that Columbus was proving to be one of the most challenging episodes in her career to date. She realised that before leaving London, she'd had no idea of Clive's love affair with Dennis and friendship with Michael, and although she was used to dealing with her boss's somewhat eccentric behaviour and mood swings, she had been very surprised by what he had become mixed up in and was impressed by his courageous plan for the next day. However, it also had to be said that she remained somewhat apprehensive about what its outcome might be and was also only too aware that her adventure in Columbus was just beginning.

While confirming their plane tickets, she reflected on how proud and fortunate she was to have Clive not only as a colleague, but also as a dear and close friend. Since losing her husband, her boss had been the only man she had ever allowed herself to get close to, and although she realised that their relationship could only ever be platonic, she was more than happy with that arrangement.

Then, having dealt with the Spoke travel arrangements, she put her shoes back on, applied a little more lipstick, and, seated in front of her dressing-table mirror, she removed the combs from her hair, which she then let roll down onto her shoulders. After she had brushed her locks into a kind of 'Veronica Lake', Shirley went and removed her shawl from the top of her packed suitcase, added a dab of Mitsouko behind her ears and from that moment on, felt ready to face Clive's remaining Columbus players.

Steve's car was parked in their hotel driveway and Shirley, now with a glamorous stole draped around her shoulders, was invited into the front seat, and she placed the shop-bought baked Alaska carefully on her lap. Clive, who sat behind carefully balancing the white Burgundy he'd selected, had insisted on that for dessert, since he told Shirley that it was Dennis's favourite pudding.

Shirley's people skills were on top form as she made polite conversation as they drove over to the German Village. Clive for his part, was mindful not to embarrass Steve by directly asking him how he was feeling in front of Shirley, and waited for an appropriate moment once they had vacated the car and were out of Shirley's earshot. He then tactfully enquired after Steve's health and the latter replied that he was feeling just fine and dandy.

Once they had reached their destination, they found Michael to be on very good form, and, wearing the Scottish sweater that Clive had given him, he gave all three of them a very warm welcome and made them feel totally at home as they joined the other three dinner party guests, who had already arrived. He proudly introduced his parents to the new arrivals, and Mr and Mrs Poledri responded in a most kindly manner, clearly delighted to meet more of their son's friends. Allen rose to his feet, greeted Clive enthusiastically and, with that cheesy smile of his, said how very pleased he was to make Shirley's acquaintance.

With the introductions completed, Michael began to serve his guests the martinis he had prepared. His father Douglas stepped in, and while his son served the drinks, he explained to all assembled that he still practised as an architect. It immediately struck Clive that Douglas's son was a dead ringer for him and thought that both Michael's mum and dad appeared to be a lot younger than he expected them to be. It was also clear where the dashing Italian good looks came from, as well as those blue-green eyes. By contrast, Gloria, Michael's mother, was a very attractive tall blonde, elegantly dressed in a discreet floral frock and, because opposites attract, Clive thought it not at all surprising that Douglas had fallen for her.

'I hope you don't mind, but I want to have a record of this important gathering.' And with that Clive whipped out his camera, and went round the room, photographing everyone and inviting them to raise their drinks in the air.

Then it was Gloria's turn to take the floor: she told Clive and Shirley that she had been a high-school teacher but had decided to take early retirement. It was apparent to the lively gathering that both parents obviously adored their son and accepted him. They also appeared to be completely relaxed about meeting more of his gay friends, but were careful to avoid any discussion about health issues, especially in front of Allen, who did appear to be a little frosty towards Steve, for reasons Clive would later discover. Shirley, astute as ever, was quick to notice how very charming Dr Allen Levitt appeared to be, but as the evening wore on, she began to understand why Clive had become so distrustful of him.

Once all were seated round the dining table, Michael announced that the gentlemen could remove their jackets and that dinner would soon be served. The food arrived and the first course was unusual: in fact Michael told them that his mum had prepared the starter: a delicious homemade mackerel brandade. Steve, who was the real foodie in the group, extolled its virtues and with that course over, the said nourishment seemed to make him look a lot better. He proposed a toast to Gloria, which was seconded by all, and got the supper party off to a rousing start, helped along by the white Burgundy so carefully chosen by Clive. Although not his dinner party, Clive decided he would get the conversation going by asking everyone around the table where they had studied and what part of America they were from.

'I hope you don't think it too cheeky of me, but because this starter is so delicious, I'm going to begin with you Gloria. Where did you study?

'I'm a local girl and went to Ohio State University, which is where I met Doug. I took English literature and he was in the School of Architecture. As a matter of fact, we got married shortly after we'd graduated and we decided to settle down here in Columbus.' Then after a slight pause she jokingly added: 'And I don't think we've ever set foot outside Ohio,' which was clearly not the case but caused much amusement round the table.

'Well, I suppose that takes care of you too, Doug,' Clive joked. 'Unless there's something you'd like to add?'

'Only that Gloria is as beautiful now as she was the first day I met her.'

'That's my dad for you', said Michael, and encouraged his guests to join him in a round of 'For He's a Jolly Good Fellow'.

'Now Michael, we all know where you studied, but Shirley doesn't.'

Michael told Shirley that because he wanted to learn to paint and sculpt, he had studied fine art and had got into Dennison University in Columbus. He joked that although the town may once have been cowboy country, it was now highly academically respectable.

'Shirley, your turn.'

'I have to be honest and admit I'm not a university lass. And, you know what? I would have preferred the cowboys,' – again causing much merriment amongst the dinner guests. 'You see, although I was sent to a private girls' school in Oxford, I didn't get into that famous university there. However, I did make it into the local polytechnic, where I took a course in secretarial studies and that's how I learnt to sit on my boss's lap.' Which last remark was certainly playing to the gallery.

'Steve, what about you? Clive continued.

'Me. Oh I was born in Wisconsin, in a little town called Spring Green.'

'Isn't that where Frank Lloyd Wright came from?' commented Douglas, which was not at all surprising, since he was the only architect round the table.

'You're absolutely correct. But I wasn't interested in architecture, and because I originally wanted to study linguistics, my parents sent me to Princeton, would you believe? But that was long before it went co-ed.'

'So there were no females to distract you,' laughed Michael.

'No! I found the other boys were distracting enough, thank you very much!'

'Now watch it! My folks may be broad-minded but…'

'Michael darling, Steve's only trying to add to the banter, don't be such a prude. And only a father can say that.'

Then Clive turned to Allen. 'So last, but by no means least, tell us what college you went to.'

Slowly straightening his tie, Allen responded in a very measured way and explained that although he was born in New York City, he had actually studied medicine at Arizona State University.

That last remark sent alarm bells across the table to where Clive was sitting, leaving him to wonder how near that college was to Tucson. Then, trying hard to conceal his anxiety, he joked: 'Oh! Doctors in the desert.'

Michael laughed, got up, and excused himself from the table, but Shirley was quick to be on her feet and offered to clear the dishes, with Gloria insisting on helping her.

During the pause between courses, there was a brief exchange between Allen and Clive about the check-up, which had been arranged for the following morning. Sensing the delicacy of the situation and in an attempt to steer the discussion away from health issues, Allen was very deft at changing the subject, and he now cleverly made Clive the central topic of conversation by claiming that he was certain everyone around the table would want to know how the Englishman had become an internationally famous theatrical agent. Once again the thought crossed Clive's mind that Allen's people skills were more than just natural. It was as if he had a master's degree in mind control and manipulation, which maybe he had also acquired in Arizona.

Douglas insisted that they wait for the ladies to rejoin them, since he was certain that Gloria would want to hear the Englishman's life story, and Clive added that he would definitely need his PA to help him relate his *histoire* and jog his memory when needed. At this point their host arrived with a splendid platter of roast guinea fowl, while Gloria brought some pan-fried salmon, which she had specially prepared for Allen, and Shirley trailed behind carrying an abundant variety of boiled and roast vegetables. What a feast!

Once all were served, Clive took it upon himself to propose one more toast: this time to Michael, and he encouraged yet another chorus of 'For He's a Jolly Good Fellow', and this time everyone sang along. The main course was going down a treat, and when a gratifying silence had descended and many delicious mouthfuls had been enjoyed, Allen deemed his timing appropriate, and he brought the subject back to Clive's glittering career. With the wine flowing freely and the atmosphere around the table being so merry, Clive had no intention of spoiling the party spirit, which was as abundant as was the delicious food so beautifully prepared by their host. So once again, using all the thespian skills he could muster, he took the floor.

'Well, I suppose that's why I asked you about where you all had gone to university. I feel that my adult life started at "uni" and, you see, I went to King's College, London University, which is slap bang in the centre of our capital city. Like so many students, I had vague dreams of becoming an actor, but I was too scared of failing, and really lacked confidence at the time. I remember one particular day when I was in my first year – you call it freshman year, I believe – I had taken a short cut to get to the Strand where my college was situated and I passed by a coffee bar, and, through the rather large old-fashioned shop windows, I saw a range of huge blow-up photographs of famous forties female Hollywood stars, like Bette

Davis, Olivia de Havilland and Joan Crawford.'

Clive told his now captivated audience that he had been tempted to go in for a quick cup of coffee and that because he was given such a warm and somewhat overpowering welcome by the owner, the Sunset Boulevard became a regular and favourite haunt of his. Although only eighteen, he explained that he had already come out to his parents and declared that the said coffee bar seemed to be just his cup of tea, if they knew what he meant? The Boolay, as he began to call it, had become a haven for like-minded young men, as well as for some rather attractive not-such-young men, if they caught his drift?

The entire gathering, including Michael's parents, greeted Clive's camp remarks with much amusement and a very positive sign of their appreciation.

'Do you know, everyone,' enthused Shirley. 'All this is such news to me. I've known Clive for a number of years now, but I've never heard him talk about his London University days nor about that period of his life before tonight.'

Shirley's remark made Clive realise that although she was perhaps his closest friend, there was a great deal that he didn't know about her life story, but he decided that this was not the right moment to put her on the spot and find out some of her secrets.

'So, tell us Clive, what has that coffee shop to do with how you became a theatrical agent?' Michael enquired.

'A great deal, actually. The owner, Bobbie Kelly, became a good friend of mine. You see, from his café, he used to run a special catering service for theatres – not for the general public, you understand, but for the people working backstage. So every day he provided meals and sandwiches for people who worked behind the scenes: for stage management as well as the performers, and he did particularly good business on matinee days. As a matter of fact, as a student I went to work for him, and in between term times, I added to my pocket money by earning rather good tips from those delivery runs.'

Michael claimed that he still couldn't see how delivering sandwiches on a matinee day made his friend one of London's leading agents.

Shirley sprang to Clive's defence and admitted that now she certainly did. 'Just give him a chance and I think you'll see the connection between Bobbie Kelly and Spoke Associates. Which for those of you who don't already know, is the name of the theatrical agency Clive currently owns.'

'Sorry, Clive. I suppose I'm so keen to know how it all happened, I'm being rather impatient,' said Michael.

'It's one of Michael's least attractive attributes, and only a mother can say so,' said Gloria, not at all unkindly.

Clive informed the gathering that eventually Bobbie got rid of his coffee shop, and set himself up in quite a different kind of business. He had made so many contacts in the theatre over the years and the Sunset Boulevard had attracted lots of people in 'the show business' as Clive liked to call his line of work. Many actors used to frequent the place during the daytime, as well as after the shows had come down at night. Clive explained that several years later, with the financial backing Bobbie gained from the sale of his catering business, coupled with his real grasp of the way that the entertainment industry worked, his friend formed his own theatrical agency. Because of his ability to spot talent he was able to persuade several actors to join him and he soon began to represent an impressive number. Within a year, the Bobbie Kelly Agency had managed to contract many promising newcomers and went from strength to strength and, with word of mouth spreading to his advantage, Bobbie's books began to fill up and his agency soon became very successful.

'And so this was the same Bobbie who had taken such a shine to you, the day you discovered that coffee shop.'

'Yes, Michael. I was a cheeky SOB, and no sooner had I graduated than I asked him for a job in his agency. I told him I was prepared to be the tea boy and do almost anything if he'd take me on.'

'Do almost anything?' interjected Steve, to everyone's amusement.

'Well, if you're suggesting that I may have been doing it with Bobbie, the truthful answer has to be in the affirmative. I mean to say, I wasn't the only new boy on the block, benefiting from the interest Bobbie used to show in all of us.'

'Clive, you really are a caution!' screamed Shirley, which caused the entire room to burst into laughter.

'And was that why he made you a partner in his firm?' asked Steve, appreciating that his line of questioning was clearly helping the evening go with a swing.

'Certainly not! Bobbie wasn't just interested in my charms, you know. Oh no, Steve! He could see that I had a similar eye for spotting talent and perhaps saw in me a much younger version of himself.'

'As your PA,' interrupted Shirley, 'I can certainly confirm that there's no denying your capacity for spotting talent when you see it, nor your ability to judge character and see through people, and detect how dishonest folks can be. I can drink to that.'

That last remark caught Allen unawares, and he almost choked on the glass of Burgundy he had just raised to his lips and he quickly covered up with: 'Hear! Hear!'

'So, yes,' Clive continued, 'and to cut a long story short, Bobbie eventually made me a partner in his firm and for a while everything went swimmingly. But I suppose I was just too ambitious, and being a good deal younger than my boss, I began to win the confidence of the less-experienced actors on his books, some of whom began to think Bobbie old-fashioned and came to me for guidance. I suppose the same thing may happen to me some day. Some of my clients might begin to think I'm old hat. What do you think, Shirley?'

But before he gave her time to respond, he quickly added: 'At any rate, things came to a head, and I decided to take the bull by the horns, leave Bobbie's agency and go it alone.'

'And truth to tell, he never looked back.' And with a good deal of pride Shirley continued, 'So Spoke Associates was born, and shortly afterwards I left Bobbie's office to join Clive's enterprise as a telephonist. I was ambitious too, you know. I didn't want to remain a secretary all my life and I slowly worked my way up to becoming Mr Spoke's PA, as I think you all know. He is much too self-deprecating to tell you about all the famous clients he has on his books to date, but I'm not.'

'Now, Mummy dearest, I think we should leave my story there. I'm sure these good people have heard enough about me and Spoke Associates for one night, don't you?'

'Whatever you say. You're the boss. And besides, I'm off to the kitchen to organise pudding.'

'Oh! Don't tell me we're having plum pudding for dessert? How absolutely *scrummy!*' exclaimed Steve.

'No, sorry to disappoint', replied Clive. 'Once again I have to say that we may all speak English, but we don't talk the same language. Pudding is just another word for dessert, and sometimes we call it "afters".'

'As I have learnt over the last week or so, our English cousins here just don't speak American.' And with that, Michael put smiles on everyone's faces.

The baked Alaska was a triumph and rounded off the meal nicely, and Clive proposed a toast to 'absent friends', which caused a slight cessation to the merriment. This prompted Michael, ever the perfect host, to bring brandy and liqueurs to the table, and he asked his dad to do the honours while, Clive suspected, he slipped away to the kitchen to dry his eyes. As Douglas poured Clive a Grand Marnier, he sidled up and gently asked him when he had first met Dennis. It was the moment Clive had been dreading all evening, but one he had naturally been prepared for. Shirley, ever attentive to her boss's needs, and sensing the delicacy of the situation, suggested that she and Douglas change places, on the pretext of her being able to sit next to his wife so that she could get to know Gloria a little better.

Clive explained that he had met Dennis in Provincetown in the late sixties and that they had remained in touch over the years, and added that Dennis wrote wonderful letters, which he had kept right up till the present day. Then he told Douglas that he'd first visited Columbus for the Bicentennial and that's when Dennis had introduced him to Michael.

'Dennis was like a son to us, you know. Gloria and I miss him terribly and we thought the world of him. AIDS is such a scary business and we feel so concerned for our Michael.'

'You're not alone there. But Michael tells me that you and Gloria have been so very supportive and I'm sure that to have such loving parents so close at hand must make a terrific difference, especially at a time like this.'

'Well, Clive, we're trying our very best to be there for him, and do as much as we can.'

'I'm rather hoping I can get him to come to London for a couple of weeks. I think a change of scene will do him good, don't you?'

'Now that's a great idea.'

And feeling that he had Michael's folks behind him, Clive decided to make his invitation more public by bringing the subject of travel into the conversation, and reminding Michael that he hoped he would come and visit London during the summer.

'Can I come too?' Steve was keen to ask.

'I don't see why not,' said Clive. And besides, it will be good for Michael to have a travel companion with him. Shirley and I will be busy at work during the daytime, so he'll definitely need company. Would you like to join them too, Allen?'

'I wish I could,' Allen was quick to reply. 'But we haven't got our summer rota at the clinic formally announced yet.'

'Well,' interrupted Shirley, 'Clive has instructed me to organise all your travel arrangements once you've sorted out your dates.

All you have to do is just give me a call at Spoke Associates. Here's our card.'

'That's most kind of you guys, but the clinic has to come first. Which reminds me, if I'm going to be on top form tomorrow morning for your check-up, Clive, I better be making tracks for home. I'm so sorry everyone, but I have to leave.' Then, as he rose to his feet, he added: 'But please don't let me break up the party.'

'No, don't you worry about that. Gloria and I want to find out more about all those movie stars Clive's agency manages. Don't we, Glor?'

'Yes. I particularly want to know all about Anthony Pollard. Michael tells me he's one of yours and I adored him in *The Butler*. What's the dirt on him, I wonder?'

'Shirley will fill you in on all the gossip on our Anthony,' Clive called out as he left the table and accompanied Allen to the back door with Michael.

Putting his jacket back on, Allen thanked Michael for including him and said what a great evening he had hosted.

'And thank you Allen, for looking after Clive tomorrow morning.'

'No problem. It's what I'm here for.' And with that he was gone.

The dinner party had been a roaring success and Clive complimented himself on how pleasantly he'd managed to behave towards Allen, hoping against hope that he'd not betrayed the genuinely suspicious feelings he was harbouring, particularly now that he knew Allen had attended Arizona State University, of all places. Clive had adored meeting Michael's charming parents and both parties made certain that addresses had been exchanged prior to bidding their fond farewells. Clive and Shirley hugged their host as they said their goodnights, and Michael confirmed that he would come to collect Clive at his hotel the following morning at nine o'clock. Steve, who was looking a lot better than when he had arrived, kindly offered to drive his new English buddies, as he called them, back to the Sheraton, for which they were most grateful. They waved goodbye to the Poledris, who joined Michael on the back porch as he wished his guests goodnight.

Shirley sat up in front with Steve and they both chatted away as they drove back to the Sheraton. Clive, on the other hand, simply switched off and reflected on how touched he'd been by Douglas's affection for Dennis. This took him back once more to his very first visit to Columbus and he once again was reminded of the deep love he had felt for his late friend and the many letters he'd received from Dennis.

Surprises can be pleasant, but can be lonely. My thoughts have been in your favour as, evidently, you have favoured me with yours. I hope you are anticipating all the best here with me and, eventually, Michael, if you want? I believe I can speak for the two of us.

Dennis wrote these carefully chosen words in a letter he posted to Clive just before their Columbus reunion in 1976. Judging from the tone of this one, and the many dozens he sent, it was not at all surprising that Clive found his penpal's turn of phrase almost poetic and why, for a while, he felt so encouraged to maintain their transatlantic relationship with such a regular exchange of correspondence.

CHAPTER FOURTEEN

DENNIS FLASHBACK

Once back at the Sheraton, Clive said goodnight to Shirley but was just too wide awake to go straight to bed. Try as he might, he just couldn't forget the moving conversation he'd had with Michael's father about Dennis and he found his mind racing back to that reunion with his Adonis when they had met up again in the Columbus airport arrivals hall in '76. He vividly remembered that his attraction for the now slightly balding 35-year-old man who stood before him was as strong as it had ever been.

Dennis still displayed that marvellous physique, those piercing steel-blue eyes and exuded just as much sex appeal as he had when they'd first met. Clive was overjoyed to see his holiday romance once more, and was certainly impressed with the car that then transported him to where Dennis lived. As they turned onto the highway, they both noticed the flashes of lightning in the far distance and they could hear the rumble of thunder coming towards them.

Finally Dennis proudly parked Benjy outside 257 Alexandria Colony Court South and asked Clive to help him put the hard top back onto the convertible, since he thought rain was imminent.

Then Dennis presented his guest with his own set of keys, warmly escorted Clive up to his front door, invited him to open up the house and said he hoped he would make himself feel completely at home.

Clive fully expected Michael to be standing on the doorstep but was told by Dennis that the pair of them had decided that it was too soon for them to move in together, and they both agreed to wait until their relationship had become more settled. Dennis explained that even though they had finally bonded, they'd decided to live in separate houses for practical reasons, which he would explain later on. Despite the fact that Clive had been unable to find a suitable partner for himself back in London, he tried not to be too jealous of Dennis's good fortune in having discovered a soulmate in Michael. Consequently, he was determined to approve of the young man and accept him as a person in his own right and not just as Dennis's new boyfriend. Clive truly hoped that, given time, he would make Michael a very close friend, which, as it transpired, was exactly what came to pass.

Clive had been amused that Dennis immediately suggested his English pal take a shower while he attended to their evening meal. Like so many Americans, he was fanatical about cleanliness, which also reminded Clive of their very first meeting on Cape Cod when Dennis always seemed so keen on them both showering. However, this time, the Englishman had to admit to himself that he'd been on the road all day and definitely did need to bathe. Now, on his second visit, it still struck Clive that bathrooms and kitchens in the States were much better designed and equipped than they were back home and, then as before, he continued to consider the portable television set on Dennis' washstand a bit over the top.

Still unable to get to sleep at the Sheraton, he was reliving his first visit to Dennis's home. Clive remembered that he had got undressed, jumped into the shower as instructed, and luxuriated for some time under the endless supply of hot running water. He always sang when he was happy, and that first night he had visited

Columbus was one of the most joyous evenings he'd spent in a long time.

Dennis, hearing his friend's loud serenade coming from upstairs, suddenly appeared and startled the Englishman by poking his head through the shower curtain. Clive retaliated by splashing water over Dennis's face in an attempt to get him to join him and he was utterly delighted when his lifeguard stripped off and climbed into the cubicle with him. As they started to soap each other down, Clive remembered paying particular attention to his shower buddy's feet, since he knew how much Dennis liked to have his toes massaged. However, on that occasion, the ex-marine was not in the least bit appreciative and although Clive was obviously excited, his lifeguard remained totally unaroused. Refusing to admit defeat, Clive began to rub himself up against his pal's soapy body in an attempt to turn Dennis on: but that approach also failed to produce the slightest response. Finally Clive took the hint, jumped out of the shower and left Dennis to complete his ablutions alone. Once towelled dry and robed, he shouted out over the loud sound of splashing water: 'Well, if I can't have you, I'll have a cocktail instead. I'd love a Bronx!' And he took himself off to the bedroom and got dressed.

'Now that's even a new one on me,' Dennis shouted back. 'What's in it?'

'Two parts gin, one part red and one part white vermouth, with a little added orange juice.'

'Sounds great – I only hope I've got all the ingredients,' Dennis replied as he got out of the shower.

'Don't worry … a Bloody Mary will suit me just fine.'

He had such fond memories of his first stay in Columbus and recalled that his friend had gone downstairs and organised the drinks: two Bloody Marys. Dennis had prepared their meal prior to driving out to the airport, and was in the middle of cooking it when Clive descended the open staircase. The dining table in the front room had been beautifully laid out with what looked like the best china, crystal and ironed napkins, and lots of candles had been lit

'Dinner won't be long,' and Dennis handed Clive a cocktail. 'Sorry, but I couldn't fix a Bronx; I just didn't have the white vermouth.' Then he added: 'To absent friends.'

Clive thought that the toast referred to Michael, so they clinked glasses and each took a sip.

Then Dennis added, 'You know, I really miss my friend, Senator Jim. I don't see so much of him any more.'

That was the very first time Clive had actually ever heard Dennis mention the mysterious Senator Jim by name, and so he asked for more information about him.

'Oh, he was one of my "regulars". I really do miss that dude, but he's now found someone closer to home … Actually, Clive, his life's quite complicated. You see, he's bi – he's married and that – and although his family are back in Illinois, in his position as a senator, he can't afford to be openly gay in Washington DC, so he leads a bit of a double life.'

'I understand where you're coming from.' Clive replied. 'I have a number of actors on my books who can't own up to being gay because it could ruin their careers – some of them even get married. Let's face it, the law in England only changed in '67 and that was barely a year before we first met; and remember how uptight I was then. But tell me more about your friend Jim … how did you two first meet?'

Dennis made no response and walked away, so Clive followed him back into the kitchen and, spotting that the salad had been chopped and prepared, offered to make the dressing. Over dinner the ever-inquisitive Clive had many pressing questions to ask but let his curiosity about Jim drop for the time being. Little was he to realise what an important role Senator James Nelson would play in his late friend's life, but Clive was to discover all about that some years later.

In any case, on that first night of their reunion, Clive was much more eager to learn all about the changes that had occurred in Dennis's world since they had met in Provincetown and, in particular, he wanted to know how he had come to meet Michael. Dennis responded by confessing that he'd come out with a vengeance since that summer on Cape Cod, and freely admitted that he was now open about the fact that he loved to be admired and was proud of his ability to captivate, either by seducing or being seduced. His newly acquired confidence had encouraged him to start what he referred to as his sideline, which turned out to be both profitable as well as enjoyable. He again mentioned that he had his 'regulars', which was how he'd come to get to know Senator Jim and why he'd frequently gone back and forth to Washington.

Clive made a further attempt at finding out more about the senator, since it was now obvious to him that the man figured large in his friend's life. However, Dennis didn't seem to want to talk about Jim and so the subject was immediately changed back to Michael, who, Clive was told, had been a student in the fine art department of Dennison University where Dennis worked as a part-time model for the life-drawing class. Dennis added that when they'd first got together, Michael found his sideline rather difficult to handle but that eventually he'd just got used to it.

'Michael's really looking forward to meeting you, you know.'

'That's nice,' Clive responded. Then hearing the lack of sincerity in his own voice, tried to cover up with: 'Oh sorry! I mean it. I really want to meet him too.' Said last remark produced what was now becoming that all-too-familiar incredulous look from Dennis, which Clive was very quick to pick up on.

'Listen, Den, you two have been together for over six years and I just wanted to congratulate Michael on his feat of endurance … that's all,' Clive added, wearing a broad grin on his face and hoping that his witty remark would cover up his faux pas.

'Look,' countered Dennis. 'I just know you two will hit it off, and I want so very much for you to become good friends. By the way, there's bottle of Almaden in the icebox. Would you mind getting it out?'

Clive made some crude remark about getting something else out, and gave Dennis a little fondle on his way over to get the wine. However, once again his pal appeared to reject his overtures and pulled away, and this total lack of interest eventually produced a numbing effect on Clive. Finally, they sat down to dine, each seated at a comfortable distance from each other, thus preventing either of them from playing footsie under the table. The food was plentiful, if a little too overcooked for Clive's palate, but the large bottle of chilled Californian red helped the meal go along with a swing. Then, with dinner over and the bottle emptied, they made for the ample sofa on the other side of the room.

More than a little tipsy by now, they threw off their shoes and Clive removed Dennis' socks and once again set about massaging his toes. This time it seemed to do the trick, and at last they cuddled up close together, bodies entwined, and gently stroked each other for a while. Then Dennis disengaged himself, closed the curtains and went and put a record on, now opting for his choice of music: he wanted to hear Albinoni's *Adagio* and not *A Chorus Line*, which Clive had given him.

'Clive, you know, it's so great to be with you again after so many years. But I'm sure you remember I'm not very good on first nights. I'll make it up to you on the second, I promise.' Then after a slight pause he asked: 'Say, do you feel like taking a sauna?'

Dennis explained that Alexandria Colony Court boasted a pool and sauna that was available to all residents. Clive reminded his pal that he wasn't a strong swimmer but said he wouldn't mind having a sauna or a quick dip.

'You'll have to loan me some trunks; I didn't bring mine.'

'Some what?'

'A bathing suit.'

'No problem. Let's go!'

They raced upstairs to Dennis' bedroom, stripped off completely and Clive tried on a selection of his friend's slim-hipped swimwear, then squeezed himself into the smallest pair of navy-blue trunks he could find. They threw on a couple of bathrobes, dashed out of the house, ran across the courtyard and made for a building that occupied a central position on the estate and served as a leisure centre.

The Colony was now silent, although there were some windows dotted around that projected small pockets of light, indicating that they were not the only people still up and about. They quietly entered the pool house and went downstairs into the basement, Clive hoping that there would be no other midnight bathers around. He had no desire to use the pool, since it was the sauna he was really after, so that he could be alone with Dennis in that warm and relaxing little room, where he hoped they could be naked. He noticed that his friend switched on the lights as they went along the corridor, encouraging Clive to assume that they were indeed the only residents down there, which added impetus to the growing excitement he was feeling.

The sauna itself was a little square wooden box built in the corner of a much bigger room that contained changing cubicles, lockers, loos and showers. Dennis adjusted the level of the heat in the sauna and once again ordered Clive to take a hot shower. Clive did as bidden, but was amused by his friend's fastidious behaviour, since he was certain that his earlier ablutions had already cleared away any vestige of travel fatigue and grime, and thought it totally unnecessary to wash himself yet again.

'I suggest you take those off too you know, before you get under the shower. I don't think anyone's gonna come down here at this time of night. And if they do, then they've got a little treat in store.' Then as he began to soap Clive down, he added, 'Mmm ... and not such a little treat, neither.'

Clive tried to turn away to hide his embarrassment, causing

Dennis to grab hold of him in one arm and scoop him up with the other, while with his free hand he switched off the shower, pushed open the sauna door, swung through and dropped Clive down onto a wooden bench.

This Tarzan-like display caused Clive to burst into peals of laughter, only to be silenced by Dennis announcing that he needed to take a crap.

When he returned, he gave Clive a tight bear hug, squeezing all the air out of his lungs and then kissed him fully on the mouth. It was what Clive had been craving ever since he arrived in Columbus, and after a certain amount of foreplay, the two men became more intimate. Sex with Dennis was always easy and very natural, causing no discomfort or pain, despite his size. He was a master at it and Clive, now very relaxed from the heat of the sauna, allowed himself to be taken with no problem at all. As Dennis bucked back and forth, filling Clive with his warmth and strength, he began to increase his rhythm and within a very short time Clive was helped to climax. While jerking spasms were still coursing through his own body, he could sense his master's pace quicken and then heard a deep groan come from the back of Dennis's throat, and at the same time, he felt a hot release pouring into him.

By now the sauna had become more like a steam room and both men felt the need for a cold shower to cool themselves down before they finally vacated the leisure centre. Dennis attended to turning down the heat in the sauna and switched off all the lights as they exited. It wasn't that late, but Clive noticed that the streets in the Colony were now deserted, making him wonder whether the entire suburb was exclusively inhabited by old-age pensioners.

Dennis invited his house guest to open the front door, and as Clive followed Dennis back into the house, he was truly contented and pleased he had come to Columbus to resume what he liked to think of as the continuation of his American 'sex education'. The obsession he had for his lifeguard had been rekindled, although that did cause him to question his own sanity.

Both men made a dive for the sofa and sprawled out for a while, somewhat exhausted. Then, with no word of explanation, Dennis quickly got up and went upstairs. Clive simply assumed that he'd gone to have a pee and must have dozed off for a while, when he suddenly woke up to find Dennis fully dressed and starring at him.

'Look Clive, it's just no good. I simply can't do it with you again.'

'But I don't understand. What have I done wrong?'

'It's not you, it's me! I feel so guilty about Michael. You see, he loves me and I love him.'

'But I need you too.'

'Need – Clive, is that all you can say? Need? I'm talking about love.'

'And do you love all the others you do it with?'

'That's business.'

'Well in that case, I'll pay for the fuck if it makes you feel better.'

With that, Dennis sprang to his feet, shaking with rage and looking really threatening. For a moment Clive thought the American was going to hit him, so he quickly curled himself up into a tight ball. Instead Dennis turned on his heels, rushed upstairs to get a coat and went storming out, slamming the front door shut as he went. It all seemed to happen in a flash, suddenly leaving Clive quite alone in a house that was foreign to him and in the middle of the suburbs of a town he was completely unfamiliar with. It made him feel most uneasy and cold, which was hardly surprising since he'd had no clothes on during the row that had just taken place.

Clive calmly went upstairs, found an old dressing gown, and sank down onto the foot of Dennis' king-sized bed. He tried to reason with himself and get his infatuation into perspective and made a serious effort to see things from Dennis's point of view. At last he was able to face up to the fact that it was foolish to believe that Dennis could think of him in the same emotional terms as he thought of Michael.

And so, having got that clearly settled in his mind, Clive went down to the kitchen, helped himself to a glass of milk, turned off the record player and switched off all the lights downstairs. Climbing back up the open staircase, he decided to try and get some sleep in the spare bedroom, congratulating himself on being such a good house guest, while at the same time chastising himself for being such a bad loser.

Much to his own surprise, he slept well that night and woke bright and early. He felt that a dark cloud had been lifted, and he was now able to face up squarely to the situation he had got himself into. As Clive showered and got dressed, he admitted to himself that it would have been far wiser to have left his hulking great lifeguard behind on that Provincetown beach years ago, instead of chasing halfway across the world after him. Sometimes in life, lessons had to be learnt the hard way and when a door closes, it's pointless to try to prise it open, even if one's teeth are strong and sharp.

Clive heard his host pottering around in the kitchen downstairs and shouted out: 'Hey, good morning, Dennis.'

'I'll bring you up some coffee,' came the reply.

'That's all right. I'll be down in a couple of minutes. Keep it warm for me.'

There had been a time when such a comment would have contained all sorts of hidden agenda, but not any more. Clive's feelings had changed overnight and with the help of his newly acquired cool and logical approach, he had been able to come to terms with the fact that his affair with Dennis was finally over and he could go downstairs and face the music, if not quite break into a foxtrot. Clive found Dennis making fresh coffee and stirring something over the stove. He looked as though he'd been up all night, but with total calm and that ever so sincere soft-spoken voice of his said: 'Clive, I really hope you slept well last night.'

'Yes, I'm afraid I did. Didn't you?'

'As a matter of fact, I haven't been to bed yet,' Dennis continued.

'I went to our local gay disco, met up with my friend Dick and made quite a night of it.'

Clive quite surprised himself by not feeling in the least bit put out and simply smiled back: 'Oh, good for you.'

'I've made some corned-beef hash. Would you like some?'

'No, thank you. But I'd love a soft-boiled egg.'

'Sure. No problem.'

There then followed a rather long silence, while both men summoned up the courage to say what was really on their minds. Finally it was Clive who broke it.

'Dennis, I've been thinking. I've decided to go back to New York ... Look, we both know this just hasn't worked out, but if it's anyone's fault, it's mine. I arrived with too many demands and the last thing I want to do is complicate your life with Michael.'

'If you really wanna go, Clive, I won't stop you.'

'Dennis, I think it's for the best. Don't you?'

'I suppose so. And I'm truly sorry.'

'Well, don't be. And, by the way, I really do want to meet Michael before I leave.'

'Yes of course. We'd both like that very much.'

There being nothing more left to say, Dennis tucked into a heaped plateful of hash and fried potato, while Clive delicately dunked his toast into his solitary boiled egg. Then with breakfast over, they climbed into Benjy and drove off to Dennison as planned. It was still surprisingly warm for April and the previous night's storm seemed to have freshened the atmosphere.

Driving through the streets of Columbus with the roof off yet again felt most exhilarating and also helped clear the air between the two of them. After Dennis's amazing performance for the art class, they grabbed a quick lunch and the star model, as Clive now thought him, announced that he wanted to stop by at Michael's house since he had a few things to collect from there. He assured Clive that he didn't expect Michael to be back from his folks till the following day, as he knew he was spending Easter with Douglas and Gloria, who lived on the other side of town.

Although Clive had decided to return to New York, he was somewhat relieved to put off his first meeting with his rival for one more day. However, imagine his total surprise to find the house occupied after all and, naturally enough, Clive suspected the ever-manipulative Dennis of having planned the entire episode. So there finally stood his competition, and Dennis made a great meal of introducing them to each other. His new host's good looks presented something of a blow to Clive's vanity, and their first meeting got off to a rather more awkward start than he had ever anticipated.

'What a cosy little house,' slipped out before Clive had a chance to stop himself and check how condescending his remark sounded.

Then to make matters worse, when Michael offered him some tea that a friend had specially brought over from London, Clive said he preferred coffee. As they chatted over biscuits and beverages, Clive began to scrutinise his new acquaintance, and on closer examination, actually found Michael's features to be quite irregular. He decided that those gorgeous green-blue eyes were in fact set too far apart, the lips a little too thin and that nose not quite straight.

Sensing tension in the air, Dennis decided to take control of what he believed had become a delicate situation, and, in an attempt to bring the focus back to himself, explained that he had decided that Michael needed space in which to practise his artwork, and that was the main reason for them living separately.

'Say, would you like to see my studio?' Michael asked.

Clive, wearing his best English manners, replied that he'd be delighted and was shown upstairs into a light and airy bedroom at the front of the house, which had been turned into the perfect place in which to paint and sculpt. A large easel occupied a central position in the room and on it stood a work in progress. There were several canvases stacked up against one of the walls and a small table nearest the window had tubes of paint spread out over it, as well as a tall glass jar containing several sets of brushes. All in all, Clive reckoned it looked like a proper artist's studio. However, when it came to having a closer look at Michael's paintings displayed throughout the house, in his heart of hearts, Clive thought that the art was only average.

Nevertheless, ever the diplomat, he felt it only polite not to be too critical when invited to comment on the paintings.

With the art inspection over, Clive asked where the toilet was, more out of the need to be alone for a while than to really use the loo. It was along the upstairs hallway and separate from the bathroom. Once he'd locked himself in, Clive sat down for a while and reflected on the events of the last twenty-four hours. Some time must have elapsed before he got up and went back to join his friends.

When he opened the lavatory door, there, to his total surprise, he found his two American friends not only embracing, but stark bollock naked. He had intended to wash his hands in the bathroom, but they were barring his way. As Clive approached them, they stood their ground and remained firmly in their clinch. Dennis reached out and pulled Clive towards him, followed by Michael, who warmly welcomed the Englishman into what had now become a trio. Clive allowed himself to be drawn into their cosy huddle, offering only a hint of resistance. Once his mate's tongues became disengaged, the two men turned, looked at Clive, smiled and simply welcomed him into their world. The meaning behind Dennis's last letter became clear as they both began to caress Clive, who by now had yielded totally. He started to fondle their two naked bodies, and his inhibitions seemed to have vanished overnight. All three hovered in the doorway to Michael's boudoir and at the time, it struck Clive that the bed it contained looked enormous and seemed out of all proportion with the size of the rest of the room. Clive attempted to disengage himself from what he thought could be a new and overpowering sexual experience, uttering that feeble line about threesomes being illegal in England, and then went off to wash his hands.

In the past, men in Clive's life had either been bright but physically unappealing, or stunning to look at, but thick as shit. Such was not the case now: experiencing a change of heart and mind, he rushed back to that enormous bed and dived on top of his Columbus boys, kissing and licking them, and exorcising all fear and inhibition. He was now having the time of his life with those two desirable, sensitive and intelligent young men. It wasn't the first time Dennis had choreographed a novel physical activity for Clive, and this threesome had introduced the Englishman to an even greater degree of sexual freedom than he'd ever experienced before.

Such were Clive's vivid memories of the time he'd had with his Columbus boys on that very first visit. He had such an amazing ability to visualise what had happened, and, although he was still wide awake after Michael's dinner party, he did finally come to his senses in that room at the Sheraton and realised that he needed to switch off and try to get some shut-eye. It was important to be well rested and ready to face up to the challenge he had set himself for the following day's visit to Allen's clinic. So, despite Clive's immensely strong powers of recall, he reached over, took one of Shirley's sleeping pills, turned off the light and was eventually able to put memories of his reunion with Dennis to one side, and willed himself to go to sleep.

CHAPTER FIFTEEN

THE CHECK-UP TUESDAY

Shirley and Clive had both requested alarm calls, were quickly washed and dressed, and, having had a light breakfast together and the imperative cup of coffee, met up again in the hotel lobby at least ten minutes prior to the arranged nine o'clock pick-up time. As agreed the night before, Michael had kindly volunteered to drive Clive over to Allen's clinic the following morning and because the check-up was to be purely routine, he appeared to be a little put out to find Shirley, fur jacketed and suitcase in hand, waiting alongside Clive by the hotel reception desk.

She explained that because she was planning to fly back to New York later that day, they'd both checked out of their rooms and, in order to kill time before her plane took off, she'd decided to go with Clive on his visit to the doctor's. Using all the charm in the world, she added that she knew Clive was looking forward to moving back into number 257 and her convincing explanation appeared to win Michael round. The two Brits once again thanked Michael for the spiffing good time they had at his dinner party, and told him how much they'd enjoyed meeting his charming parents. Over dinner the previous evening, it had become abundantly obvious to the assembled guests that the two Brits were not only very close colleagues but also inseparable friends, which further helped persuade Michael that it was hardly surprising that Shirley wanted to accompany her boss to the clinic. However, it was hopefully also apparent that Michael had absolutely no idea that there was any ulterior motive in her going along for Clive's check-up and, more importantly, neither did either of the two Londoners believe that Michael had a clue about the plot they'd hatched the previous day.

Shirley also explained that as well as booking her own flight home, she had taken care of Clive's travel arrangements back to London via New York for the following day. Michael more than understood that the two had pressing commitments in both cities, and accepted that their Columbus sojourn would have to come to an end at some time or another. He'd been invited to join them both at Le Gai Paris for a late lunch before Shirley got her plane, and he was looking forward to what he knew would be a jolly threesome. He left them at the clinic in good time, and told them that he was going to look in on Steve and perform his angel of mercy's good deed for that day, and reminded them that he would be back to collect them in about half an hour.

Clive had never actually been inside the clinic, having only ever seen it from a distance, and he felt that the single-storey modern building that housed it looked rather like an English bungalow. It was completely detached from the adjacent and larger Columbus General Hospital, and set back in its own grounds at the end of a long drive that turned off from the gates of the main entrance to the hospital and wound round to its own independent front door. Once inside, it felt not unlike other similar institutionalised buildings he'd frequented back home and, as he and Shirley took stock of the general layout of the rooms and the central corridor leading off from the entrance, they felt that there would be no problem beating the hasty retreat they had rehearsed, should that become at all necessary.

The two of them were greeted by a very efficient-looking nurse, who sat behind a long curved desk placed to one side of the waiting area, which was devoid of other patients. Sporting a badge bearing her name, Nurse Edith Grant invited them to take a seat and assured them that since Mr Spoke had an appointment to see the doctor, it was unlikely that he would be kept waiting. In no time at all, Allen emerged from one of three doors that faced the six rows of vacant chairs opposite, wearing a typical long white clinician's coat as well as that broad, beaming grin of his.

He was somewhat surprised to find Shirley sitting beside Clive, but nonetheless greeted the Brits in a friendly manner, and introduced them both to Nurse Edith. He said how much he'd enjoyed the dinner party the previous evening and how well he thought Michael was doing, considering what he'd been through over the last three months. The greetings now over, he politely took his leave of Shirley, guided Clive to his office doorway and ushered his patient in.

On closing the door behind them, he began his examination with a fine display of traditional old and well-trusted bedside manners, which began with him inviting Clive to take a seat, remove his raincoat, and make himself comfortable. So, with such formalities over, the check-up began.

'Now Clive, when did your doctor last give you a thorough examination?'

'Honestly Allen, I really can't remember. But it must have been ages ago.' And knocking gently on the wooden desk in front of him, he continued: 'I really don't feel the need to see him much these days because I'm in reasonably good health … I think!'

'Well, yes, I must say you look pretty fit to me.'

As Clive took in the room, he noted that there were a number of glass-doored cabinets fitted along one of the walls, and since he was on the lookout for the much-detested needles, he hoped that they might be housed there. The plan was well-rehearsed in his brain; he knew what he was looking for, and assumed that any toxin would be kept in the fridge, so he was keen to spot where that might be located. Outside in the waiting area, Shirley had brought a book to read, which appeared to engross her completely, but her mind was elsewhere and she was equally well prepared to play her part in the deception. It was essential to get Allen called away and leave Clive alone in the doctor's office, totally free to rummage around and find the evidence they were sorely in need of finding, speed being of the utmost importance for both their sakes.

There was a slight pause in the proceedings in the doctor's office while Allen put pen to paper and Clive enquired whether he should pay before the examination began. Dr Levitt explained that would not be necessary, since Clive needed to settle the account with his nurse on leaving the surgery.

Then Clive revealed a genuine hint of nervousness as he asked the doctor whether he should get undressed.

'I think you're gonna have to if I'm to give you a thorough examination.'

Removing his cardigan and then undoing the buttons of his pristine white shirt, Clive reflected that he felt nowhere near as shy undressing in the surgery he went to back home as he did now in front of Dr Allen Levitt. But then he also had to admit to himself that his GP in London was most certainly not a sexy young man, nor, for that matter, was Dr Gilmore gay. As he slowly removed his brogues, grey flannel trousers and underwear, he also realised that he had no definite proof of Allen's sexual orientation, since for some time now, he had begun to entertain second thoughts about Allen's repeated assertions that he was homosexual. His Spoke intuition was starting to doubt all that Dr Allen Levitt actually stood for and, not unsurprisingly, this line of reasoning made undressing in front of him become a great deal easier.

Allen sat while Clive now stood naked in front of him and he began his close examination by running his hands up and down Clive's body. He clearly appeared to know what he was looking for and at least that left Clive in no doubt as to the veracity of his medical credentials. He put pressure on various parts of Clive's anatomy and even gently squeezed his skin in several places as he looked for signs of a blemish or rough surface.

'Allen, do you mind giving my left foot a closer look. You see there's a small purple patch on it which has been troubling me and causing me some concern since your lecture the other evening.'

'Of course, lift it up.'

He gave the mark a gentle squeeze. 'Not to worry about that. It's only a birthmark. But could you now please open wide.' And with that, he looked into his new patient's mouth and down his throat. 'Well, I'm glad to say that there's no sign of thrush.'

'I should hope not!' responded Clive once his mouth was free.

'You know, you'd be amazed how common it is. The problem is that you can have it but not realise. Like a lot of these damn things.'

He went on to look inside Clive's ears and up his nose: 'There don't appear to be any nasty little blotches there either ... or there.'

'That's a huge relief. I haven't had such a complete overhaul in years. I'm most grateful to you, Allen.'

'You know I always advise people to have a yearly check-up, not just because of this AIDS scare, but as a general health precaution. Nowadays it's highly advisable, since there are so many nasty things about, and the detection of early warning signs would save so much illness and misery in the long run. I mean, that's why you're here, isn't it?'

'Yes, of course,' replied Clive, lying through his teeth. 'You know, Allen, back home, it's compulsory for our actors to have a thorough medical examination prior to signing a movie contract. Film companies need to be assured that their leading man – or woman, for that matter – isn't going to peg out halfway through the filming and bring everything to a standstill. Having to find a replacement can cost them a fortune and then there is the additional expense of a reshoot, which just creates a huge amount of unnecessary extra work for all of us at Spoke Associates.'

'Well, that makes total sense. By the way, I didn't ask you where your office is located in London.'

Clive attached little importance to Allen's enquiry at the time and told him that Spoke Associates was just off Saint Martin's Lane, in a charming little pedestrian precinct called Cecil Court, in the heart of London's theatre district.

'That sounds delightful, and so convenient for your work.' Then Allen asked Clive to move over onto the medical couch located on the other side of the room, causing his patient to show more than a little amusement.

'Yes, what is it about the good old casting couch? It never fails to raise a smile with even the most nervous of patients. I bet I know what's running through that wicked mind of yours, Clive!'

Clive hoped in hell that he didn't and, laughing off Allen's remark, he asked: 'I couldn't have a glass of water, could I?'

'Yes, of course! Still or sparkling?'

'Sparkling, please.' And sure enough, it was kept in the fridge.

The Brits had decided to go into action after twelve minutes of Clive having been admitted into the doctor's office and, naturally, it was imperative that Allen knew nothing. After the agreed time had elapsed, Shirley would set about feigning her fainting fit, which she hoped would so alarm the nurse at the admissions desk, it would cause the young woman to alert Allen to the unfortunate situation. It was to be expected that this would make the doctor leave his office and come immediately to Shirley's rescue, thus leaving Clive alone, enabling him to go into action. Then, when Shirley had come to and was stable, Clive's check-up could continue, and once things had returned back to normal, they would both leave the building as though nothing had happened.

However, as the examination progressed, Clive's imagination ran riot. What if Allen held an ace card; one that he and Shirley had not bargained for? What if, in setting up his clinic, Allen had been fully prepared by his mentors in Tucson or Washington or wherever the hell he'd been conditioned, and had been briefed that in the likelihood of his cover being blown, he would have to ensure that not a trace of his involvement could ever be discovered? Clive believed that men like Allen were thorough professionals: they were enlisted voluntarily, and, although you might say that they had been brainwashed, it was also obvious that they were totally aware of the deadly game they were playing. Not for one moment did Clive think that a posh car or an expensive wristwatch could be sufficient compensation for what Allen might be assigned to do.

This once again provoked him to consider the enigma of the Allen's motivation and made him question why Allen had become involved in this ghastly business in the first place. As Dr Levitt raised Clive's left leg and squeezed the calf muscle, his patient tried to get his head around what might be the root cause of Allen's disaffection with the gay community. He was aware that, for religious reasons, Allen claimed to be conflicted by his own homosexuality, but Clive felt that this was hardly sufficient motive to trigger the degree of hatred which would have led him to play such a destructive role and be the instrument of so much suffering and cruelty. He knew that being Jewish, Allen would be familiar with the Old Testament and the severe teachings in Leviticus: 'God will bring sudden terror on detestable practices, wasting diseases that will destroy sight and sap such men of their strength.'

AIDS had certainly done that all right, and if Allen really believed that being queer was truly an abomination punishable by death, that would have contributed to his murderous actions. If found guilty of Dennis's demise, then he most certainly had blood on his hands, but the whys and wherefores behind Allen's behaviour were somewhat irrelevant. What mattered now was to put a stop to it all, much in the same way that Allen had put a stop to Dennis's life, as well as numerous other Columbus casualties.

'I hope I'm not squeezing too hard?'

Allen's slightly suggestive remark had not thrown Clive in

the least and he used all his thespian skills to counter it with the performance of a lifetime. 'Oh, come on Allen, you can see I fancy you rotten. I did from the moment I first set eyes on you when I opened the door for you at Den's house.'

'Clive, let's get one thing straight, shall we? I may be gay, but I really don't believe in mixing business with pleasure. I'm honestly not in the habit of seducing every attractive male patient who walks into my surgery, even if they are charming and from London – I'm sorry!'

It was exactly the kind of reply Clive had expected and for which he was totally prepared: 'And I'm sorry if I've embarrassed you.'

'Apology not needed. Then,' Allen firmly enquired, 'shall we continue?'

'Of course.'

'Good. Now Clive, please turn over.'

Clive knew it was coming, and he was equally prepared for it. This certainly was not the first time a doctor had inserted something up his back passage and so he tried to relax. He supposed that Allen was having a good look around the entry wall as well as inside the cavity of his anus, and thought he would probably be taking a smear, which would be sent for analysis at a laboratory.

'Everything all right down there?'

'Seems that way. I'm just inserting a swab. I won't get the final answer until the results come back from the lab in a few days' time.' Then, once that part of the examination was completed, Allen asked Clive to turn onto his back again.

'This is similar to the kind of examination we get at our VD clinic in London.'

'I suppose it must be, although we're on the lookout for possibilities other than gonorrhoea and syphilis; though we do find them too, you know. Now, this one's always a bit more painful.'

Then, as he was about to insert a smaller narrow swab into the aperture of Clive's penis, he added: 'Please sit up.'

At this point, all hell seemed to break loose in the waiting room and there was a loud knocking on his surgery door which, fortunately for Clive, interrupted the examination. It was Nurse Edith shouting for Allen to come quickly to the reception area.

'Sorry about this, Clive, but I better go and see what on earth's going on out there.' And with that, he swiftly left the room, at last leaving Clive alone and able to accomplish his mission.

Nurse Edith quickly explained that not only had Shirley passed out, but she appeared to be in a great deal of pain. The nurse apologised profusely for interrupting Allen's examination, but since the Englishwoman had arrived with Mr Spoke, she felt it necessary to let them both know what had happened. She said that she'd tried to make the lady as comfortable as possible on the floor in the recovery position and had covered her with a couple of blankets.

Allen immediately took Shirley's pulse, and after giving her a very cursory examination, announced to Nurse Edith that she had done absolutely the right thing in calling him away from his patient, although he hinted that it had somewhat complicated matters. Shirley, still pretending to have passed out, had picked up on his last remark but remained quite still. Then Allen announced to Nurse Edith that he felt he could leave Shirley in her more than capable hands for a minute or two, while he returned to his patient and explained what had happened. Meanwhile, Clive had lost no time in setting to work and made a quick search of the fridge and grabbed a small container of what he hoped might be the deadly toxin. Next he went over to the cabinets he had spotted on entering Allen's office, but the first he tried contained plasters, bandages and a collection of hand towels. He had greater success with the second cabinet, where he found a tray of needles in the top drawer, along with several rows of plastic capsules in the drawer below, which he supposed were used to store blood samples, probably obtained from unsuspecting patients. He carefully wrapped six of each in two large handkerchiefs he had secreted in the inside pocket of his raincoat as quickly as he could and then replaced the remainder.

He was just about to close the cabinet when Allen walked in on him and as the office door swung open, it nearly knocked Clive over. Fortunately, Allen's mission to inform Clive of what had happened to Shirley temporarily distracted the doctor from noticing that one of the cabinet doors had been left ajar.

'Clive, I'm sorry for the interruption, but I'm afraid it's Shirley. She seems to have fainted.'

'Oh my God! I was afraid this might happen.' And he began to make for the door, then realised he was stark naked. He went back just for his raincoat and before Allen could stop him, headed for the waiting-room area, where Shirley was lying on the floor.

'Tell me Clive,' said Allen, quickly following behind him, 'does this happen often?'

But rather than waste time answering, and now playing the role of an anxious friend, he rushed out of the examination room, putting his coat on as he headed for where he could see a nurse's uniform bending over a person lying prostrate on the floor.

'Shirley, darling.' Kneeling down beside her, he took hold of her hand. 'It's me, Clive. What's wrong? Tell me!'

Shirley murmured something indistinguishable, and slowly opened one of her eyes.

'It's OK, darling, I'm here.' And he stroked the back of her hand, gently kissing it. 'You see Allen, she's diabetic and her blood sugar level must have dropped. She probably needs to eat something.'

Then as Shirley slowly appeared to come to, she tried to sit up, but Allen smartly intervened and firmly told her to lie still for a minute or two, and warned her that under no circumstances was she to attempt to stand up. Finally she slowly uttered: 'Where … am … I?'

Clive made no attempt to answer that particular question, but Allen stepped in quickly, telling her that she had fainted, that he was a doctor, and left Clive to reassure her that she was in safe hands. Indeed, it appeared that both protagonists had given such credible performances that they had successfully convinced both Allen and Nurse Edith that Shirley had indeed had a diabetic attack.

Clive asked whether they should give her some chocolate, which he knew she always kept in her handbag for similar emergencies or whether they should try to get her to the Columbus General Hospital next door. Allen thought that hospital would not be necessary until he had conducted a complete and thorough examination. However, he agreed that chocolate seemed to be the right course of action for the time being. Clive was just about to get Shirley's handbag when suddenly, and for no apparent reason, Allen quickly rose to his feet, and without excusing himself, headed straight back to his office. Clive simply thought he'd probably gone to get a stethoscope or medical bag or something, and felt it more plausible to stay with Shirley rather than follow Allen. So he remained by her side, assured her she was going to be fine and persuaded her to eat a small square of dark chocolate. At the same time, he was more than aware that he had not had sufficient time to close one of the cabinet doors and wondered whether Allen would notice whether there was anything missing.

In no time at all, Allen came charging out of his office into the reception area, and, completely out of character and appearing slightly out of control, started shouting abuse at Clive, which even caused Nurse Edith to back off from the English visitors.

'What the fuck's going on? Do you mind telling me what you were doing in my office, Clive?'

'I don't know what you're talking about. I was waiting for you to come back.'

'Yes, you were waiting for me, all right. But what were you up to while you were waiting? What were you looking for in my cabinets? Look, some of my needles are missing, and I believe you've taken them. Do you mind telling me what exactly you two are doing here?'

Shirley, now seeming to come to, slowly asked: 'Clive, why is the doctor shouting at us? Is it my fault?'

'Shirley's diabetic you see, and sometimes she does forget to take her medication,' Clive shouted back at him. 'That's why she always keeps a bar of chocolate in her handbag.'

'Never mind her. Or her fucking handbag! Where are my needles, Clive? I want them back.'

And with that, Clive uttered '*sortie*' under his breath, which was the password for the exit strategy the two Brits had rehearsed earlier that day. This caused Shirley to go into action and suddenly grab onto Clive's outstretched hand, leap to her feet, and at the same time push the poor and the somewhat confused Nurse Edith to the ground. Then our two intrepid detectives made for the exit sign, both shoeless, both scared shitless, and both running for their lives, with Clive grabbing hold of a chair as he tried to leave the building.

Allen was quick off the mark too and immediately chased after them, but they had a hair's start. Clive took a chance however, and stood behind the main exit door with the chair raised in the air while Shirley, clutching her mink jacket, ran screaming towards Michael's waiting car. Fortunately, Clive's timing was impeccable and as soon as Allen's head appeared round the door, Clive brought the chair down heavily on it with all his might, knocking him over, and then rushed towards the brown sedan as fast as his two naked feet would carry him, and joined Shirley on the back seat.

Michael's eyes were popping out of his head by now, since, to his utter astonishment, he'd witnessed the couple's deranged flight from the clinic towards his waiting car and could see Nurse Edith struggling to get the poor doctor back on his feet. Once inside the car, there was no time to explain what was going on and, fortunately for them, Michael simply followed the chorus of their monosyllabic instruction, which they shouted from the back seat.

'Go!' 'Go!' 'Go!'

As Michael put the car into gear, Clive and Shirley turned around and watched Allen and his nurse stagger back inside the building. The tree-lined drive seemed a lot longer than when they arrived, and although Michael accelerated as much as his brown sedan allowed, they begged him to go faster. Then, as the car gathered speed, they heard the sound of sirens coming from the bungalow and just before clearing the hospital gates, Michael pulled into the kerb and came to a sudden halt.

'Sorry. But do you two mind telling me what the hell is going on?'

'Yes, of course. We will explain', said Shirley. 'But Michael, please drive on!'

'No! Not until you tell me what the fuck is happening. I've just witnessed you two running like a pair of banshees from the clinic where, Clive, I saw you hit Allen over the head with a chair, leaving him lying on the ground while you both came tearing towards my car. I think you owe me some sort of explanation. Why did you attack Allen in that way? Do you mind telling me what this is all about?'

'You're quite right. I apologise, I do owe you an explanation. I'm sorry to say that I got into a bit of a disagreement with Allen over the test he wanted to give me. You see, I'm terrified of needles, I have a real phobia: and I just didn't want to let him take a sample of my blood.'

'Now don't you play games with me. Allen's a really dear friend of mine and a damned good doctor. I seriously don't believe that's why you slugged him and left him lying on the floor like that. And tell me, did you set the fire alarms off too?'

'Well, as a matter of fact, *I* did. You see,' continued Shirley, 'Allen got so aggressive with Clive that I had to find a way of distracting him.'

And so once again the ever-dependable Shirley had come to the rescue and backed up Clive's story 100 per cent. She now claimed that the row coming from the doctor's office had disturbed her so much that she decided to knock on Allen's door and try to interrupt the examination. She told Michael that, for some reason or other, Allen then violently turned on her, which so surprised the two of them that they had no choice but to get out of the building as quickly as possible. Then when Allen chased after them, she came up with the bright idea of setting off one of the fire alarms, which she hoped would delay him as they ran for the exit, though this didn't exactly explain why she was shoeless.

Michael sat listening somewhat incredulously to Shirley but still claimed he didn't understand why Clive had knocked Allen to the ground. Suddenly, they heard the most enormous explosion come from behind them and a shock wave hit their parked car. Michael now took total control of the situation and decided to swing the car round and head back along the drive towards the clinic, where they could see flames pouring out of the bungalow. As they got nearer, there were a series of minor explosions that seemed to blow the building completely apart. Now with all three of them in a total state of shock, Michael suddenly jammed on his brakes, keeping a good distance from the burning building. It was all totally surreal and the bungalow appeared to be ripped to pieces and collapse in a matter of minutes.

'Am I seeing straight or what?' shouted Michael. 'Did your row also make you blow up the building?'

And before they had the chance to answer, a couple of fire engines arrived on the scene and three stocky firefighters tried to take control of what appeared to be a lost cause.

'Michael, honestly, trust us,' said Clive. 'We've really got nothing to do with what's happening. Why on earth would we want to blow up Allen's clinic? Listen, the sooner we get out of here the better! Let's get back to the safety of the Colony, where we can both tell you what we think might have happened.'

'I think Clive's right.' And with that, Shirley uttered more of a command than a polite request: 'Let's just get out of here, right now! We may all be in grave danger.'

'OK! OK!'

And with that, Michael, realising that there was no point in arguing, swung the car round again and headed for the hospital gates once more, passing a number of white-coated people running towards the burning building.

CHAPTER SIXTEEN

THE AFTERMATH TUESDAY

All three sat in absolute silence as they drove over to Dennis's house, and once on the freeway, they noticed a police car come racing towards them on the other side of the road, presumably on its way to the clinic. Michael kept his decision to drive back via Allen's house to himself, but not being that familiar with Columbus, his two passengers simply assumed that they were on their way over to number 257. However, as Michael drew nearer to where Allen lived, he could see another police car parked outside the house, and for fear of his brown sedan being recognised, he pulled up, reversed and drove off again in the opposite direction.

Clive broke the silence. 'Now *you* need to tell *us* what's going on. Why have you done an about-turn and where are we, anyway?'

'Sorry, guys, but I took the liberty of driving past Allen's house on our way over to Den's. I was just curious to know whether his car was parked outside and if he was at home. But when I saw the police outside and no sign of his car, I decided to turn back and hightail it out of here.'

Clive camouflaged his true feelings and stated that he was not in the least bit surprised that the police were at Allen's house, and thought it only natural that they would want to question him and find out if he was all right. Deep down he couldn't help but think that Michael had become far too closely attached to Allen, which was beginning to cause him some concern.

'Clive's right,' agreed Shirley. 'It's only to be expected that they'd check to see if he was still in one piece. I mean, that's only normal.'

Michael added that in his opinion, it was well known that Allen was bound to be on duty on a Tuesday morning and he was concerned for Allen's safety, since he felt that there was obviously little chance of anyone possibly surviving such an explosion.

'Unless, of course, Allen and that nurse of his escaped before the place was blown to pieces,' suggested Shirley.

This produced no response from Michael, causing another silence to descend as they got back on the highway and made for what they hoped would be a safe haven. Unfortunately, their plan was to be thwarted yet again, since no sooner had they turned into Alexandria Colony Court South, and began to approach number 257, they spotted two black saloon cars parked outside Dennis's house. Michael ordered Clive and Shirley to quickly duck down and cover themselves over with the car rug on the back seat and, as he calmly drove past, he counted three men in suits, lounging around outside the house, while its front door remained wide open.

'They must be on to us too!' Michael whispered under his breath as he drove on.

'Who are?' Shirley whispered back.

'Judging by the cars, it looks like it's the FBI and they're bound to be armed,' replied Michael. 'That means we can't go back to my place either.'

Then from under the rug Clive muttered: 'We better go over to Steve's house. It's our only option.'

'I think you're right. I've only just left him and I'm sure he's still bound to be at home.'

Fortunately, this time they were not to be disappointed and there were no signs of anyone loitering outside their next port of call. Steve quickly came to his front door and although somewhat surprised to see the three of them standing on his doorstep, he warmly welcomed them in, while Michael, displaying a great deal of agitation, led the way into the sitting room.

Before their host had a chance to utter a word, Clive exclaimed: 'Steve, I know this is going to sound like a very odd request, but do you happen to have a spare set of pyjamas I can borrow? You see, I'm wearing absolutely nothing under my raincoat. I'll explain later…'

'No need. I dunno! You Brits!' Steve was for once almost speechless as he climbed the stairs up to his bedroom, breaking into peals of laughter as he went. 'You English really are such an eccentric lot, you know. What have you been up to?' And before giving Clive the chance to reply, he continued: 'Clive, you better come up with me and see if I've got anything that's small enough for you to wear.' Then he shouted down over his shoulder: 'Michael, please offer Shirley a drink. We'll be with you in a couple of minutes.'

Shirley was more than grateful for the Scotch that Michael placed into her shaking hand, then he poured himself one as they both stood silent, just staring at each other, and waited to be joined by the two upstairs. Eventually Clive appeared in an ample pair of red stripy pyjamas, some borrowed slippers, and his raincoat swung over his shoulders, with Steve in tow, giggling like some maid of honour at a bizarre wedding.

'This is no laughing matter, Steve! You won't believe this, but we've just come from Allen's clinic, which we saw blown to pieces right before our very eyes.'

'What! Michael, are you serious? What are you talking about? Clive, you didn't say anything about that upstairs. What's been going on? Y'all better sit down. Now I think I need a drink … Was anyone hurt?'

'I fail to see how anyone could have escaped alive,' said Michael.

Then, turning to Clive, he raised his voice. 'But, Clive, you were in the clinic. How many people were in there with you and Shirley?' Then, without waiting for a reply, he calmed down and fixed on Clive. 'Now, I think this has been going on long enough. You both owe us an explanation. Do you mind telling Steve and me what the fuck this is all about?'

'OK OK I'll tell you everything I know. But you have to understand, this was all my idea, and Shirley only got involved because I insisted.'

'You mean you did blow the clinic up!' shouted Michael.

'Don't be ridiculous,' Shirley intervened. 'Of course he didn't. But our visit there may have caused Allen to take what appears to be a drastic course of action.'

Now it was Steve's turn to get flustered. 'What in God's name do you mean? None of this is making sense to me.'

'No. You're quite right, Steve. I need to start at the beginning.'

Clive then explained how he and Shirley had gone to the clinic that morning with a plan because, amazing as it might seem, they had begun to believe that Allen Levitt was involved in a major form of espionage. He confessed that the more he got to know Dr Levitt, the more he became convinced that the good doctor, as Clive now liked to call him, was responsible for causing the premature deaths of some of his own patients.

Judging from his stunned reaction, Clive realised that Michael was finding it difficult to come to terms with what he was hearing. The situation got worse when Clive stated that he believed Allen wasn't the kindly and supportive young gay doctor some people thought him to be, but was in fact working as an undercover agent, probably for the Federal Bureau of Investigation. Despite Michael's reaction of disbelief, Clive maintained that he was sure that beneath the doctor's rather genial and benevolent facade, there lurked a cruel and deceitful murderer who he truly thought had been brainwashed, programmed and posted to Columbus with a mission. He reminded them that in *The Manchurian Candidate,* which he hoped the Americans had seen, a subject susceptible to being hypnotised could be brainwashed into committing an act that might violate that individual's own moral code. And in their post-hypnotic state they would have virtually no recollection whatsoever of what they had done.

Michael was unable to hold his silence any longer and burst out: 'What! You're nuts! Both of you! That was a movie. Things like that don't happen in real life. I think you and Shirley are in cloud cuckoo land. You've both been working in "the show business" for far too many years.'

Clive kept his cool, agreed that it all might sound unbelievable, but explained that their real intention had been of finding some sort of proof positive to confirm his theory. He then admitted that they had completely underestimated Allen's ability to strike back.

Together they related the clinic drama to Michael, and Shirley concluded: 'Whether you believe him or not, Clive is now certain that Allen has been injecting the AIDS virus into the men who, in all innocence, have been coming to see him for a check-up and blood test.'

'And,' add Clive, 'I'm sorry to have to say this, Michael, but I truly think that Dennis was his first and most important victim.'

Michael simply sat speechless and, after a while, Steve broke the uncomfortable silence. He told them that he did remember the movie Clive mentioned and that he could understand his line of reasoning and believed in the power of hypnotism. He also confessed that he'd actually been 'put under' once himself and knew for a fact that the CIA had launched Project Bluebird way back in 1950 when they started experimenting with hypnosis. He told them he was fascinated by hypnosis and that he'd read up about it, and explained that he'd learnt that, at the time, it could only be administered to a subject by an authorised member of the Central Intelligence Agency.

He added that he was still finding it hard to come to terms with what Clive and Shirley thought Allen had become mixed up in. But, after a pause, he continued: 'Although I have to admit –reluctantly – that just recently I've begun to harbour my own concerns about our medical friend.'

'Well you've been keeping your cards very close to your chest, Steve!' Michael almost exploded. 'You've never mentioned your suspicions about Allen to me before.'

'You're quite right and I'm sorry to upset you,' apologised Steve. 'But with Dennis's passing and all, I just felt it wasn't the right moment to share my views about Allen with you. In fact, if it hadn't been for these two, I'm not sure I would have even broached the subject at all. But just lately I've become a little suspicious of Allen. I'd even go so far as to say that I have recently declined a blood test from him myself since I just felt that, even though he was my doctor, I was putting myself in unsafe hands.'

'Well, this is all news to me,' Michael insisted. 'I can't believe I'm hearing this coming from you!'

'Yes I realise that, but it was just an uncomfortable feeling I had about him which I needed to keep to myself. I also had to find an excuse for not having a goddamn injection when I last visited him. Allen wouldn't take no for an answer, although – like you Clive – I tried to convince him I had a phobia of needles. So I threw a hissy fit and just charged out of his surgery before he had the chance to inject me. I know my behaviour didn't exactly endear me to him, which is why he was so frosty with me at your dinner party, Michael … and I was really surprised that he came round on Sunday to try to see me.'

'Well I'm not,' admitted Clive. 'You see, I'm afraid, when questioned by Allen last Saturday after his talk-in, I now realise I unwittingly endangered you, Steve, by revealing it was you who told me all about Dennis's wipe-out theory.'

Clearly this proved more than Michael could stand and he

erupted. 'Now just listen, all of you! Allen has been a terrific friend to me and he's a great doctor. I don't believe for one moment that he tried to kill Dennis. You remember how hard he fought to save his life, for fuck's sake. And anyway, what's all this business about Den's wipe-out theory?'

Steve then explained to Michael how Dennis had come up with his theory, and how, just before he died, he'd confided in Steve. Steve then finally came clean and stated that he was not at all surprised by what he was learning from his English friends, and confessed that they had finally persuaded him that Allen could have had something to do with the spread of the deadly virus in Columbus.

With that, Michael suddenly rose to his feet in an emotional outburst: 'I've had enough! I just can't stand much more of this. You both owe me an apology and I think I have the right to know exactly what Dennis told you, Steve, and what you think he had become mixed up in. Remember, he was my partner, for fuck's sake.'

Shirley, ever the pacifier, immediately sprung into action and calmly took control. She urged Steve and Clive to level with Michael and bring him up to speed with what they had found out. She also suggested that they all needed another whisky to calm their nerves. Once Michael was seated, with a fresh drink in his hand, Steve told the story, and explained that Dennis had deliberately not wanted Michael to know any of the details in case he also became too involved in what could turn out to be an equally dangerous situation for him.

Michael, seeming to have calmed down a bit, admitted that he did remember Dennis trying to tell him something when he went into hospital for the last time, but because he was so ill, and barely able to get his words out, Michael urged him to save his energy. Now he slowly turned to Clive and asked: 'So what exactly did you take from Allen's office?'

Clive reached into the inside pocket of his raincoat. 'These!'

Steve rose from his seat and walked towards Clive's outstretched hands, and then unwrapped the handkerchiefs, which held what had been taken.

'And this. And if it contains what I think it does, it could be the toxin that is the key to spreading the deadly AIDS virus.'

'Oh my God!' Steve exclaimed. 'That's incredible.'

Shirley once again took command. 'In a way,' she said, 'getting the evidence was the easy bit. What we do with it now is much more of a challenge. Clive darling, I think my handbag would be a far safer place to store these precious objects than your raincoat pocket, don't you?'

'As always, Mummy dearest, you know best.' And with that he carefully handed over his booty into her charge.

After a short pause Steve announced that he really hadn't been thinking straight. He suggested that the first thing they all ought to do was call the Men's Center, which was just round the corner from the hospital. His friend Shane was usually on duty there and that he might know the latest on what had happened at the clinic, and whether there were any fatalities or not.

'Good thinking, Steve,' said Clive. 'Anyway, I can't walk around in your pyjamas all day long and Michael has brought our bags in from the car. You see, we checked out of the Sheraton and Shirley is due to fly back to New York tonight.'

'Clive darling,' interjected Shirley. 'Now I'm none too sure about that … I don't feel I can leave quite yet.'

Steve rang Shane, but after a while he turned to the others. 'It's no good. The line's constantly busy. I just don't seem to be able to get through.'

Michael, who'd remained silent during the last exchange suddenly stood up. 'Why don't we just go there and then we'll find out the latest from Shane in person.'

Steve felt that wasn't a good idea at all. 'Michael, I don't think any of us should be seen around town.'

'At least let me call my dad and ask him to drop by the Men's

Center and talk to Shane.'

'Go ahead, Michael. Please use the phone in the hall.'

Shirley sat and examined the stolen goods in her handbag. 'You know boys, we really do need to get this situation into some sort of perspective, and distance ourselves from what has happened and think more rationally.'

'Shirley, you're absolutely right,' agreed Steve, 'and I also have to admit that I think we are all in very great danger. I'm sure you have a Secret Service back home, but you've got no idea what our FBI is capable of.'

'No, I suppose not. But Steve, strangely enough, just recently I met a gentleman called Peter Wright, who was a key figure in British intelligence. He came to me with a play he'd written about Soviet espionage and about how our counter-intelligence got involved with the Russians in the seventies. I seem to remember that one of the characters in his play was your J. Edgar Hoover and at the time I thought it quite a good idea for…'

'Sorry to butt in,' interrupted Michael. 'Dad said he would go straight over and talk to Shane. I didn't go into too much detail, but said we thought there had been a problem at the clinic. You know, I really do need to talk to Douglas. He's always so wise in an emergency and I'm sure he'll give us all some sound advice. By the way, would you two like to check back into your hotel? I could drive you there on my way over to see my folks?'

'Now, listen everybody! No one's going anywhere for a minute.' Steve 's voice grew louder as he became quite overheated. 'Let's all just sit down and calmly try to talk this thing through. Although I didn't see the clinic being blown up like you guys did, the whole thing sounds very sinister to me … Michael, they cannot possibly go back to their hotel and if Allen is who we think he is, he must already have told his superiors what Clive and Shirley have stolen from his office. I believe they are in great danger – we all are! For all we know, the FBI might be planning to blow up the Sheraton.

I really think, because Clive gave details of your residence when he filled in his immigration details, it's also dangerous for you to return home too, Michael. They could be outside your door and waiting to arrest our English buddies or bump them off.'

'Oh, don't worry, I've already thought about that. I intend to stay with my folks tonight and the family house is registered in Gloria's maiden name, since it originally belonged to her parents.'

'Well, that's a relief. At least the FBI can't trace it to the Poledris. And I suppose if you really do need to see them, you'd better go straight away. I won't try to stop you. But please be sure to come back in an hour's time, packed and ready to leave Columbus. We've all got to get out of this town. And sharp's the word! Just tell your folks you're going off to Florida with your new beau for a few days.'

It was pointless for Michael to say that his folks knew he didn't have a new boyfriend, but he did assure Steve that he would be back within the hour.

Once Michael had driven off, Shirley pointed out that it was well past their lunchtime and, her diabetes aside, they should all try to eat something. Fortunately, Steve, ever the foodie of the group, had his refrigerator well stocked and quickly offered to prepare some sandwiches, which he suggested could be helped down with a few bottles of beer. Shirley also pointed out that she needed to cancel her flight back to New York, since she now had every intention of staying one more night in Columbus. Steve told her to go ahead and use the phone in the hallway and, while their host was in the kitchen, Clive retrieved the stolen items from Shirley's handbag and proceeded to wrap his precious evidence in some hand towels he'd found in Steve's bathroom and lock it away in his small suitcase.

The two Brits had not had time to discuss what to do with what they had removed from Allen's office that morning, and once Shirley had rejoined Clive, he freely admitted that although he knew everything he'd stolen required rigorous forensic examination, the problem was that he didn't know how to organise such a procedure.

Shirley suggested that perhaps once he got back to London, he should discuss the matter with his own doctor back in Hammersmith.

Now alone with Shirley for the first time since their escape from the clinic, Clive confessed that he was also beginning to have a change of heart, and wondered whether he should hand everything over to Steve to deal with. Shirley felt that wasn't quite fair, but suggested that they divide everything in two, except for what might be the toxin, of course. Since Clive valued her advice above anyone else's, and believed that she normally knew what to do for the best, he decided that it was an excellent suggestion and confessed that she had solved his dilemma. So they set about retrieving all their stolen evidence from his locked case and started to divide their booty.

'Shirley, I'm so sorry I've got you involved in all this. I had no idea it would all turn out so drastically.'

'Remember, Clive, I offered to fly out to Columbus. You didn't force me. And you know what? I'm really glad I decided to come.'

'Me too. But it's not over yet.'

'I know what you mean. Even Michael believes that the FBI is on to us and that's why they had gone to Den's house. But darling, presumably having come this far, you do want to go through with it all? I mean to say, without even knowing about what happened to Allen and that poor nurse of his, you do want to get to the bottom of what we're dealing with, don't you? And by the way, now I come to think about it, I remember Allen whispered something under his breath to Nurse Edith when I was lying on the floor – about how my fainting had somewhat complicated matters. I bet that they were working as a team.'

'That doesn't surprise me in the least. But I dearly hope there were no other staff or patients in the other rooms and I'm praying that there were no casualties. I know you feel it's more than likely that Allen and his nurse probably escaped the blast, but you know what? I feel like I'm sitting on a Columbus time bomb and I'm not sure I have enough stamina to cope with much more of this. I now just want to get out of here, get back home and have my share of this stuff analysed.'

'This really doesn't sound like you. We can't simply walk out on Steve and Michael and leave them to deal with the aftermath.'

Then coughing rather loudly, she changed tack. 'That looks delicious!'

Steve emerged from the kitchen bearing a huge platter of sandwiches and a tray of beers. All three sat silently, munching their way through their picnic lunch in a very tense atmosphere. After a while, Steve pointed out that there was no point in trying to phone Shane again, although he had to admit that he was longing to know if there was any news about Allen. 'You know, I'm still finding it hard to take in all that's happened.'

The others agreed.

This may be a somewhat indelicate question on my behalf,' said Clive, 'but you don't think Michael has got too close to Allen, do you Steve?'

'Well Clive, I'm not quite sure what you're driving at.'

'I realise he's Allen's patient and they spend a lot of time together… please don't be offended by what I'm about to say, but do you think we can really trust Michael?'

'Well, to be honest, the thought has never crossed my mind.'

'Oh, I suppose with all that's happened, I'm just getting a bit paranoid, that's all. Perhaps Michael's right, I have been making too many movies lately!'

'His Spoke nose can get things wrong, you know,' joked Shirley, in an attempt to try to salvage another awkward moment.

'Guys, while I was in the kitchen making the sandwiches, I had a few thoughts of my own. Please don't misunderstand what I'm about to say, but I really think you both have simply got to disappear.'

Clive and Shirley put their beers down, speechless.

'Oh, don't get me wrong, you two, I'm not going to bump you

off. I just want to help you both get away from here in one piece.'

'But how?' Shirley asked.

'For starters, you've both got to go into hiding. Was the Sheraton booking made in your name Clive?'

'Actually Steve, I made the reservations,' Shirley stated. 'I was going to book it under Spoke Associates, then I changed my mind at the last minute and used my own credit card.'

'But you had to show your passports, which were surely photocopied?'

'Well, yes.'

'Don't you see that the CIA will try to trace your whereabouts, and prevent either of you from leaving the country. They must have found out what you've stolen by now, and it's in their interest to put an end to this wipe-out conspiracy theory for once and for all.'

Now, so very unlike her, it was Shirley's turn to get agitated.

'Steve, before we came here, we did go back to Dennis's house, but Michael saw that the place was crawling with men in dark suits, so they may have been looking for us there. Do you seriously think that those people will really try to wipe us out too?'

And before Steve had a chance to reply, Clive turned to Shirley: 'Darling, I've also been doing a lot of thinking. I believe it's high time we gave ourselves up before anything else gets blown up. Don't you, Steve?'

'That's not what I'm suggesting,' Steve insisted. 'We've just got to get you both out of Columbus as soon as Michael comes back; we'll all get across the border and into Canada. With British passports, you won't need visas, and once out of the USA, it will be much more difficult for any of our government agents to track you both down.'

'You know, I really didn't think this thing through, did I? It honestly never occurred to me that I was putting all our lives in such grave danger when we went to the clinic this morning.'

'What's done can't be undone, and anyway, we can't put the clock back. Speaking of which, Michael will be here shortly, and we need to think of making a move.'

'But I'm still in your pyjamas.'

'And I'm shoeless,' added Shirley.

'I was thinking about that while making the sandwiches. My younger brother Adam comes to visit often and always leaves a change of clothes here. Clive, I think you're his size and I'm sure we can find a pair of slippers you can get into Shirley – that is, for the time being. Come on, let's go upstairs.'

Clive pointed out that because they had checked out of the Sheraton, they both had their overnight bags with them, and so they would both be fine.

'And luckily,' Shirley added, 'I know I've packed a spare pair of heels in my bag. But, I don't know about you Clive, I really wouldn't mind freshening up a little.'

Steve was quick to suggest that they went ahead and used the showers. 'There's one off my bedroom and one in the spare bathroom, and there's tons of hot water.'

'Now you're sounding just like Dennis. He was always on at me for not showering enough. Come on Shirley, why don't you use the one in Steve's bedroom?'

While he left them to it, Steve double-checked, and found the spare set of keys to a chum's house just outside of Toledo where he often used to house-sit. Ron was on sabbatical in California, but out of courtesy, Steve put a call through to him and told him he would be going north for a few days with some friends and asked if it was convenient for them to stay at his house for a few nights. Ron was more than happy with that arrangement, and so, as he put the phone down, Steve smiled to himself and felt that his escape plan was really going to work.

CHAPTER SEVENTEEN

THE SUMMIT TUESDAY

Shirley lost no time at all, was soon in and out of the shower and, having obviously decided not to wash her hair, had tied her locks back in a ponytail. Wearing black slacks and a navy-blue Sonia Rykiel twinset, she also sported dark glasses and wore a headscarf in an attempt at camouflage. Clive was out of Steve's pyjamas in a flash, showered, and was quickly changed and ready to go. He quite obviously had not shaved and was now wearing a dark shadow, indicating that he was trying to grow a beard.

Shirley pointed out that was rather too obvious a form of disguise and revealed that she had another idea for Clive's transformation, which she hoped he might find much more amusing. So once again she took command of the situation, advised him to shave, and he did as bidden. She was now convinced that it was imperative for Clive to travel totally incognito and so she'd laid out a printed cotton frock, a pair of tights, her hairpiece and a headscarf, which she was sure would come in handy later and finish the job off nicely.

Now back downstairs and waiting, from the large bay window in the lounge, all three saw Michael, punctual as ever, arrive and get out of a different car. Once through the front door, he told them that he had driven past the hospital on his way over to meet his folks and described how as he approached, he could smell the stench of burning debris through his open car window. From a distance he could see that the little that remained of the bungalow was still smouldering and he confirmed that there was virtually nothing left of what had been Allen's clinic. He said his dad had quickly gone over to the Men's Center after he had phoned him, and had indeed found Shane manning the reception desk. What he didn't tell them however, was that he had decided to telephone Allen from his parents' house and that since there was no reply, he'd left a message for him on his office answering service, which he hoped he would somehow pick up.

'You know, I trust my dad implicitly and I was genuinely curious to find out what he would do, were he in my shoes. After all, he treated Dennis like a son, and has got to know Allen real well. And, by the way, my folks more than enjoyed meeting you both last night and they know that Den was like family to you too, Clive.'

'Well, I appreciate that, Michael,' Clive responded. 'But what did Douglas actually find out at the Men's Center?'

Michael's dad had told him that the place was packed to the rafters with a very good turnout from the Columbus gay community, as well as many press and media people, including a team from the local television station. Douglas had pushed his way through the crowded reception area and finally got Shane's attention.

'I have to admit, guys, it's just as you predicted,' Michael continued. There are no survivors and no one seems to know how the fire started nor who was responsible. Shane told my dad that the police had taken statements from him and some of the other guys who were at the Center when it first opened this morning, but apparently there were no witnesses at the clinic.'

Steve admitted that he was glad to hear that, and he was relieved to learn that no one had seen Michael drop the Brits off there for

Clive's appointment, since he felt that the last thing they all needed was for that brown sedan of his to have been recognised as it drove away from the clinic.

'By the way,' Michael added, 'from now on I'm using my mom's car.'

Steve said he'd noticed and thought it a very smart move. He was also curious to know how many people it could take.

'Five I should think. It's an estate. She uses it for getting the groceries. Why?'

'I'll let you know later. Carry on telling us what Shane said.'

Shane had told Michael's dad that the police believed that Allen and the nurse had been on the premises earlier this morning, but that there were no signs of them now. According to Shane, one of the firefighters had been badly injured trying to deal with the burning building, but the flames had become so intense that he had had to abandon the site.

'Were there any charred human remains, do you know?' Clive was keen to ask.

'Apparently not. The police thought that the building had been evacuated.'

'That's a blessed relief,' Shirley volunteered. 'I don't suppose for one moment that anyone could have possibly survived that explosion. And so is there any news of where Allen and Edith are?'

'For what it's worth,' Clive added, 'my Spoke nose tells me that the two of them were blown to bits.'

'But Clive, I don't think it's as simple as that,' Steve insisted. 'I'll come clean with you all. I realised that after Den had told me what he had learnt from Jim, there was a very strong possibility that his life was also in danger. Then, when he got sick after the blood test Allen gave him, I started to get suspicious. The more I began to find out about Dr Levitt, the more I started to distrust him. And now, to tell you the truth, after what you two guys have found at his clinic, if I were Allen, that's exactly what I would want the whole world to believe: that I had been blown out of existence.'

And although Steve was demonstrating his somewhat unsympathetic colours again, Clive welcomed his line of reasoning. 'You mean, simply disappear into thin air? Now that's very interesting, Steve. I suppose that makes total sense.'

'Well, put yourself in Allen's shoes,' Steve continued, 'and remember his story. He arrives in Columbus, a young and attractive fully trained medic. Little is known about him, and then he becomes totally committed to helping the AIDS cause. On arrival, he claims to be gay but for religious reasons, he's troubled by his sexual orientation and no one has ever seen him with a boyfriend or even a trick in tow.'

'That's perfectly true, Steve. And guys,' admitted Shirley, 'surely that's a little weird.

'And how come he can afford a Cadillac on a local doctor's salary?' Clive chimed in.

'We've already been over that one,' Shirley reminded Clive. 'He's probably inherited his money.'

Steve agreed with Shirley and pointed out that his wealth wasn't important but everything else about Allen was concerning. After all, Allen knew all about Den's involvement with that senator friend of his, because Dennis had told Allen what Jim had discovered in Tucson. He concluded: 'Dennis had to be got rid of and Allen has to be inextricably involved.'

Then Clive turned to Michael, who was clearly not liking Steve's last remarks and, in an attempt to change the subject somewhat, asked him if Allen had ever discussed his family background with him.

'Well as a matter of fact, he did. One night, when we were getting slaughtered, he told me that he had rather a difficult relationship with his stepfather.'

'Do you think he was abused by him as a child?' Clive responded.

'He didn't imply that much. Allen simply said that he had a

problem with his stepdad, that's all. And remember, we'd both had rather a lot to drink.'

Clive simply admitted that he was just trying to understand what caused Allen to hate homosexuals to the extent that he had allowed himself to be brainwashed, 'put under' and been driven to become a serial killer.

Steve agreed that it was all food for thought, but added that if Allen had been programmed, it was therefore not in the least bit surprising that he would have been prepared for eventually being found out.

Clive agreed with Steve and claimed he now firmly believed that if Dr Levitt was part of a national conspiracy plot, he would have been briefed and prepared by his bosses for any eventuality and would most definitely have had a a an escape strategy up his sleeve.

Shirley pointed out that Allen already had more than four hours to escape since the explosion at the clinic had occurred, and thought that was enough time for him to try to get out of the country and be well on his way to Mexico.

'I bet he'll soon be across the border, go into hiding and simply disappear,' Shirley stated. 'And who knows? He may even have Nurse Edith with him as a decoy. Well, am I right, boys?'

'I think Nurse Edith is more than a decoy: I think they're doing it and I don't believe he is gay at all! That's just a cover up, he's as straight as a die.'

'I think he's a real smart alec,' Steve continued, 'and, wherever he is, I think that he must have informed the FBI about what was stolen from his office, and I now believe we're all in great danger.'

Michael had sat silent during this discussion and looked very troubled by what he was hearing, and then suddenly shouted: 'Listen, all of you, if you think we're in so much danger, then do you mind telling me what the fuck we're doing just sitting around like this?'

'Michael, you're absolutely right,' agreed Clive. 'But we all have to keep calm.'

Shirley turned to them and told them that she felt it was now turning into a summit meeting.

'It sure is, Shirley,' agreed Clive. 'I feel we should not approach the local police until we've had the opportunity to talk all this through together. I do realise this may appear somewhat cowardly on my part, but after all, we have no proof that Allen did actually booby-trap his clinic.'

'Clive's right,' added Shirley, 'and because of us, you two have both now become heavily implicated.'

'Let's face it, guys, we're running out of time, said Clive. 'And what worries me is that a visit to the police would involve me having to return the evidence I managed to acquire and divulge the real purpose of our visit to the clinic. And that's before we've had the opportunity to get this precious stuff scientifically scrutinised.'

'And do you think the local police would believe our conspiracy theory anyway? I mean to say,' Shirley continued, 'how much communication do you think really goes on between the FBI and those local police officers of yours?'

'Well, I would imagine a good deal,' affirmed Michael.

The thought again flashed through Clive's mind that Michael did perhaps know a little too much about such matters. However, again using all his thespian skills, he calmly continued, 'I know that I can speak for Shirley when I say that we may have been the catalyst for Allen's actions. I sincerely believe that if we were to turn ourselves in to the local police, they might just take us for a couple of "potty Brits". We would rather get back home and have this stuff looked at by the appropriate authorities in London who I'm sure would contact your police force should they discover anything untoward.'

'And judging from what I read about President Kennedy's assassination and the business of the three bullets,' added Shirley, 'I gather the crime laboratory department of the American police force is not currently held in the highest esteem. I for one would certainly not want to hand anything over to them. So, what do you say, guys? Can I go ahead and make our flight reservations from Canada?'

'Michael, what do you think?'

'I'm sorry to say that I'm really not sure.' And then, after a long pause and showing more than a certain amount of embarrassment, Michael finally came clean.

'I'm not a hundred per cent convinced that you would be doing the right thing. I told my folks everything I know and I'm afraid Douglas thought we should all go to the police here in Columbus and come clean with them. He even volunteered to come with us.'

'So you told your dad that you took us to the clinic this morning?'

'I'm afraid I did, Clive, and I trust my dad totally. He thinks we should be a little more proactive, as do I.'

'Well,' said Clive throwing a quick glance at Shirley, 'I suppose that's clear enough.'

'You see, that's why I drove past Allen's house this morning,' continued Michael. 'I thought if he'd been at home, I would have gone in and had it out with him, and tried to get to the bottom of all this.'

Camouflaging his true feelings and convinced that Michael may have indeed tried to get in touch with Allen, Clive responded. 'I must say Michael, I think that would have been very brave of you. Steve, why don't you tell us what you're thinking? You know how much we all value your judgement.'

'I can see both sides of the coin,' said Steve. 'I fully understand why Douglas thinks we should face up to the police here; but I can also see why you two feel you don't want to pursue matters further on this side of the pond.'

'Well, that's all very Switzerland of you, Steve. But it doesn't answer my question. Do you really think we should go to the local police and tell them that we went to the clinic to steal this evidence?'

'Actually,' Steve responded, 'you know, while I was making the sandwiches, I decided that I was prepared to go to them myself, and tell them that it was me who went there this morning, on my own, and stole the needles and stuff. But then I changed my mind.'

Even Clive was thrown to hear this coming from Steve, and his last statement reversed any feelings of doubt he might have had about him. So with one knowing glance from her boss, Shirley was now assured that she could trust Steve and also treat him as an ally.

'That would have been most courageous of you, too,' Shirley announced, 'and your loyalty is quite overwhelming.'

'But,' Clive resumed, 'you both have to know that we would never have left either of you in any impending trouble with your police. We wouldn't dream of letting you cover for us. Would we, Shirley?'

'Clive's absolutely right,' confirmed Shirley.

Michael broke the silence. 'Honestly Clive, you need to know that when I called your office in London, I had no intention of getting you mixed up in any of this. At the time, I really had not realised what Dennis had discovered and what it might all lead to. I simply wanted you to know that we had both lost him and that Dennis was dead. But as for Allen, you have to understand that he has become a very good friend of mine and I have developed a very trusting relationship with him.'

As Michael uttered these words, Clive had one of his Spoke premonitions. He experienced an uncanny feeling that he was right about Michael after all. He noticed how much Michael defended Allen, and wondered whether he might even be an accomplice and in communication with the good doctor. So, in an attempt to cover up his true feelings, he changed the subject back to Dennis.

'You do know Michael, I just wanted to come here to comfort you and be near you, and pay my respects to Dennis. It's I who should be apologising. I should never have taken matters into my own hands. But you see, I kept thinking of Dennis and what he had found out and somehow I just couldn't help myself. I couldn't bear the thought that he died for nothing.

'And I have to take a share of the blame too,' added Shirley. 'I really think my coming to Columbus added fuel to fire, since I encouraged Clive to go to the clinic this morning, and remember, my role in the deception was just as great as his.'

Then Clive rose to his feet. 'I realise we mustn't waste any more time, but there is one more thing Shirley and I want to discuss with you. We both think we should share what we removed from Allen's office and have taken the liberty of dividing the stolen goods in half. The capsule, which we think may contain the deadly toxin, is sealed and cannot possibly be tampered with and I am more than happy to assume full responsibility for that. But you must both discuss what you do with your share and decide whether to pursue the matter here in the United States or do absolutely nothing about it. Shirley and I leave that totally up to you. I have every intention of bringing our half of the samples back to London and placing them all in the appropriate scientific hands and getting them analysed under the strictest supervision, as soon as possible.'

Then he handed some of the stolen goods over: 'Here Steve, please take this; I've wrapped everything up in a hand towel I found in your bathroom.'

'Now I appreciate that very much indeed. I'll hang on to these if you don't mind, Michael, and lock them away for the time being.'

Michael on the other hand, thought that they should get the stuff over to Douglas immediately, for safekeeping, which only served to increase Clive's feelings of distrust for Dennis's partner.

Steve suddenly took command of the situation. 'Michael, I really don't think that will be necessary. Look, I'm going to bring this pow-wow to a close. We're wasting very valuable time and I think the most important thing now is for us to get out of Columbus as soon as possible. Are we all agreed?'

'Whatever you say, Steve.'

'Thank you, Clive. And you, Shirley?'

'Absolutely.'

Then Michael added, 'I'll go with the majority!'

'Good. Now I know we're all in total agreement, I can tell you my plan. But there's just one thing before we leave. Shirley, I'm impressed with your attempt at disguise, but Clive, I'm afraid you have to change your appearance more radically until we cross over into Canada.'

Shirley informed Steve that she'd already thought about that and explained that she'd set out some of her own clothes for Clive to wear but added that she was concerned about what he'd wear on his feet. Apart from that, she was convinced that no one would recognise him once she'd finished with him, and maintained that it would then appear that her Columbus boys were travelling with two female companions. Shirley explained that she and Clive needed to get cracking, so they went back upstairs and she assured Steve that they wouldn't take long.

'Go ahead, you two! I need to explain our route to Michael, since he's going to be doing most of the driving.' And much to Steve's amusement, the two Brits hurried back up to his bedroom to organise Clive's transformation.

'Michael, those two never cease to amaze me. I suppose that's what comes of working in "the show business", as they call it.'

'Yes', Michael somewhat grudgingly agreed. 'I suppose you're right … they sure as hell are full of surprises.'

The two Americans sat for some time and pored over the map which Steve had carefully marked out, and after a while it was decided that, rather than stay on the highways, they should opt to go cross-country in order to keep a low profile. Steve thought that by doing so, they would be able to tell whether they were being tailed or not. He explained that they were going to drive north and stay just outside Toledo in his friend Ron's house.

'Our objective is to get across the border and into Canada, and Toledo is en route. We have to make for the Great Lakes and, once on Canadian soil, Clive and Shirley will be out of American jurisdiction, relatively safe, and will quickly be able to get back to England. Then you and I can make our way out to the west coast, where I've got some other friends and we can stay with them on Vancouver Island.'

'You seem to have friends everywhere,' said Michael. 'But how exactly are we going to get across the border?'

'There is a transit system that operates on the Lakes: it goes back and forth on the Saint Lawrence Seaway between the States and Canada. We'll catch a ferry from Lake Erie and end up in Toronto.'

'Steve, that sounds like an excellent plan. But aren't we still forgetting one thing? Our Federal Bureau of Investigation.'

'No Michael, I'm not. That's why we've got to get going right now. I better go and give those two a shout.'

And, just as he got up to fetch them, Clive made the most unbelievable entrance, which neither of the two Americans were ready for. Shirley's printed cotton dress had the most dazzling effect and the Chanel headscarf, keeping a fringe in place, was the icing on the cake: the entire ensemble created a very convincing new female travelling companion, apart from a pair of plimsolls on Clive's feet.

Michael was speechless but Steve was able to utter: 'Words fail me. Clive … you look unbelievable!'

'Well, why wouldn't I?' Clive giggled. 'I've got the most amazing costume designer and make-up artist.'

'I haven't had time to fix his face properly, but I figured we could do that in the car.'

'Shirley, you most certainly can. But we should set off right away.' Steve explained that he thought they needed to use two cars to start with, just to check they were not being followed. 'Michael, I'll take the Brits and you should take a downtown direction. Let's meet up at Columbus Cares in half an hour and we can change cars there. I can leave mine in our car park and no one will think there's anything odd about that.'

'Just one moment!' commanded Shirley. 'I was just telling Clive while we were upstairs, there's one thing that troubles me, Steve. How do we know your car is safe? When did you last use it?'

'To drive back home after Michael's dinner party.'

'But that was last night,' observed Shirley. 'And how do we know it hasn't been tampered with while you were sleeping? And what's more, don't you all think it's a little odd that there's been no policemen crawling around your house, Steve?'

'Or men in dark suits?' added Clive.

'Yes, Clive, I have to admit it is a bit strange that we've been left undisturbed.'

'Exactly,' continued Shirley. 'I had to spend some time in Northern Ireland during the Troubles, back in the seventies. I was between jobs, and my Auntie Flo had got me a temporary job stage-managing. Every time we set off from a gig, we used a mirror device to search below our vehicles in order to check that the IRA hadn't placed explosives underneath them.'

'You're surely not suggesting that the FBI have booby-trapped Steve's car?' Michael asked.

'Why the hell not? You know that they are perfectly capable of doing such a thing,' responded Steve. 'And that would eliminate all of us, except of course you, Michael.'

CHAPTER EIGHTEEN

THE ESCAPE TUESDAY, WEDNESDAY, THURSDAY

They left Steve's house with great caution looking around for Allen and Edith as they stepped outside the front door. They could be lurking anywhere just waiting to shoot them all dead. Once they were satisfied that this was not the case, the boys made a quick getaway and went to the car whilst Shirley was placed on lookout duty on the front porch. It was her job to keep a watchful eye up and down the street and raise the alarm should either the police or men in dark suits suddenly appear. Michael took charge of unlocking the boot of his mother"s vehicle, and was also on guard while Clive and Steve loaded up the luggage in Gloria's roomy estate car. As navigator, Steve sat up in front and, having worked out their route, he kept a detailed map of Ohio State and the Great Lakes on his lap. Clive and Shirley shared the back seat but, as all four finally drove off, they were well aware that there was an all-pervading smell of apprehension throughout the car and it wasn't till they were finally on their way and those all-too-familiar Columbus skyscrapers receded into the distance that the heavy silence was broken by Steve.

'That's right, Michael, just keep going north towards Delaware.

Once we've reached the outskirts of Marion, I'll take over the wheel.'

After an hour's fast driving, they began to approach the outskirts of the town of Worthington, Ohio, where they branched off and took a side road to Delaware. As they drove along, Michael pointed out that, by going cross-country, he hoped that it would make it difficult for them to be trailed. Then he added: 'Unless of course a hidden tracking device has been attached to Mom's car.'

Michael's remark once again fuelled Clive's suspicions about him, but Clive decided to change the subject and drew everyone's attention to the local architecture.

They headed on until they passed a signpost showing that Marion was not far away, and then Steve changed places with Michael. Although the light was beginning to fade, as they approached the street where Steve's friend Ron lived, they could see that the dwellings were by no means modest in size. They finally turned into a driveway and parked, and Steve quickly got out of the car and opened up the house while Shirley and Michael went back to the end of the drive and kept a lookout for dark limousines. Steve waved them back, they each retrieved their overnight bag out of the car, and eventually made their way to bed. Before finally going to their rooms, Steve apologised for reminding them that they would be making a very early start and told them that he wanted to be on the road by six-thirty the next morning. He added that he knew a place where they could stop off for breakfast, at a junction just before they headed towards Toledo.

The following morning, his well-disciplined guests were all punctual and ready and waiting downstairs as requested. Steve locked up the house and as they set off, he explained they were first making for Fostoria before heading towards Toledo on Lake Erie, where they would take a ferry to Port Stanley, which lies on the Canadian side of the lake.

'Well, we both know Port Stanley, don't we, Clive?' grinned

Shirley. 'But that's the one in the Falkland Islands, off Argentina.'

'Yes, Shirley, thanks for the geography lesson. Only joking, darling.'

'And Clive, darling, just because you're in drag, you don't have to get all bitchy.'

'No, Shirley, you're quite right.' And in an attempt to alleviate the growing tension they were all now feeling, Clive continued. 'I just love the fact that there are always so many English place names in the United States, and they do make us feel at home, don't they, Shirl?'

'I'm glad about that,' responded Michael. 'And look at you! You do still look amazing, by the way.'

'Don't say that, Michael. I might get too attached to cross-dressing all the time.'

'What are you two Brits like?' burst out Steve. 'You should both know that Michael and I are sure gonna miss having you two theatricals around. You've certainly livened things up for us over here, I can tell you. I just wished it hadn't all ended up like this and you could have stayed on for a bit longer.'

'And I'm sure I speak for Shirley when I say that we'll miss you both. But I know you understand that we do now have to leave the States and get back to London. Apart from the dangerous situation I've thrown us all into over here, I desperately need to get this stuff analysed as soon as possible. I also have to admit we've been neglecting Spoke Associates somewhat of late, and we do have a pile of work to catch up on. Don't we, Shirl?'

"It has certainly been grand getting to know you Columbus boys,' said Shirley, 'but we really do have to get back home. I really want you both to know that your support and trust means a very great deal to us, doesn't it Clive?'

'It most certainly does,' agreed Clive.

'Michael, don't miss the turn-off to Fostoria,' Steve interrupted.

'Thanks – but I can see it coming up.'

The car swerved off to the right at the next junction, still heading north, and a further silence descended. They all knew that they were still in danger but there was no option except to sit back, watch the countryside dash past and succumb to the long journey ahead of them, hoping against hope that they weren't being followed. After a while, it was Clive who, trying not to sound too pessimistic, got everyone's attention again.

'And if we ever get out of this in one piece, Shirley, remember that the boys have promised to visit us in England once this is all over.'

'Of course we're gonna get out of this OK,' Steve firmly stated. 'And, by the way, we really are planning on coming to stay with you, aren't we, Michael?'

'We sure are. Just checking, but do I take the next turn off to Upper Sandusky?'

'Well-remembered,' the navigator replied.

'What a curious name. Is it American-Indian?' Shirley asked.

Steve told Shirley that he thought it was Polish in origin and explained that there were many Europeans who had settled in this part of the States.

'So many who came to this Land of the Free. Well, I suppose it hasn't been such a liberating experience for us this time, has it, Shirl?', Clive admitted.

Shirley steered the conversation in a more positive direction. 'And to get back to your visit, guys, you know there's lots of theatre in London that I can arrange tickets for.'

'And then there's the little cottage I rent by the sea in Kent: it's even cosy in the winter. St Margaret's Bay isn't in quite the same league as Provincetown, if you know what I mean, but it's a charming little seaside resort on the south coast of England and I feel sure you'll love it there as much as we do. There are lots of like-minded people for you to meet in this delightful Kentish hamlet, if you get my drift?'

Shirley confirmed that there certainly were, and described the great social life they led down there because they had made so many very good friends in St Margaret's. Although she also made it clear that although she had no intention of contradicting her boss, she felt she had to inform them that Clive was being terribly modest about what he had referred to as a 'little cottage'. She went on to assure them that it was actually more like a mansion, with five bedrooms, an enormous garden and stunning sea views. On a clear day it was possible to see France and that they could easily pop over to Calais for lunch.

'London's only a hop away,' she said. 'All you have to do is to let me know when you plan to arrive, and I'll go ahead and book your flights.'

'You're both welcome to stay as long as you like', added Clive. 'Just call the office.'

'Clive, I'm sure I speak for Michael when I say that's most kind and very generous of you. But at the moment,' Steve continued, 'I just want to get us all onto Canadian soil and to Toronto airport in particular. I think we'll have to put all thoughts about London on a back burner just for the time being.'

'Speaking of which,' Shirley remarked. 'Did you see the signpost we just passed. It said London.'

'Well spotted! But that's London, Ontario,' announced the navigator. 'And that's in the opposite direction. We now need to head for Genoa and then ultimately arrive in Toledo.'

'You know, Steve,' Clive remarked, 'I still just can't get over all these other European place names too, from Italy and Spain, as well as the UK.'

And so the small talk went on, hiding their pent-up anxiety, until they eventually reached the last stop on that day's journey, and they pulled into the driveway of a Holiday Inn quite near to where the ferries left from the dockside in Toledo. Steve made straight for the lobby, while Michael parked the car and the Brits got the overnight bags out of the boot. Steve booked a room for him and Michael and asked the hotel desk clerk where they could purchase their ferry tickets for the following morning, and the young man kindly offered to assist him.

It was clear that they had all started to unwind and were obviously feeling a lot safer now that they had left Columbus far behind them. However Clive, realising that they were not completely out of the woods, went back to the car park and also double-checked that there were no ominous black saloons parked along the driveway up to their hotel. Shirley followed him outside, commented on the fact that their pursuers could easily be tailing them in a very nondescript jalopy for all they knew, and then smartly escorted Clive into the ladies' room where she stood guard while he changed back into his male attire so that they could book their rooms and have their passports inspected.

All four of our intrepid travellers having now safely checked in, went to their separate rooms, which were conveniently adjacent, and tried to settle in after the trials of the previous explosive day. They decided to meet up in the hotel lounge after an hour and treat themselves to a nightcap before finally turning in. It was apparent that they desperately needed to get some shut-eye in anticipation of what they knew was going to be another equally stressful day.

Once they had reunited, back down in the hotel lobby, a rather more subdued mood had set in and, making their way to the bar, they all admitted that they were most thankful that so far there had been no sign of Allen, or that nurse of his.

Although not as glamorous as at the Sheraton several evenings ago, Shirley still cut a striking figure and the dark glasses she sported added a certain *je ne sais quoi* to her appearance. She now wore a pair of jeans, a blue blouse and navy cardigan, and had decided to let her hair down. As for Clive, much to his own relief, he was back in mufti and also wearing jeans. After the waiter had taken their orders, and disappeared to fetch their drinks, it was Michael who broke into conversation.

'I did tell my folks I was going to Florida, by the way.'

'And let's hope nobody knows we're staying the night here. Just outside Upper Sandusky, did you say it was?'

'That was a few miles back', Michael replied. 'I think we're nearer to Toledo. Am I right, Steve?'

'Yes, Michael, I would say so,' Steve quietly responded.

At this point their drinks arrived to quench their anxiety, and Clive decided to propose a toast to Dennis, which, although he hadn't meant to, cast a further shadow over the proceedings.

Steve broke the mood of introspection with some more practical information relating to their itinerary and told them that their travel arrangements were all taken care of. He'd purchased the ferry tickets, and announced that they had to get to the dockside by nine-thirty, a good half hour before embarkation. He went on to suggest that they all had an early breakfast, and to be on the safe side, they needed to leave the hotel shortly after eight o'clock at the latest, since he wasn't entirely sure where their ferry left from.

'That's fine with us, isn't it, Shirl?'

'Absolutely.'

'Have you ever gone to Toronto this way before?' Clive asked Steve.

'No Clive, to be perfectly honest I haven't. It's all quite an adventure and the sooner we cross over into Canada, the better I'm sure we'll all feel.'

'I couldn't agree more', Michael added.

Although their late-night drinks somewhat helped ease the obvious tension they were all feeling, it was quite apparent that a terrible malaise had set in. Indeed, Shirley's sleeping pills were going to come in very handy, providing there was a loud morning alarm call, which she had been sure to request for both herself and her boss.

Nevertheless, she decided it was time to break up the party and so she rose and excused herself in her usual politest of ways: 'Listen, boys, I don't wish to appear rude, but this drink is not going down too well and I really feel I have to turn in, so I do hope you'll all excuse me.'

As her three escorts stood up, Clive was quick to respond. 'Shirley, I think that's a very shrewd move on your part, and I feel we should all follow your wise example.'

And with that, our four weary travellers downed their drinks, bade farewell to each other most fondly, and went to their rooms to try to get a good night's sleep.

Breakfast was a hasty affair and they were soon on their way to catch the ferry, with Steve at the wheel this time, in order to give Michael a break from all the driving he'd done. Once they pulled up at the dockside, and in order to lessen the tension they were all feeling, Shirley remarked that she thought that their ship resembled one of those Scottish MacBrayne steamers she had once taken when she sailed to the Outer Hebrides from Oban, to visit the Isle of Lewis.

All four of them showed a good deal of apprehension as they approached the US official at the quayside. But to their total astonishment they managed to clear customs with not a hint of difficulty which, naturally enough, had been the one thing they were all really dreading. The ease of the procedure began to concern Clive as they drove up the ferry ramp and down into the ship's hold, since he acknowledged that leaving the United States had been relatively effortless, but he had to admit to himself that it left him feeling more suspicious than ever. He just couldn't understand why he and Shirley had not been apprehended, nor could he help but think that they were being tailed after all, and were probably under surveillance and consequently still in a good deal of danger: but he decided not to share such thoughts with the others.

Once on board, and with their car carefully stowed away on the bottom deck, they heard the engines of their vessel spring into action, which was a huge relief for our four uneasy travellers. This encouraged them to go up on deck, joining many of the other passengers and watch their ship finally cast off and see it slowly drift away from the shores of the United States of America, leaving them all feeling most relieved.

After a while, it was Shirley who said that she'd kill for a cup of coffee and Steve felt the same way. Clive, who only smoked Sobranies when under stress, announced that he really needed a 'fag' now that he had begun to relax a little, which caused some amusement amongst his American buddies. Michael, though not a confirmed smoker, said he'd love to try one and so he remained on deck with Clive while the other two went below and looked for the cafeteria.

As the two men stood there watching the US coastline slowly disappear into the middle distance, Clive offered Michael one of his Black Russians, which was graciously accepted, and the Englishman set about lighting it up for him. Michael took a few puffs but then said he found it rather strong, apologised for wasting it and threw it overboard. He then broke an awkward silence by announcing that he felt totally shattered and said that if Clive didn't mind, he needed to turn in, find his cabin and have a lie-down.

'Michael, I'm not the least bit surprised you're tired. You must be exhausted from all that driving. Look, you go ahead and get some rest. I'll stay here and finish my cigarette.'

As Clive stood there alone, staring out across the vastness of the lake, he breathed in the fresh air and at last, as the realisation that they had been able to safely leave the USA finally began to sink in, he started to unwind and felt a little more secure. He must have been standing there for some time, leaning over the rail, quietly enjoying his cigarette, when quite suddenly a disturbing sensation sent a shiver down his spine, and he was overcome by the idea that an ominous presence was behind him, which made him turn around quickly. Imagine the shock he got when he saw Dr Allen Levitt coming straight towards him, glaring at him with that awful cheesy grin of his.

'Great to see you, Clive – welcome aboard. Now I can finish my examination.'

'Why, you son of a bitch!' Clive retaliated. 'Oh no you don't! … I know who you really are and who you've been working for. And if you think you're going to get away with it, you've got another—'

But before he could finish the sentence, he quite suddenly received the most almighty shove to his shoulder from behind, and, without being able to stop himself, was propelled head first over the side of the ship, and down into the murky waters of Lake Erie. He'd quite obviously not been aware that Nurse Edith had crept up behind him, and, at the right moment, she had used all her strength to push him overboard. The two Americans, now with their mission accomplished, and believing their deed had gone unnoticed, nonchalantly turned on their heels, and, arm in arm, calmly sauntered back to the far end of the deck, smiling and chatting away as they went, as though nothing at all had happened.

Fortunately for Clive, further along on the starboard side there was a young couple who had also been enjoying the fresh air and had been staring out into the same middle distance as him. They were quick to respond to what they saw happen and it was this Mr and Mrs Green who alarmed everyone by shouting: 'Help! Come quickly! Help! There's someone in the water! Help! Help!

In no time at all, two members of the crew came out on deck to see what the commotion was all about, and immediately sprang into action, shouting, 'Man overboard! Man overboard!'

One of the crew went off straight away to raise the alarm and inform the captain on the bridge about what had occurred, while the other firmly stood his ground, focusing on the person who'd gone overboard and pointing in Clive's direction, since it was crucial to monitor his exact position. Once notified, the captain then pressed the man overboard device, which immediately shut down the ship's engines in order to avoid colliding with the unfortunate passenger in the water. Time was of the essence, and the engines were soon started up again and the ferry went into an Anderson turn, hard starboard, so as to circle round the person and avoid causing an undertow. At the same time there were three long blasts of a whistle and then the Oscar flag, red and yellow squares, was raised.

More crew appeared on deck, and the officer of the watch, knowing the position of the floundering passenger, automatically released safety rings, and a life raft was launched into the lake, which contained a float emitting orange smoke to guide the person in the water towards it. Then two other crew members clambered into a rescue boat, which was very carefully lowered down into Lake Erie.

In all the confusion and concern for the person they were trying to rescue, no one seemed in the least bit interested in Clive's two assailants, who, once again, seemed to have vanished into thin air. In fact, Allen and Nurse Edith created their own disappearing act by both managing to quickly escape in a motor launch that had pulled up on the port side of the ferry when the ship's engines had been shut down, and because of all the commotion on the starboard side, their speedy escape drew not the least bit of attention.

By now, many of the other passengers had arrived on the scene, including Steve and Shirley, who, like everyone else, had responded to the alarm and, in common with all on board, were more than anxious to know who had fallen into the lake. From where they leaned over, they couldn't quite make out who was in the water, but that didn't impede their curiosity. Meanwhile, poor Clive, who Allen had cleverly discovered was not a strong swimmer at the best of times, had struggled to keep afloat for a short while, but was able to grab hold of a safety ring and just about managed to reach the life raft and haul himself onto it. Then the two crewman in the rescue boat, obviously well trained and fully prepared for such an eventuality, managed to come to the assistance of their passenger and pulled him on board their vessel.

They immediately attached a life jacket to Clive and covered him with thermal blankets, since he was now at risk of hypothermia and could lose consciousness. One of the two seamen also administered some artificial respiration, which caused those on deck who could see the team in action to break into lively applause. This display of sincere admiration for the crew's ability to rescue the poor fellow helped alleviate the extreme anxiety amongst those passengers who had witnessed the drama.

As Steve and Shirley drew nearer to the rescue scene, they were flabbergasted to discover that it was one of their travelling companions who was being unceremoniously fished out of the water. Shirley lost no time at all in rushing towards the rescue boat as it was hauled safely back onto the deck. By now the chief officer was in command and once Clive had been carefully lifted out of the boat, a path was cleared for him as he was taken to the safety of a cabin. Shirley watched her dear friend being carried through the crowd on deck and she saw that poor Clive, with his heart probably going like the clappers, was now wrapped up like a papoose.

Displaying all the determination in the world, Shirley eventually pushed her way forward and managed to get the attention of the purser and explained she was travelling with the man who had just been rescued. She lost no time informing the gentleman that her main aim was to be by Clive's side and attend to him; she rambled on somewhat, informing the young man that this was only what he had done for her at Allen's clinic.

'The difference this time is that I know he's not faking anything,' claimed Shirley.

The purser, not fully understanding what Shirley was going on about, did however realise that the poor lady was obviously also in a mild state of shock herself, since she appeared to be babbling on incoherently. He begged her to calm down and informed her that as soon as he was given the OK, he would arrange for her to see her travelling companion. In the meantime, he called another member of the first-aid team over to deal with Shirley and made sure that she was given something to steady her nerves.

Steve stood close by Shirley's side throughout the proceedings, also tried to calm her down, and was clearly very distressed by what he'd witnessed. Then he took it upon himself to double-check with the medical officer now attending Shirley that Clive was out of danger. It was explained that although hypothermia was still a risk, Clive was doing fine and was recovering as well as could be expected. They would be sent for and allowed to visit Clive as soon as he was in a stable condition. However, the officer warned Steve that once the patient was released, and because he was probably still in shock, the strict medical advice was that Clive should take it very easy for the next few days and not to exert himself in any way.

In all the hullabaloo that had occurred, neither Steve nor Shirley had noticed that Michael was nowhere to be seen. It was only when they had finished consulting with the medical officer that it dawned upon the two of them that their other fellow traveller had not made an appearance. In fact, Mr Poledri had indeed gone back to his cabin to have a lie-down, and later claimed to have fallen fast asleep despite all the pandemonium. Steve declared that he wondered where in hell his room-mate could have got to, but Shirley believed that Michael must have been so exhausted from all the driving that he'd probably retired early and had left Clive alone on deck. Although she also had to confess that she did think it a little odd that he had not responded to the loud alarm that had sounded throughout the ship. Steve agreed with her, and was clearly a lot more worried by Michael's disappearance but, for the time being, decided to keep the deep misgivings he was beginning to harbour about his old friend to himself.

At any rate they both felt that there was no point in wasting time discussing Michael's whereabouts. The important thing now was to get to see Clive and make sure he was well on the road to recovery and so, when Shirley and Steve were finally admitted into the warmth of the first-aid room, they were relieved to find Clive all wrapped up in blankets and fast asleep.

However, as they drew near, one of the first aid team explained that their friend was still in a great deal of discomfort, which was hardly surprising, since he was recovering from shock, had obviously swallowed a heck of a lot of unclean water and had nearly frozen to death. As Shirley gently stroked Clive's hand, she explained to the crew that she was his personal assistant and was keen to show how indebted both she and Steve were to all the gallant seaman who had rescued Clive.

Steve volunteered to go down to the car and bring up Clive's overnight bag so that he could have fresh clothes. The medical officer in charge explained that for the moment it was not advisable to remove his layers, since they wanted to keep their patient as warm as possible, but he hoped that before they docked it would be possible to dress him in dry clothing.

On his way to the car, Steve reflected that he had never told his English companions that he always travelled armed. Of course, like so many fellow Americans, he naturally possessed a licence for the revolver that he usually kept on his person, in his inside jacket pocket. He had not carried his gun on him during their journey, but had kept it more safely stored down below, in his locked luggage. It was in his mind to retrieve that while going down to collect Clive's overnight bag out of the car. As he approached the vehicle, he couldn't help but wonder where Michael might have disappeared to and so, with that thought in mind, he decided that once back on deck, he would excuse himself, return to his cabin and try to find the missing Mr Poledri.

As Steve re-entered the first-aid room, trying hard to conceal his revolver, he noticed that Clive was breathing more easily and was now a little more conscious. Shirley, on the other hand, was deep in conversation with a young couple he'd never met before and when he approached the group, he was introduced to Mr and Mrs Green. It appeared that they had both seen how Clive had fallen into the lake and they had come over to see if there was anything they could do to help. Soon recognising that they should not crowd the patient, they excused themselves and told Shirley and Steve that they needed to go and also inform the chief officer what they had witnessed on deck.

'Shirley darling, what was all that about?,' exclaimed Steve.

'Steve, I'm so glad you're here now. I've got something amazing to tell you.'

And as she got Clive's change of clothes out of his overnight bag, Shirley repeated what the couple had just told her.

'Clive didn't fall – he was pushed! And the Greens said they saw who did it.'

Steve was dumbfounded when Shirley told him that the couple said that they had seen Clive on deck smoking alone, but that he'd then been joined by a man with whom he appeared to be having an altercation. The Greens claimed that they suddenly saw Clive being pushed overboard from behind by a woman and when they described the two people in question, to her fearful amazement, their description matched those of Allen and Nurse Edith.

She quietly ushered Steve away from Clive's bed, and continued. 'I don't understand how it was possible for those two villains to follow us once we had left Columbus without our realising it. They clearly intended to kill Clive … I just can't get my head around it all. And I bet Dr Levitt and that damned nurse of his are also trying to bump us off as well. And it's all because of that conspiracy theory and of what we stole from Allen's clinic.'

Steve was clearly nonplussed. He just stared at her with an incredulous look on his face and took her hand in an attempt to pacify her. Then he slowly whispered: 'I can't believe I'm saying this, but I think we have a spy in our group. Michael must be in cahoots with Allen after all, and somehow tipped him off. I bet there was some sort of tracking device fitted to his mother's car – I can't think there can be any other explanation, can you? And where the hell is he, anyway?'

'Steve, he's one of your oldest friends and I've only just got to know him. I just can't believe he would want to grass on us and, after all's said and done, he was Dennis's lover … I'm trying to understand why on earth he would want to ally himself to Allen if he knew he was the cause of Den's death. And, more importantly, why would he want to help get Clive killed. None of this is making sense to me.'

'Me neither. Except there was something Clive said about Michael yesterday that made me wonder whether young Mr Poledri was to be totally trusted.'

'That Spoke nose is usually very accurate. But if Michael really is in cahoots with Allen, that would suggest that he has also been working for the FBI all along and I'm also trying hard to believe that.'

'You know, with all that has happened in the last few days, I don't know what to believe any more. What I do know for sure is that as well as Clive, you and I are also in danger; and without wanting to scare you too much, I have to tell you that I'm now carrying a revolver.'

To his surprise, Shirley admitted that she felt all the safer for it, and claimed that if Clive were to be more conscious, he would no doubt welcome the presence of an armed guard. She further admitted that she wasn't nearly so troubled by the men in dark suits as she was by Dr Levitt and Nurse Edith. Steve said shared her views and was also deeply concerned about where all three villains might have disappeared to. More importantly, he confessed that he thought of Allen as a dangerous murderer and wondered whether Shirley was the next to be eliminated or was it now his turn. Having come clean with her, a silence descended upon them as they nervously waited and kept vigil.

After a certain amount of time had elapsed, their attention was drawn to the figure of an official they'd not met before making his way towards them, and Steve broke their introspective mood by announcing that Shirley was not to be alarmed, since he thought that the fellow might be the ship's chief officer.

CHAPTER NINETEEN

HOMEWARD BOUND THURSDAY AND FRIDAY

Much to their relief, the uniformed gentleman introduced himself to them both as Chief Officer Thomas, and told them that he wanted to check up on how his unfortunate passenger was doing and whether his companions were all right. They welcomed his concern for Clive's welfare as well as for their own, and assured him that their poor friend seemed to be better than expected, though they had been warned that he was not completely out of danger. Then Officer Thomas invited them to step outside the first-aid room, and informed them that Mr and Mrs Green had given him a detailed account of what they had witnessed on deck, which he had made sure was registered in the ship's logbook. Our two compliant travellers told Officer Thomas that the Greens had also paid them a visit, and that the man and woman they described were probably an American couple they were sure they knew from Columbus, Ohio.

Officer Thomas said he was taking the matter very seriously indeed, since it looked to him like a case of attempted murder, and warned them not to hold back any information. He invited Shirley to immediately make as detailed a description as possible of the two people in question, and she set about physically describing them. She further explained that Dr Allen Levitt and Nurse Edith Grant had given them rather a hard time a few days ago in the USA but deliberately didn't go into great depth about what had actually occurred. She also confessed that neither Steve nor she had any idea that they had been followed on board the ferry by the said couple and admitted that she was extremely shocked by what had happened to Clive.

Shirley also explained that their other travelling companion, Mr Poledri, was causing them a good deal of concern since he seemed to have disappeared, but Steve added that with all that had occurred, neither he nor Shirley had had the time to search for him. Officer Thomas offered to be of any future assistance, should they require his help, but stated that he did not want to question them further for the time being. However, he made it quite clear that he needed to take a statement from Clive, once he was feeling able to answer questions.

Officer Thomas went on to tell them that there would be a thorough search on board to find the two missing suspects and that, in the meantime, he suggested that they return to their cabins to see if Mr Poledri was anywhere to be found. He instructed them to take Clive to his own quarters as soon as the first-aid team had released him, pointing out that he and his men could keep a better protective eye on all of them there, just in case their Columbus acquaintances turned up again and started causing any more trouble.

Officer Thomas's departure left Shirley more agitated than ever, and once again it was Steve who now became the pacifier of the two, and tried to assure her that they should try to keep calm and do as bidden, since he felt they would all be a lot safer in the officers' area. But first he felt he needed to go to his cabin and see if Michael was anywhere to be found. However, before doing so, he just wanted to check that his revolver didn't protrude too much, and Shirley assured him that his double-breasted jacket seemed to conceal it admirably.

Just as they were about to part company, they were stopped in their tracks by Michael, who made a sudden appearance on deck and started walking towards them. He declared that he was amazed to have found out that a man had gone overboard but claimed to have gone back to his cabin, had passed out and slept through the entire incident. He appeared to be astonished when Steve told him that the man in the lake was Clive, and Michael was manifestly dumbfounded to learn that the two people seen pushing him in were none other than Dr Allen Levitt and Nurse Edith Grant.

'Michael, we're not making any of this up, you know,' said Steve, going on to tell Michael all the details.

'Those two so-called friends of ours are just not to be trusted,' he continued. 'They must certainly have been tailing us all along and I'd like to know how.'

'Never mind them – what about Clive?

'But Michael, this is serious: Allen and Edith are dangerous, and now I think they're out to get us too!'

'So you damn well keep telling me. But I'm much more worried about Clive. Tell me, Shirley, how is he doing?'

'Well the medics keep using the same jargon, "as well as well as can be expected", which you know really doesn't tell us very much,' she responded.

Then, in an attempt to hide his true feelings, Steve added: 'We appreciate how worried you are about Clive, don't we Shirley?'

Shirley played along with Steve, thanked Michael for his concern, adding that Clive seemed to be making better progress than they'd expected, and suggested that they all went to the first-aid room together.

An awkward silence followed as all three stood at Clive's bedside and waited for him to stir, and as soon as Clive finally came to, there was a joyous reunion between all four of them. Shirley and Steve were clearly thrilled to bits by Clive's amazing recovery, while Michael also appeared to be visibly relieved. They again expressed their heartfelt thanks to the entire medical team and, slowly but surely, poor Clive began to revive, was able to sit up in bed, and finally began to utter his first words. He put on a brave face, and insisted that he was feeling a lot better, which caused the medical team to spring into action. Clive's visitors were requested to step outside, as it was explained that the first-aid team needed to make further examinations before their patient could possibly be released.

After a thorough going-over and once Clive was able to assure the medics that he could stand up unassisted, he was finally allowed to change into a fresh set of clothes and made to drink some water. It was decided that he was definitely well on the road to recovery and his attendant friends were summoned back in and Clive was finally liberated. Nevertheless, Shirley, still showing a great deal of concern, repeated the medics' strict instructions, much to their approval: that although Clive stated he was feeling better, he was to take things very gently for the next few days.

Steve then told Clive that they had all been invited to join the chief officer in his quarters, since there were a few questions that Clive needed to answer now that he was up to it. A young officer arrived to escort them, and they were warmly welcomed into the officer's quarters. Clive was told he could sit on the bunk bed or lie down if he wanted. Clive assured Officer Thomas that he was feeling much better and was pleased to answer any questions he might need to ask him.

Judging from his answers, it was quite apparent to them all that Clive had only a hazy recollection of how he came to end up in the lake, although he did remember going out on deck to have a smoke and being astonished to see Dr Allen Levitt walking towards him. However, he didn't see who pushed him. The Chief Officer made a note of his statement and also pointed out that Clive was more than likely suffering from a mild case of amnesia, which he was advised to have checked out as soon as they arrived on dry land. Steve was then asked to step outside for a moment because Officer Thomas, now clearly also armed, needed to know exactly where they'd parked the car they had been travelling in.

As they descended into the hold, accompanied by another armed officer, Steve was informed that 'the Columbus Couple', as Allen and Edith had now been named, were so far nowhere to be found on board, and that before disembarking it would be necessary to check every single car in order to be sure they weren't hiding in someone's boot. As he approached Michael's mother's car, Steve produced the appropriate key, but before opening up, he involuntarily felt for the inside of his jacket pocket. The young officer with them was quick to jump in, look under the seats and give the car a thorough search. When the boot was opened, Steve was relieved to find that there was no sign of either Allen nor Nurse Edith, but he couldn't help but notice Michael's small suitcase right on top of his own. It did cross his mind that there might be some sort of tracking device locked away inside it, and for a moment, he was tempted to surrender it over to Officer Thomas.

However, he decided to put negative thoughts regarding Michael to one side for the moment. What was much more pressing was the fact that somehow Dr Allen Levitt and Edith Grant had turned up on board ship out of the blue and then disappeared into thin air. Or had they? That was the burning question.

Steve watched the officers as they flashed torches into some of the nearby cars, still searching for the missing couple, and was troubled by how Allen and Nurse Edith had been able to follow them all the way to Toledo and then, without any of them noticing, board the ferry they were on. He was now more convinced than ever that those two must have had an accomplice. His vivid imagination also led him on to think that in all the carry-on, they might even have actually been airlifted by helicopter to the safety of dry land, aided by the FBI, of course. However, what still remained a fact was that he felt that all of them were probably still under constant surveillance and in danger, and that led him on to wonder whether there might indeed be something sinister hidden away in Michael's bag.

Steve mentioned the great concern he felt for Clive's safety and asked one of the officers whether it might be possible to let their car off the ferry first once they had docked. The officer said that the location of their car on the bottom deck meant they would have to wait their turn. He went on to explain that there would be a cordon placed on the top deck and manned at the end of the ramp so that all vehicles could be given another search before being allowed to leave the ship. The helpful officer also said he would do his very best to give them priority, since their vehicle had already been thoroughly investigated and told Steve that there would be a public announcement to all passengers over the loudspeaker saying disembarkation would be delayed by one hour.

Steve and his escorts soon returned aloft and it was not long before they could see the Canadian shoreline coming into sharp focus. In no time at all, the ferry was soon docking in Port Stanley and their ship had reached its final destination. Our four brave travellers were now ready to set off and attempt the next and hopefully final stage of their journey and get to Toronto airport. With their farewells to Chief Officer Thomas and his crew completed, they were warmly wished *bon voyage* and in return, they once again graciously expressed their sincere thanks to the crew for taking such good care of them.

As they approached the car, Steve unbuttoned his jacket and felt for his gun as he double-checked the boot once more. It was decided that Clive should take the back seat so that he could spread out more comfortably, which would help him recuperate, and Michael was to squeeze to the other side of him. This time Shirley was to be in charge of the map.

After several three-point turns and a certain amount of manoeuvring, they drove up the ferry ramp and were allowed to pass through the temporary barrier, ahead of some of the other cars. The Canadian officials inspected their passports and waved them through without hesitation. However, before leaving the harbour,

Steve briefly pulled to one side and stopped the car's engine.

'Well, guys,' he said, 'I know we need to have another summit meeting, but we simply don't have the time. We must get on our way as soon as possible and take advantage of the little headway we've been given. I dread to think what Allen and Nurse Edith might be planning to do next, but I don't want to hang around to find out.'

'That's fine with us, isn't it Clive?' said Shirley.

Clive agreed and as they drove off he added: 'I have been considering a few ideas about those two, but we can discuss them on our journey to Toronto, can't we?'

'As a matter of fact, I've got another idea,' Steve announced. 'I don't think it's wise to stick to our original plan any more, for obvious reasons. So I've decided we should head for a different Canadian airport.'

'Anything you say is fine with us, isn't it, Clive?' averred Shirley.

'You bet, Shirley!'

As they drove along, Steve told them that when he went down to the car with the chief officer, he'd brought the road map back with him and checked how far they were from Ottawa airport. Michael, who had remained silent thus far, questioned Steve's sudden change of plan and seemed to be more than a little bit put out by the different choice of destination. This clearly made his travel companions feel even more uncomfortable, and Clive tried to resolve what had turned into a rather awkward moment. He gently suggested that Steve had probably done the right thing, since he felt that there was a strong possibility that they were still being tailed by Allen. Clive revealed that he'd searched the boot just in case the Columbus Couple had tampered with their car and planted explosives in the boot, the kind that could be detonated from a distance, which last remark made Shirley utter an expletive and go quite cold.

Steve said he was convinced that there was no harm in changing their plans and heading a little further north to be on the safe side, and the two Brits were in complete accord. He maintained that his different choice of airport was worth the extra hundred or so miles of driving but explained that they might have to stay one more night in a hotel. Shirley and Clive said they had no problem with another day's travel and Shirley even volunteered to become the chauffeur, which Steve insisted would not be at all necessary.

Then, after a while, Shirley remarked: 'There is just one thing that still worries me.'

'What about, exactly?' Michael asked.

'Actually Michael, about your mum's car … I don't think for one moment that we're carrying explosives but Steve, you don't suppose it has some sort of tracking device fitted to it?'

'I've already thought about that. Even if it doesn't, I think we should try and dump it as soon as possible. Let's all be on the lookout for a car-hire centre, so that we can change vehicles. The more we can camouflage our movements, the better.'

'And maybe we should go for something very ordinary and unobtrusive, like a Ford,' suggested Shirley.

Clive was slowly beginning to feel like his old self again and, although still in a mild state of shock, started to make a mental list of the concerns he harboured about their safety. Shirley, always so in tune with her boss, must have been reading Clive's thoughts, but before she had the chance to start the long-overdue discussion about the possible whereabouts of Allen and Edith, Michael announced that he had something important he wanted to say, which made his travelling companions wonder whether they were about to hear a confessional.

'I'm not sure I can stand much more of this', he said, seeming to get quite emotional. 'I really think I should drop you all off at the airport and then head back home to Columbus. If the FBI have fitted a tracking device to mom's car, then let them all follow me. The most important thing now is to get you two Brits back to England safe and sound and as quickly as possible. What do you think, Steve?'

Before having the chance to answer Michael's question, Steve spotted a garage that he thought looked promising. Steve was quick to hop out, and without much delay he had completed all the necessary paperwork and hired a very discreet little grey saloon. Then they drove into the adjacent car park, and in no time at all, changed vehicles. Steve said they would make for Ottawa airport, leaving Michael free to go ahead and drive his mother's car back home, if that was really what he wanted to do.

Steve removed all the luggage from Gloria's car and it was Michael who appeared to be the most upset by the leave-taking. As he stood holding his hand luggage, he advised Clive to take great good care of himself and try not to overdo things until he had fully recovered. He hugged Shirley and promised to visit London in the not too distant future, and he and Steve even kissed each other, expressing the fondest of farewells. The two Americans agreed to keep in touch via telephone but would allow a few days for them both to reach their destinations before doing so. Michael's solitary figure stood with what appeared were genuine tears rolling down his cheeks as he waved a lonely goodbye at the grey hired Ford until it had left the car park.

It was Steve who broke the silence that had descended in the newly hired car: 'I've changed my thoughts about our route. Let them all believe we're driving towards Ottawa Airport, but I hope you don't mind, I think we should head for Toronto after all. It is much nearer and now we're in this hired car, let's hope there's no tracking device on board.'

'I think that's very smart on your part, Steve,' said Clive. 'The sooner we can get on a plane, the better.' Then after a short pause: 'I know what I have to say may appear somewhat unkind, but I for one am relieved by Michael's decision to quit and return home. But let's not forget that if he has been grassing on us, he could still pass on the details of our new hired car to the authorities.'

Shirley totally agreed with Clive, and volunteered that since the incident on the ferry, she had felt most uncomfortable about the thought of having Michael around anyway. She reminded the boys that Michael had been the one who had wanted to go to the local Columbus police in the first place, and she now declared that there was little wonder about that! She just could not forget that remark of his about how their so-called friend believed that 'there was a good deal of communication between the police and the FBI'.

'You're so right, Shirley,' admitted Clive. 'At the time it didn't mean that much to me, but thinking about it now, it sounds as though he really was much more in the know we previously suspected.'

Steve repeated that he now strongly believed that there was a lot more to Michael's friendship with Allen than was ever owned up to. 'And I don't just mean all that "caring young doctor' stuff" … Well, am I right? And you see, after Den died, Michael and Allen sure used to hang around together.'

Steve continued that, on reflection, he had to admit that Michael had been the first to mention the notion of tracking devices and that Steve had personally become more than a little too suspicious of him when he heard him suggest that he take their share of the stolen evidence over to his Dad's house. He now believed that it would have provided Michael with the perfect opportunity to deliver the goods straight back into the hands of the FBI, should he have been in cahoots with Allen.

'Steve, you know I would really like to give him the benefit of the doubt,' Clive confessed. 'But on the other hand, I wouldn't be at all surprised if Allen was more than capable of putting Michael under some kind of hypnosis while they were hanging out together, and that's how he managed to recruit him.'

'There's a thought … and then, once hypnotised,' Steve suggested, 'Michael really couldn't be held responsible for his actions when he was conscious. Allen may even have conditioned him to bump all three of us off!'

'Now, Steve darling', interjected Shirley, 'don't you think you're getting a little too carried away? Really! This is all beginning to sound a little too far-fetched.'

Fortunately Steve had overestimated the time their journey would take and they reached Toronto Airport sooner than expected. He said he had also changed his own travel plans and, rather than fly out west to Vancouver, he'd decided to visit some other friends he had up in Montreal. He would have loved Clive, whom he knew to be a French speaker, to have joined him in Quebec, but was well aware that his English pals needed to get back to London as soon as possible.

There was a British Overseas Airways Corporation flight departing for Heathrow at seven o'clock that evening and Shirley immediately booked two first-class tickets on it while Clive and Steve kept a lookout in the airport for Allen and Edith. Their reservations now made, it still left them more than enough time to have a final farewell drink in the bar before Steve made tracks for Montreal.

'You know, Steve,' said Clive, 'we both just want you to know how terrific we think you are and can't thank you enough for getting us safely to this airport. You've got the telephone number for Spoke Associates, so be sure to call us in a few days and tell us how you're doing.'

Then, echoing the words of Bobby Kennedy, Steve responded with: 'Let's drink a toast to love and wisdom and compassion towards one another.'

'And one final toast to Dennis,' added Clive.

'To Dennis!'

All three found saying their goodbyes very emotional and it was with a feeling of the greatest sadness that Clive and Shirley waved a final farewell to their last remaining 'Columbus boy', to whom they would always be indebted and eternally grateful.

They had their passports checked and were surprised and

relieved to be able to check their luggage through Toronto Customs without any difficulty at all which left them enough time to enjoy a light snack in the departure lounge before their BOAC flight was called.

Shirley excused herself on the pretext of powdering her nose, but in fact there was an urgent matter she had to deal with. She was desperate to put a call through to London and contact her brother-in-law, which she managed to do before the flight was called. Then, once she had rejoined Clive, and just before boarding their plane, they both had to admit to each other that they had been jolly lucky to get out of Columbus in one piece. The 'Rainbow Conspiracy' had certainly brought the two friends closer together than ever before, and although fearful of what the Columbus Couple might attempt next, they both agreed that it was time to get back to work at Spoke Associates.

CHAPTER TWENTY

LONDON FRIDAY

Flight BOAC 212 was on time and Clive and Shirley finally boarded their aeroplane to London, via New York. They were both suitably impressed by the rather handsome air steward who showed them to their seats and although Clive still experienced a certain amount of his usual anxiety as he fastened his seatbelt, more pressing matters fortunately distracted him from the take-off. Once their plane had reached the horizontal, the two Brits placed their orders for two Manhattans with their charming airline attendant and tried to settle back for what they knew was to be a long journey home.

After they had almost downed their cocktails, Shirley was the first to break the silence. She confessed that although she realised that they were both exhausted, she had a very important matter to discuss. Clive admitted that he was somewhat worn out by it all, but was more than happy to let her go ahead. Shirley quickly set about getting the attention of the young attendant to order more drinks. While the steward went off to do as bidden, his two passengers drifted off into their own worlds as they waited for their martinis to be replenished, and once the fresh drinks were in their hands,

Shirley felt prepared enough to be able to resume.

'I'm sure things have been weighing heavily on your mind too, and although I realise that Michael's behaviour has caused both of us a great deal of concern, I feel his possible involvement with Allen is not worth losing much sleep over … although it does leave us with rather an unsolved Poledri conundrum.' Then without giving Clive the chance to comment on her last remark, she focused her attention on Dr Levitt. 'I feel that Allen is quite another kettle of fish, however. After what he tried to attempt on board that ferry, I'm now more convinced than ever that he's going to turn up in London and strike again!'

Clive agreed, and remembered that, during his check-up, Allen had actually asked him where the Spoke Associates office was in London. He told Shirley that at the time, he had not attached that much importance to Allen's question, but now, in the light of what had happened on the ferry, he admitted that they should consider it as a warning.

'All joking apart,' continued Clive, 'I wouldn't be at all surprised if he wasn't already in St Martin's Lane with Nurse Edith Grant in tow, keeping a watchful eye on number fourteen Cecil Court, and waiting to bump us both off!'

Shirley pretended to be amused by Clive's last remark and told her boss that was exactly what she wanted to talk to him about. However before addressing their current problem, Miss Morris declared that she needed to open up to Clive a little more about her private life and he would soon understand why. She revealed that although he knew that she had only been married once, for professional reasons she had always used her maiden name. Without wanting to go into too much detail, she told Clive that her late husband, Roger Rowlands, had not died in some ordinary car crash – he'd actually been killed in a car chase while trying to catch a criminal. 'You see, Roger was a police officer and was killed while on active duty.'

Clive was truly surprised by Shirley's revelation, but his manners, as impeccable as ever, prompted him to tell her how very sorry he was to finally learn about her loss, and so he took hold of her free hand to demonstrate the depth of his sincerity. She said that although the tragic event felt like a lifetime ago, she had continued to remain in contact with her brother-in-law, Peter, who was also a member of the constabulary. With a good deal of pride she went on to inform Clive that Peter Rowlands was now a chief inspector in central London, and although she only met up with him for the occasional drink, he had always made it quite clear that if ever she was in any sort of trouble he would always be there to help in any way he could. Up until now she had never felt the need to call upon his services, but because she trusted Peter implicitly, believed that this might be the right time to get in touch with him.

Clive sat patiently listening to what Shirley had to tell him but that Spoke nose of his knew what was coming next, and so he beat her to it. 'So, own up, Shirley darling: you've contacted him and told him about what's just happened to us, haven't you?'

From the tone of her boss's voice, Shirley deduced that he didn't sound at all cross or too put out about what she might have done, and although she thought she might have crossed the line yet again, this time she made it quite clear and openly admitted that she only had their best interests at heart.

'Clive, I'm so glad you think I've done the right thing: after all, this is an emergency. We both think Allen and that nurse of his are more than likely tailing us and therefore I felt that it was essential to get some sort of protection in place before our plane touched down in London.'

She finally confessed that she had called her brother-in-law before they had left Toronto and that Peter, who thought he knew Shirley quite well, had sounded astonished to learn what had taken place in Columbus. Although he knew Shirley to be somewhat theatrical, she felt that he had realised that she couldn't possibly have fabricated such a series of events. Knowing that it wasn't like her to come to him for assistance, he had immediately volunteered to help in any way he could.

Before letting Shirley add one more word, Clive announced: 'So you've organised an armed escort to meet us at Heathrow. Well, Shirley darling, I think that's a splendid idea!'

Their plane landed safely in New York and there was a quick turnaround before they set off from Kennedy Airport. More passengers had now joined their flight and as was customary when travelling on a night flight, their seats were adjusted into the horizontal, and the onboard team recommended that all passengers try to get some sleep, which is what Clive and Shirley endeavoured to do. As they lay side by side, Clive joked with his travelling companion about how it was the nearest they'd ever got to sharing a bedroom! At the same time he confessed that it had also crossed his mind that Allen and his nurse might have boarded their plane, which made falling asleep rather difficult for both of them.

Our two weary British protagonists finally touched down at Heathrow the following day just after midday and as they came through customs and kept a sharp lookout for the two Americans, Shirley was relieved and delighted to find her brother-in-law waiting for her in the arrivals hall with his posse, although clearly the police presence alarmed some of the other passengers. She lost no time in introducing Peter to Clive, and with such formalities over, our intrepid travellers were escorted by their armed guard back into the customs area.

Chief Inspector Rowlands explained that before leaving the airport, he and his colleagues had a few questions to ask, and so they were duly shown into a small room. Clive provided Peter with a brief resumé of what had happened and another police officer, whom they later discovered was Peter's assistant, took copious notes while the chief inspector informed Shirley that he needed to know exactly what the two Americans looked like, although they could easily have decided to disguise themselves once they had had their passports stamped and passed through customs.

Clive handed over the film with the negatives of the photographs he'd taken at Michael's dinner party, and went to great lengths to try to give an accurate description of Dr Levitt and Edith Grant. As the police interrogation proceeded, Clive began to unwind and not for the first time the thought crossed Clive's mind that he was truly blessed in having Shirley as his PA.

The last and most important detail that remained for Clive to reveal was his account of their visit to Allen's clinic and the description of what he had removed from Dr Levitt's office. With that accomplished, he handed over the stolen contents, which he had managed to get through customs.

Once they had left the airport building, with umbrellas raised to avoid the pouring rain, they were finally escorted to a waiting police car. Eventually, as they both approached the Hogarth Roundabout, they breathed in the London air and then simultaneously exhaled a huge sigh of relief. However, there just remained the important matter of the Columbus Couple, who were now their major preoccupation, since they were both convinced that they would show up at some point and strike one more time.

Before driving down St Martin's Lane, Chief Inspector Rowlands ordered their car to a standstill and told them that he wanted them to know what his plan of action was. He explained that they would be under strict surveillance from now on in by two plainclothes officers, whom they wouldn't even realise were tailing them. Once out of the police vehicle, he assured them, they would be closely followed and would only have to walk a few blocks carrying some of their luggage before turning into Cecil Court and entering the Spoke office building.

Clive said that he knew he was speaking for Shirley when he told Peter that they were both most indebted to him and his men for taking such good care of them. He also confirmed that they had absolutely no objections to the chief Inspector's plan. It was decided that they drive round the block one more time, and our two protagonists were deposited on the corner of Old Compton Street and left to make their own way to Charing Cross Road. Peter advised them that it was very important that they appear as relaxed as possible and were in no way to be on the lookout for the Americans. However, should the Columbus Couple make an appearance, Clive and Shirley were to set off the tiny silent pocket alarm device that they had each been given. It would not only alert the two plainclothes officers close by, but would also warn the backup team installed by Peter, and then they would also spring into action.

Before Clive and Shirley attempted to walk through their familiar neighbourhood, they turned to each other and admitted that they had both never been through an ordeal quite like the current one before and, though using all their thespian skills to cover up their true feelings, they both declared that, underneath it all, they were scared shitless. Having got that off their chests, they put on brave faces and made for Spoke Associates.

They crossed Cambridge Circus, made for Seven Dials, walked down Monmouth Street and finally reached St Martin's Lane. As they approached the Albery Theatre, they almost came to a standstill and tried hard to keep going. They just couldn't believe their eyes as they caught a glimpse of Dr Levitt and Nurse Edith having a cigarette outside the Salisbury pub, on the corner of St Martin's Court. Pressing their devices, they immediately let their armed escort know that Dr Levitt and Nurse Grant were in the vicinity. As they walked on past the pub and approached Cecil Court, they appeared engrossed in animated conversation and laughter. As they drew nearer to their office, they just hoped that they had convinced the two Americans that they had not noticed them and had consequently not given the game away.

Within ten yards of reaching their destination, they heard the sound of a scuffle and raised voices come from behind them and, as they turned around to see what was going on, they witnessed Allen and Edith being taken away. The Columbus villains were finally bundled into a police car, and Clive and Shirley watched as they were driven away.

Then, not for the first time in the last twenty-four hours, they breathed an immense sigh of relief as Chief Inspector Rowlands came walking towards them and informed them that once they had deposited their bags in their office, they needed to accompany him to police headquarters near Charing Cross Station, where Dr Levitt and Nurse Edith had been taken.

As they sat in the police waiting room, not far from Trafalgar Square, Clive reached out for Shirley's hand.

'Shirley I've been thinking. Now that all this *mishigas* is nearly over, I have something important to say to you.'

'Now surely you're not going to propose to me at long last, after all these years?'

'Don't be silly! Seriously, now – I have another proposition. I think it's high time I made you a partner in the firm. What do you think?'

'Clive, I don't know what to say...'

'Everyone knows you're fifty per cent of the business, so I think it's high time I made it official. Your promotion is long overdue.'

'That's really most generous of you. I'm truly gobsmacked, and these are tears of joy, by the way.'

'I think that from now on we should call the agency Spoke and Morris: we don't need "Associates: any more. I'll get our graphics design team on to it first thing in the morning, because we're going to need a new logo.'

'Clive, now I've got something to say to you.' Then, in the most eloquent of Spoke-speak, Shirley turned to her boss and announced: 'Clive, darling, what more is there that I could ever possibly say?'

A NOTE ON THE AUTHOR

Stuart Hopps is an eminent, award-winning choreographer. He has worked on many major feature films with directors such as Kenneth Branagh, Derek Jarman and Ang Lee. He has also produced work for the Royal Opera House and Welsh National Opera and has taken his own work to the Edinburgh Festival. He lives in Deal, Kent and this is his first novel.